Dating For Decades

Tracy Krimmer

For Stephanie
Thank you for believing in this book.

Dating For Decades

Chapter One

I just plucked six hairs from my chin. Hairs! *From my chin.* I'm going to pretend I don't even see the stray grays intertwining with my auburn strands. My fortieth birthday isn't for almost eight months, and I'm already transitioning into an old maid. The top of the hill is in my sight, and as soon as I cross over, I'm sure I'll collapse and spin down until I crash into a wall. Can I stop this?

There's no time to worry about that right now. I'm waltzing down this aisle in fifteen minutes whether I'm ready or not. These gray hairs will be a shiny accessory, matching the platinum bracelet hanging from my wrist and necklace plunging down between my cleavage. Gosh, I never noticed in all my fittings how much my boobs were exposed. I hope they're not the main event.

"Time to line up!" The wedding planner, Hillary, gathers us all, spinning and straightening us until we're right where she wants us. "Cassie, hold your flowers closer to your chest." She shoves the bouquet against my dress, nearly snagging it in the process.

We're all behind the shut double doors of the church and the groomsmen are lined up on the other side waiting. I'm not the least bit nervous, except for the testosterone that has taken over my face. Will anyone notice? They won't grow throughout the day, will they? If they do, I'm in trouble.

A few latecomers slip past us and find their seats, trying not to bring attention to themselves. The ceremony should take less than an hour and after pictures, I can kick off these godforsaken shoes and change into something more comfortable. I'm looking forward to the ballet flats waiting for me in my car. These shoes seemed like a great idea at first, but now that I've been standing in them for an hour, I can barely feel my toes. I love heels, but these are more like suction cups with sticks on the bottom. Whoever made these *hates* women.

Hillary claps to grab our attention like we're a class of five-year-olds. She runs through the instructions again, as though walking down an aisle requires a ton of direction. She hands me my flowers and I take a quick whiff. These were a great choice. The purples and whites complement each other and really pop against the gowns. I personally would have gone with a purple dress and put yellows and ivories in the arrangement, but that's me, and I'm not a florist. Sasha is.

The music begins playing, which is our cue to begin our parade down the aisle. Four others go before me. Four, which means I'm fifth in a line of seven, which equates to a total of fourteen people, sixteen if you add the ring bearer and flower girl. I don't even know how we'll all fit into one frame in a picture, but that's the photographer's problem, not mine. By the time we're all up front and squared away on our appropriate sides, it feels as though a full thirty minutes has passed.

I take a deep breath as everyone stands and the doors open again, this time, a glowing, confident, beautiful woman stepping through in a flowing, white gown. My young cousin, Sasha, commands the room as she takes my Uncle Ray's arm and makes her way down the aisle to her groom.

Twenty-five years old and starting her life with her husband. Almost fifteen years younger than me and settling down with the man she loves. Soon she'll be thinking about babies and family photos and trips to the zoo. Here I am, almost forty and no prospects in sight.

How does the saying go? Because it fits me perfectly.

Always the bridesmaid, never the bride.

•••

What an amazing dinner! The tender chicken is doused in marsala sauce, which runs like a river into my mashed potatoes. I splurge on a piece of chocolate cake. My waistline keeps me in check and I don't usually eat sweets outside of events like this. I worked my ass off to fit into this dress and I fully intend to stay this size, but after the sixty-minute ceremony and another hour of posing for photos in chilly weather, I'm stuffing myself.

The rain didn't start until dinner, so we managed to finish the pictures without a problem. They say April showers bring May flowers, but the precipitation was sparse last month. The rain is very welcome because my perennial garden could use some water after last year's drought. I can do without the below average temperatures.

My favorite part of a wedding is always the dancing. This time, though, I'm a bridesmaid, so I'm required to do the bridal party dance. I prefer the fast songs to the slow and to dance by myself. Sasha paired me up with Phil, her new husband's stepbrother. At only twenty-two years old he loves to drink and by the time we arrive on the dance floor, he's already pretty drunk.

Sasha selected "That's What Friends Are For" by Dionne Warwick for the dance. I guess the choice is appropriate — all of her friends and family coming together on this special day. When Phil wraps his hand around mine, he squeezes and a smile spreads across his face.

"I've been eyeing you up all day." I could probably get drunk off his breath alone.

His left-hand slides further down my side than I'm comfortable. He winks, and though I want to roll my eyes, I instead move his hand up so it's nestled on my waist. "The ceremony was beautiful."

"As are you."

I'm tempted to stick my finger down my throat but refrain from the childish act. I extend a thank you and push through the song. Once the last note is played, I rush off the dance floor to the bar. I need a drink. Now.

The couple went all out with an open bar. A risky move, if you ask me. One thing I've learned about allowing the alcohol to flow free is that people tend to drink things they normally wouldn't, and usually it's the more expensive alcohol. I order a beer. As much as I want to get as shit-faced as Phil, I left that stage of my life back in my twenties.

"Sorry about my stepbrother."

I turn to Garrett, my cousin's new husband, who is leaning up against the bar. "Oh, don't be. He's young."

He smiles at my remark, and I know this is because he's young, too. I forget I'm the old lady in the bunch of this wedding party. I never expected to be a thirty-nine-year-old bridesmaid. Sasha and I are more than cousins, though. We're friends. I like having such a young cousin in some ways. We're actually into some of the same music, and we've even gone to a few concerts together. Of course, I've done the same with her mom, my Aunt Dorothy. In fact, I'm closer in age with my aunt than I am with my cousin.

Now with this realization, I could have a daughter almost Sasha's age. My stomach lurches at the thought.

"I hope you're having fun." Garrett orders a beer for himself.

"Yeah, I am. This is a very nice wedding." And it is. Although I never intend to have one, I still like attending and viewing the spectacular gown the bride picked out, listening to the music that is sometimes too loud, and people watching. I've already taken note of the group of girls who can't take enough selfies, witnessed a man bitching that the wedding is during a Brewers game, and a couple who is displaying way too much PDA. A creative mind could go crazy here. Good stuff.

"Thanks. All the credit goes to Sasha and Hillary, though."

"Hillary," I laugh. "She's a character all right." And by character I mean psychotic wedding planner.

Garrett and I look beyond each other, not sure of where to head with our conversation. While we've met multiple times, our only commonality is Sasha.

"Well, I better get back to my wife."

His face glows when he says the word wife. He and Sasha had a whirlwind romance, and within a year of meeting, are now married. A real-life fairy tale if I've ever seen one. "Yeah. You don't want to keep your new bride waiting." We clink our bottles of beer together in a quick toast before he heads off.

"So, Cassie..." I cringe at the voice of my great Aunt Ella coming up behind me. Before I can make a run for the door, she has me by the elbow. "When are we getting an invitation to your wedding?"

Of course I couldn't avoid this. Here I thought I'd make it through an entire event with no one mentioning my spinster status. What an idiot I am! Why is this always the focus? Why doesn't anyone ever ask about my job? Everything comes back to a man.

"Hi, Aunt Ella." The cigarette stench radiates from her clothes. "No time soon, unfortunately." I add the unfortunately for her benefit because, to be honest, I'm really not too bothered by it.

"Aren't you dating anyone? Didn't you bring a nice boy to the wedding with you?" Her pink lipstick is on a little too thick, and when she smiles, the color is transferring to her teeth. Is that hair above her lip? I touch my finger just below my nose. Whew. I'm safe. No mustache starting, only the chin hair, but that's bad enough.

"No, I didn't." I wouldn't drag a date here and introduce him to my crazy family. Even if I *had* brought someone, I'd neglect him the entire time anyway because I'm required to be in so many places as a wedding party participant. That wouldn't be fair.

"Maybe you'll meet a nice boy here."

"No offense, Aunt Ella, but I don't want to meet a boy. If I meet anyone, it'll be a *man*, and no one here interests me. I think they're all too young, or family."

She crinkles her nose and scans the room, dropping her glasses down as though that helps her vision. "There are a few good-looking fellows here."

Hey, I'm not denying these boys are cute, but they're just that — *boys*. I'm a grown woman. I'm not getting involved with someone in his twenties. "Yes, there are some attractive guys here." I down the rest of my beer. "I think Sasha is about to toss the bouquet, so I better head out. Nice seeing you, Aunt Ella."

"You too, dear. I hope you meet someone soon."

I give her a quick peck on the cheek as I find my way back to the dance floor. My goal is to make it through the remainder of this night without commentary on my dating status.

The garter toss is annoyingly graphic for me. I'm clueless as to why men insist on using their teeth to retrieve it. I really don't want a peek under my cousin's dress. I watch as he tosses the piece of fabric and the best man, Garrett's closest friend, catches it.

Next is the bouquet toss. I don't want to participate, but Sasha gave me a lecture at her bachelorette party about how I'm one of the only single people that will be here, and she'll be so embarrassed if no one participates. Sadly, this is true. The circle consists of me, my second cousin Megan, a couple of other little girls I don't recognize (probably from Garrett's side), and one other woman who is maybe in her twenties.

This isn't embarrassing for Sasha, but I'm humiliated to be singled out and part of this! But today is about her, not me, so I suck it up.

Garrett covers Sasha's eyes with his hands as they slowly begin to spin in a circle. Those of us surrounding her start our march opposite her. Everyone in the crowd is watching us and clapping their hands together. Aunt Ella waves at me and I roll my eyes. When will this be over? I hope one of these little girls catches it. I know when I was that age, I would have loved it. I'll need to make sure it's easy for them.

The music stops and Garrett halts Sasha. She dips down and whips the bouquet back, which is coming right for me. I glance around and the little girls have their arms in the air. There's no avoiding the inevitable, though. I can either dodge it and let the flowers hit the floor, or I give in and make the catch. If I miss on purpose, I'll never hear the end of it from Sasha. As much as I'm annoyed to do so, I put my arms out and it lands right there as though meant to be.

The crowd cheers and the groomsman who caught the garter is eyeing my cleavage. This will be a fun dance.

The DJ announces us and puts on a Luther Vandross song. Once this dance is over, I'm headed for the bar again. And I don't think I'll ever be a bridesmaid again.

Chapter Two

One Month Later

I can't handle another meeting right now. My lunch consisted of the crappy coffee in the break room and a fortune cookie left out on the table in between meetings. No wonder I'm able to keep my figure. My boss, Terrence, has pulled me every which way he can, from conference room to conference room, and I need to catch up on my own stuff. Sometimes being the manager really sucks.

It's already three o'clock, and if I don't find a real meal soon, I may pass out. Terrence scheduled this meeting yesterday, though, and if I ask to reschedule, he won't be happy. An unhappy boss equals overloaded Cassie because he'll drop everything on me.

I knock on his door and wait for him to invite me into his office. I have my own space as well, but since he's the Director of IT, he gets a window view of Lake Michigan. I may be able to relax a little if I had this view to look at every single day. His desk is slanted into the corner, and the entire back wall is nothing but windows. The wall to the left is filled with diplomas and certificates he's earned throughout his career. One day I'll be in *this* office. One day.

"You wanted to see me?"

"Yes, Cassie. Thanks for coming." He sticks his pen back into the holder and locks down his computer. We all learned to do that once the help desk decided it would be fun to play pranks on people who walked away from their computers without locking their screen. Juvenile, perhaps, but a little horseplay is good for the office. Terrence and I choose not to participate, and even if we did, it would take quite the balls for the staff to mess with us. We've got a sense of humor, but screwing with the bosses is a no-no. Still, better safe than sorry.

"Take a seat." He motions to the maroon chair in front of his desk.

I sit, thankful for the lake view before me. I take a mental picture and file it. I can use it when I try to fall asleep tonight. "I hope your day is going well." Terrence enjoys small talk. He's softer then.

"Fairly well, thanks. I've probably been in and out of about as many meetings as you today, but I can't complain."

He always takes an hour lunch and usually goes to some swanky restaurant. I'm sure his belly is full and he can concentrate. Too bad I can't say the same.

He straightens a photograph of his wife so it's angled toward him. Maya is gorgeous and a sweetheart to boot. We've met a handful of times, and she often brings sweets to the office. Working at a bakery and fudge shop offers that advantage. I try not to partake too much. I've been down that path before and it doesn't end pretty.

"Now, I know you've been working very hard on the Pilot Project. Let's just say I'm glad I don't pay you overtime because you might run the company out of business." He folds his hands in front of him, a noticeable twitch in the corner of his eye.

I smile at him because we both know the truth of that statement. I love being salaried, but when it comes to all of the after hours I work, I certainly don't see immediate benefit from that. My year-end bonus is always awesome, though. Last year I finally bought the Louis Vuitton pumps that entered my dreams for six months straight. I don't splurge often, but when I do, I do it right.

"That project is about all I can focus my time on right now. I pushed everything else to the back burner."

He rubs the scruff on his face. "Actually, that's what I need to talk with you about. The Pilot Project is the biggest thing on your plate at the moment, but we can't allow the smaller projects to suffer."

"Oh, I didn't mean to imply that I'm not getting other things done." I live and breathe this job. If *he* ever came into *my* office, he'd see the to-do list I keep at my desk. My laptop comes home with me every single night, and if I'm out and about, I always keep my iPad Mini with me in case I need to access the network.

He waves his hand at me in opposition. "You're a great worker and an even better manager. However, it's important to recognize when to delegate."

Delegation. This may be the most obscene word in the English language. It's not that I don't delegate *any* tasks, but if something needs to be done right, I do it myself. Let's be serious here. While a wonderful team supports me, almost all are new college graduates. Not *brand-new* graduates (those kids work like horses because they want to impress me), but the ones with about three years under their belts. They do enough but are finding ways to slack off. I'm well aware of who they are (Kimmy, Julian, and Trevor). They don't fool me one bit. Every review I receive, Terrence and I discuss delegation. And every year we agree I will try my hardest to divide up projects so I'm not taking on everything. I delegate one to two projects a year, but a majority of the time I work my tail off to do everything myself.

"I don't think I need to give the team any of the work I'm doing." I don't want to, either. I have a routine and like to keep busy.

"We really need to push play on the Pilot Project. The Board of Directors has given November first as a deadline."

"I can do that." At least I hope I can since I just committed to it. Quite a lot still needs to be done, including coming up with a plan.

"Cassie, I'm sure you would find a way to make it work, but I need this to be a top-notch production. I'm bringing in another person to help you out with the job."

"Excuse me?" My voice squeaks like a teenager, and in my head, I'm already across the desk with my hands around his throat. This is *my* project. *I* suggested we do it, and *I* presented it to the board. I'll be damned if Terrence is taking it away from me.

He releases his hands and sets them gently on his desk. "His name is Lucas, and I think you two will get along fine."

I don't really care if I mesh with this guy because I'm not looking for a friend. "You've already hired somebody?" Terrence went ahead and posted the position and interviewed people? Why did he keep me in the dark about this? He and I — we're a team. We discuss these things and make decisions together.

"He graduated last month, and I think he'll be a great asset. He can take the lead on the project, and you can help out when needed."

"Wait. *Just* graduated? As in, he's never even stepped foot into a real environment and you're going to put him on the Pilot Project? What is he, like your nephew or something?"

"Actually, he is."

What the hell? Right now I can't decipher if I'm shaking from the lack of carbohydrates and sugar in my system or the bubbling anger building inside of me. His nephew? A family member? This is completely unfair.

"Cassie, I didn't hire him because he's my nephew. He's good and really knows his stuff."

"So do I. I can do this on my own." I'm stern with him, holding onto any bit of confidence I have left. I'm not having some young kid come in and upstage me. Especially not someone who got the job because of blood. My blood runs through this company, too, and in my opinion, in a much more deserving way.

He taps his fingers on the desk before standing and walking to the window. He puts his hands in his pockets and stares out onto the lake. "One of the reasons I think you're such a great worker is your desire to succeed. You don't let anything stand in your way and, most times, complete the job on your own."

"Thank you." So far, completely true. I feel a but coming on.

"But." There it is. "Sometimes certain deadlines get in the way, and you need to ask for assistance." He turns and meets my eyes. "There isn't any shame in asking for help."

"I'm not ashamed, Terrence. I just don't need any." I stop before he can interrupt and insult me any further. "But, if you feel I need to step back, fine." See? I can throw buts around, too.

"Thank you, Cassie, because you and Lucas will be co-managers."

Did I hear him correctly? "Wait. He's going to be *management*?" I've been at this company for seven years. It took me five to raise up to the management ranks. This hot shot kid is straight out of college and he's a *manager*? On *my* level?

"Trust me, Cassie. He's smart. Brilliant, actually."

He grins like that of an uncle would do. I'm sure my Uncle Ray would say the same about me, if I kept in contact with any of my family other than weddings.

It's no use. He's already hired Lucas, and it's not like he's going to fire his nephew on account of me. My eyes glaze over and I realize I'm shaking my head. If Terrence notices, he doesn't say anything. "So, when do I meet this guy?" Can I tell my Aunt Ella I've met a man? Does this count?

Terrence presses a button on his phone. "Monica, please send Lucas in."

Great. He's already here? He's probably been here all day

observing me. Why didn't he discuss this with me right away in the morning? The day is almost over, and I've probably passed him in the hall a zillion times.

Okay, Cassie, game face on for this know-it-all. Even though he technically is going to be a boss as well, I need to make my position clear, but at the same time be friendly. If he respects me straight out of the gate, we shouldn't have a problem.

A knock on the door redirects my focus. Confidence. I need to exude confidence. This isn't some Joe Blow off the street. This is Terrence's nephew. Someone who knows my boss better than I do, and if I act or say something wrong, my mistakes will most certainly make it back to him.

The door opens and a tall, slender, toned man waltzes in. His black hair is buzzed, leaving little knots at the top. His green eyes pop against his dark skin. *This* is Terrence's nephew? I expected someone a little less slick and a lot more nerdy. Terrence doesn't exactly resemble the classy guy he pretends to be. Sure, he's polite and professional, but he fits the typical stereotype of an IT geek, even at his age. Lucas is in his early twenties and has pulled together a sleek look with his dress slacks and button up shirt. A tie would complete the look, but he'd come across as much too elegant and sexy for the position. Wait — sexy? No. I check my hormones and redirect my pulsating body from admiration to anger. I hate this guy.

"Lucas, I'd like you to meet Cassie, my secondhand person at the firm."

Good thing I'm a woman because if I were a man I don't think I'd be able to stand for a few moments, or be in search of a book to put in front of my lap. "A pleasure meeting you," I politely say as I firmly shake his hand, his soft, *soft* hand.

"The pleasure is all mine."

I'm so taken with his eyes. They're pulling me in, and I'm drowning. He probably sweet-talked his way into this job. Those eyes can hypnotize anyone.

I sit back down, and he takes the chair next to me. Now it's time to make nice.

"Your uncle tells me you're a recent college grad."

"Yes. I received a Bachelor of Science in Computer Networking and I graduated with top honors."

"That's wonderful." Top honors. Impressive. Almost as

impressive as his beautiful face.

"And while we're on the subject, I would prefer not to call Terrence my uncle during working hours. I want to prove myself here without everyone thinking it had something to do with our family."

Do I want to commend Lucas for his professionalism, or stick my finger down my throat for his blatant attempt to suck up and look like a better person? He may be drop-dead gorgeous (there's a cliché if I've ever heard one), but it doesn't change the fact that I'm still pissed off about the whole situation.

"Fair enough. Did Terrence bring you up to speed on the Pilot Project?"

"Yes, he has. I'm very familiar with it and want to share some ideas with you."

I'm not sure why he thinks any of his ideas would sway any of mine, but whatever. I'll push through this, let him present his thoughts, and make him think he's the one coming up with the final plan.

"Sounds great." My stomach grumbles. If I don't feed this belly of mine, I'll be passed out in Lucas' lap. "I have a meeting," I lie, "but let's chat soon."

I thank Terrence and let myself out. Once back in my office, I slump over my desk. This can't be happening. A hot, young professional has come in to prove he can do a better job than me. I'm damn good at what I do, but I can't compete with a fresh graduate who has learned the latest and greatest technology. I yank open my center drawer. Chocolate. Where is it? There has to be a piece in here somewhere. A little refueling will help me through this. I find what I'm looking for and rip apart the wrapper, snapping off a bite.

Co-managers. You've got to be kidding me.

Chapter Three

I'm not sure how Shannon gets anything done around her house. With a ten and a twelve-year-old boy, her house reaches obnoxiously loud decibels. She's sitting on her couch, coffee in hand, her legs pulled up on the cushion, and I'm on the sofa, my legs crossed, furiously working on my iPad. Meanwhile, Jake and Jordan are wrestling on the floor in front of us. Her house is like a second home to me, and I don't hesitate to make myself comfortable.

"How do you do this?" I ask, glancing at the battling boys as I swipe through my emails.

"I let them work out their differences on their own."

Soon one of them will kill the other, I'm certain. Kids never were on my radar and they still aren't. I never felt a motherly urge my entire life. Maybe the fact that my mother wasn't much of one contributed to that. I work. I don't mother. Jake screams, which Shannon ignores. "How can you even think?" I much prefer silence to work. Well, at least library quiet, not yelling kids.

She laughs and sips her coffee, letting out a loud "Aah." I'm wording an email and trying to type as she responds. "After a few years, you drown it all out. The shouting and stuff puts me at ease. If they're not making noise, that's when I need to worry."

A message comes through that one of our servers is down. I don't want to deal with this right now. I came over with the full intent of enjoying Shannon's company, but, as usual, work calls. I forward the email onto the supervisor, Julian, at the help desk with detailed instructions on how to handle the situation. Yes, I'm aware my supervisor can manage this without my assistance, that's why I hired him, but I don't want to have to end up going into the office to fix this if he misses a step. I ask him to email me when he's done.

"Do you ever put that thing down, Cassie?"

"What? My iPad? Sure." I open a few more emails before deleting them. Then I toss my tablet on the seat next to me.

"Don't."

"Don't what?" I reach for my purse, which is on the couch.

"Don't get your phone. You're trading your iPad for your phone, which, honestly, is basically the same thing. Shut down every once in a while. *Unplug*." She pulls her dark hair back and twirls it to one side.

"I do. From about midnight to five." I dig in my purse and pull out the phone.

Shannon pushes off the couch and grabs my cell from me, not saying a word as she tosses it back into my purse. With her free hand, she picks up my purse and brings it back to the sofa with her, clutching it at her side.

"What are you doing?" I need my cell. If I can't stay connected to work, something can go wrong and I can't fix it. That device is my lifeline.

"Taking control. Shutting you off. Take a half-hour to unplug. Please. I didn't invite you over to visit with the top of your head."

She's right. My job requires me to be available and online, but I can take a minute to appease her. "Okay. Sorry. Let's chat." I place my hands on my lap like an attentive student, though my mind keeps racing, wondering if Julian has responded to my email yet, or even seen it for that matter.

Shannon places her coffee on the arm of the sofa, her hand gripped around it. "This is a little weird, now, I must admit. Your devices are like an additional limb on your body."

Am I *that* bad? Everyone is like this these days. People take their phones everywhere. The bathroom, shopping, out to dinner. I even witness joggers checking their phone. Shannon is a rarity — *I'm* the norm.

"My boss hired another manager this week. Well, his fresh out of college nephew who's supposed to help me with the big project I've been devoted to for the past three months."

"I hope you held yourself together."

"I did. I'm *really* pissed, though." She knows me so well. I'm sure she expects me to paint a picture of myself as a fire-breathing dragon, but even I can tame my emotions when necessary.

Shannon shushes me and points over to her boys, who are still wrestling.

"Mom, we know that word," Jake unlatches from his brother to say. "We've heard you use it plenty of times."

"What! I have not!"

I smile at her. Busted. She used to have a mouth like a trucker, but when she had the boys, she cleaned it up. She doesn't fool me, though. She still uses her fair amount of f-bombs and other not suitable for children words.

"You two go upstairs. Now. Let me visit with Aunt Cassie."

I'm actually not their aunt, but I've known Shannon since high school, so I might as well be. She's like the sister I never had. "Bye, guys." I wait as they race each other up the stairs.

"You need to limit your phone time. Put it down. Find a hobby, for God's sake."

Are we back on this again? First, Aunt Ella corners me with the insatiable need to marry me off, and now Shannon insists I shut down my technology. "I *do* have a hobby."

"Walking on the treadmill while you watch TV on your iPad is not a hobby. Put yourself out there and *do* something. You might meet a guy."

"I meet plenty of guys." I'm not shy about dating. At all. It's June and I have five relationships under my belt. Of course, by relationships, I mean hook-ups. All nice men. All ready to commit. I'm too busy for something serious. Who wants to deal with a clingy man who has to spend all his time with me? My personal space is important to me. Casual hookups are the best. No commitment. No one gets hurt. Especially me.

She puts the coffee down again. "Look. Enough with your one-night-stands or whatever they are. Find someone to marry already."

"Maybe I don't want to get married."

Her eyes widen like this is the first time she's hearing this. "Who doesn't want to get *married*? A huge wedding and a flowing gown? Everyone's attention on you for the entire day? And presents. Lots of presents."

"Plenty of people. Take George Clooney, for example."

"He *is* married."

"Yeah, but consider how long it took him. I've got at least ten or fifteen more years before I'm his age." Committing to another human being for the rest of my life? No. That's not natural.

"I'm not saying you need to meet the guy you're going to marry, but Cassie, stay with one person for a while. You're kind of ..."

"Kind of what?" I know what she's thinking, but I want her to say it.

"Well, if I'm being honest –"

"Please, be honest." *Do it. Say it. I dare you.*

"Trampy."

And she said it. Even if I was sure that was what she was thinking, hearing the actual words sting a little. "I'm thirty-nine years old, Shannon. I'm not some high school hussy who slept with the entire football team."

"It's been *at least* a football team."

"So you're judging me now?" I never brag about the guys I meet, but I always sensed a bit of jealousy from her. She met Ben in college and they got married right after graduation. But commitment is her thing, not mine. She always wanted to have a Prince Charming and become a suburban housewife.

"No. Not at all. I think you're married to your work, though, and you may be a little less stressed out if you stayed with a guy a little longer than a few weeks. Isn't that why you started that support group?"

"I created the group to meet other women like me. And along the way, I realize I'm happy how things are. I keep it going for the others." Even though I don't want to commit to a man, I commit to other things in my life. When I started Dating for Decades a handful of ladies joined and they need me and each other. I can't let my girls down.

"Well, that's great then. But why not do something else with your free time? I mean, keep the group going, but maybe do some volunteering? Something in your field."

The thought crossed my mind before. For one, it would spice up my resume. I'm not looking to switch jobs, but in the event I do, this will only push my visibility. Second, I love technology and this gives me another reason to work with my passion.

"I've got an idea!" Shannon practically jumps from the couch. "The library. I always see flyers with people teaching things there. Why not teach some sort of a class?"

"I guess I can do something like that." I shrug and take a drink of my coffee. It's not as sweet as I'd like, but I'll force the java down. "What could I teach, though?"

"Why don't you go to the library and talk with someone there? I'm sure they can help you."

I could use a distraction from my situation at work and this may prove a good way to do that. I can't deny the possibility that I may learn something, too.

"When, though? My weeknights are usually jam packed with work and on Saturdays I have yoga."

"So move yoga to Sunday. Problem solved."

Of course she had an answer ready. Shannon will do anything or say anything to push me out of my comfort zone. She always has. Not a visit goes by where she doesn't try to pop my work bubble and get me to do something else.

"Fine. I'll try it." She smiles and her eyes light up. "For you."

"Thank you. You'll *love* doing something for someone else."

Maybe, but I've spent my entire life focusing on me and bettering who *I* am. Do I even *know* how to help someone else?

I guess I'll find out.

•••

The last time I set foot in a public library I waited for hours for my mom to come pick me up. She dropped me on a Thursday after school and told me she had to work and would be there by eight to pick me up. The books kept me busy for a while, then by 7:45 I began to worry. What if she didn't come back for me? What if one of her "boyfriends" convinced her to be with him and leave me behind? She told me never to call the police if she ran late. Just wait.

So I did. Three minutes before the library closed, and about thirty seconds before the librarian planned to call the police, my mom strolled through the revolving door, her hair a ratted mess and her lipstick faded and smeared onto her skin. She apologized and explained her shift at the restaurant ran late because someone didn't arrive on time. I knew she wasn't working. Her appearance told me all I needed to know about why she almost forgot about me.

I haven't been to a public library since.

The library sure changed since the last time I was in one. I'm impressed by how they've moved forward with technology. There's a self-checkout station, a big screen television showing events they're putting on, and even a security checkpoint so books aren't stolen. Do people steal books? Is this an ongoing problem?

In my sightline, I notice a four-tier shelf with books for sale at a quarter apiece. A woman with a backpack searches through the DVDs to the left. It seems you can find everything here.

A librarian sits behind the circulation desk typing on the computer. I wonder if she's checking in books, or surfing the internet. I'm not sure what else she could be doing.

"Excuse me?" I interrupt her.

Without a second thought, she stops typing. "What can I help you with today?"

Her name tag says Sophie. She's younger than me, and her hair is short and in spikes. "Hello. I want to speak with someone about teaching a class here." I swallow and my saliva catches in my throat. Approaching people comes naturally to me, so why is this so difficult?

She smiles widely. "Sure! I'll page Mr. Lin. He'll be excited a community member wants to help out."

She's too perky for my taste, but I'm glad she thinks this Mr. Lin man will be on board with my teaching a class. Sophie picks up her phone and pages for him to come to the circulation desk. I wait patiently until a middle-aged, Asian gentleman approaches me.

"Good evening. I'm Bryan Lin. What can I do for you?" He has a welcoming smile and a full head of graying hair. I touch my hand to the back of my hair. Are my grays noticeable yet?

"I want to discuss the possibility of volunteering some of my time here."

"I'm always happy when someone wants to help out." He turns and waves me with him. "Walk with me."

I meet his stride and he leads me up the stairs. I don't consider myself out of shape, but the two sets of stairs do me in. I catch my breath when we reach the top. Bookcases go on for ages to my left and to the right a few tables are set up on a balcony overlooking the circulation desk where Sophie sits. Directly in front of us is another librarian.

"That's Kiki, our Adult Fiction librarian."

When I was a kid I remember there were children's books and novels. Now everything is divided into juvenile, middle-grade, teen, young adult, *upper* young adult, adult, new adult. I can't keep up. Since when did we feel the need to segregate all the books? In my eyes, a book is a book.

"We have a lot of different programs here. Since I took over as director, we have added reading sessions for children, story building courses for young writers, and genealogy instruction, which is probably our most popular course. They're all free to library members." Mr. Lin continues his tour as we move past Kiki.

Before moving through the aisles of books, we pass a roundtable filled with computers. Almost every station is occupied. I glance at the screen of a young man as we walk and he's playing some sort of a game. People come to the library to play video games?

We reach a large room with double doors. "This is one of our community rooms, which is handicap accessible via the elevator. We try to hold children's programs downstairs and adult upstairs. This way it's quieter."

The library has an elevator? Why didn't we take that? My legs are begging me to use it on the way back down.

We enter the room and it's clearly set up for the genealogy class. Poster boards are scattered around the room with different old-time pictures, and a white board lists different search engines. Computers outline the area.

"This is a huge room. How many are in this class?"

"About twenty. We can't have more than thirty in the room. So, what sort of skill do you want to volunteer?"

I walk the room observing everything around me. All I need access to is a computer. "I'm not certain. I work in IT and would like to do something with that."

"We receive a lot of requests for teaching the Internet to those over sixty-five. Most people want to use Facebook."

Facebook. I'm a high-level manager and I'm supposed to teach old people *Facebook*? Why are they on there anyway? What is there for them to do?

"Well, I know the ins and outs pretty well, but do you receive any requests on how to use spreadsheets or anything like that? Maybe even security issues?" I'm a whiz at Excel and enjoy showing others the incredible things you can do with the program. I can't think of what someone in his or her seventies would *use* Excel for, but learning it may be a fun experience.

He thinks for a moment, crossing his arms and running his thumb against his jaw. "I'm sure we receive *some*, but I'd love to utilize you where your skills are needed most. This is what our patrons have requested. Do you think you're interested?"

Shannon is in my ear telling me to do it. I'm patient (for the most part) and I know I should. But teaching old people to use social media? I'd have an easier time giving up technology altogether. Yeah, right. Who am I kidding?

My mind wanders back to the office and Lucas is barging through my door, pulling me out of my chair, and demanding my desk. If I don't do this, I'll let the anger fester on the weekend and may blow up at work. This will pass the time, and, who knows, it *could* be fun. "Sure. When do you need me to teach?"

"Saturdays. Either from 9:00 to 10:30 or 1:00 to 2:30."

Hm. Yoga is in the afternoon. I like the late session because in the off-chance I go out the night before, I can sleep in and work off any hangover I may have. But, this is all about helping others. I can move my yoga to the morning and be mindful in the evenings so I don't stay out too late. I can do this. I need to do this, or Shannon will have my head on a platter. "How about the p.m. session?"

"Great. You can start the first Saturday in July."

We shake hands and as he leaves the room I'm left standing amongst these photos of older generations — people who never experienced a computer in their lives. The people I'll be teaching aren't far behind them, really. I hope I didn't put myself in a situation that will frustrate me more than I can handle, or I may finally break.

Chapter Four

I return home to an abundance of mail overflowing in my mailbox. Did the post office hold everything for the entire week and decide to deliver it today? I grab a bottle of water from the refrigerator and sit down at my kitchen table to begin sorting.

A bill, another bill, junk mail. Does it ever end? I should pay everything online. The fact that I don't doesn't make much sense. I'll add that to my running list of things to do along with this work project.

Beyond my bank statement and balance due notices, I toss aside credit card solicitations. A donation request hops to the top of the pile. I love sending money to charities I support, so I set it aside to write a check later.

I'm surprised when an envelope with my cousin's return address is buried among the bills. I can't believe Sasha sent her thank you's this soon. No one in my family is that fast at something like that. Heck, over half my relatives don't even know what an RSVP is, much less a thank-you note. I'm sure she returned from her honeymoon not too long ago. I think writing thank you cards would be last on my priorities after a few weeks in Italy. Lucky girl.

I peel open the envelope, pulling out a small letter instead of a thank you card. She never sends me letters. I recall she mailed me one once when she was a little girl as part of a school project, but that's it. I even wrote back. Who writes letters anymore? Doesn't everyone text or email these days? I think if I sat down and attempted to use a pen, my brain would go haywire from the confusion. I rack my brain trying to recall the last time I used ink for something longer than a grocery list. Heck, I even use my phone for that now, too.

I wonder what requires a handwritten letter. Perhaps she wants to thank me for being in the wedding and her three-hundred dollar monetary gift. I'll admit, a handwritten thank you is nice.

I unfold the paper, anticipation winning out. I'm anxious for what this is about. Before I can begin reading the words, my eyes divert to the signature. "Mom."

My heart tightens and stomach gurgles. I suck in air as I try to expand my lungs. *Breathe, Cassie. Breathe.* I remind myself to push the air back out to exhale. Pressure builds in my chest as I work my way through my yoga breath, or ujjayi breath as my instructor calls it. If yoga is teaching me anything, it's importance of steady and rhythmic breathing.

I close my eyes and my nose whistles as I breathe in and out. Why is my chest aching so much? Is this what a heart that's already broken feels like when it shatters even more? My mom hasn't crossed my mind in more than a passing thought in years. *Why* is she writing me? And why is this coming from my cousin's house? I keep inhaling and exhaling, allowing my breath to take control. Finally, after about five minutes, I'm ready.

My eyes open and my attention immediately goes back to her signature. I can't do this. I slap my hands on the table as I rise and march to my corner cabinet. This is where I keep the good stuff. The cabinet door slams against the one next to it as I yank it open. Damn it. I put the chocolate up high so I wouldn't be tempted like I am now. Out of sight, out of mind, right? When you're short like me, everything is out of sight. I wipe my sweaty palms against my pants, grip the countertop, and hoist myself up. I start to slip but balance myself before plunging to the floor. Once I'm on my knees, I have a better view of the top shelf. Snickers, Milky Way, Twix. Where is my Butterfinger? This is what I need right now. I push bar after bar aside and then remember that I ate the last one right before Sasha's wedding.

What am I doing? I can't go down this rabbit hole. I press my hand to my stomach and imagine myself 40 pounds heavier. That wasn't a good time in my life, and I don't want to go back there. I know I shouldn't even keep the temptation in the house, but I'm usually fairly good at allowing myself to treat in moderation. I know very well this wouldn't be in moderation. I want more than anything to devour every single piece of chocolate in that cabinet. I shut the door and hop back down. I'm better than this.

I pull the kitchen chair out farther and take my time sitting back down. A couple of deep breaths later, I think maybe I can do this. I may be better off not knowing what she wants. This woman, who has the audacity to sign something to me as "Mom," hasn't done anything good for me in my life. How I survived my childhood is beyond me. If I even knew who my dad was, maybe he could've been a better force in my life. But nope, my absent dad is one of the random guys she hooked up with in her teens. I don't have a clue if he's alive, healthy, or in jail. I'm sure my mom doesn't, either.

I gulp down the rest of my water, my hand shaking as I set the bottle on the table. I close my eyes and open them again before turning the letter over and beginning to read.

Dear Cassie,

I'm very glad you're reading this, if you, in fact, are. I've struggled for years deciding if I should contact you. I realize it's been a long time. I hope you're glad I'm writing. I've been wondering about you.

I stop reading. She's been wondering about me? No contact in over twenty years and she's *wondering* about me? That's rich. I barely think about her. Life is better that way, honestly. My palms start sticking to the paper, some of the ink transferring to my skin.

I used Sasha's address so you'd open this. I want to tell you I'm clean now. I mean it. Six years now. I checked myself into rehab and I'm done.

She's said that before. Not to mention it's been *six years* and she hasn't thought once to contact me in that time? Really, *Mother?* Contact from her is the last thing I want, but waiting this long to reach out is unbelievable to me.

I hope you're proud of me. I am. I'm so sorry for all the years I put you through so much pain. I should have been clean and sober and taking care of you and spending every minute with you. Instead, I lived my life high and with any man I could find. That's why I'm contacting you.

So she's not writing to tell me she's clean? She has a sick desire to tell me everything wrong she did in my life like I don't have a running list in my head.

I'm sick, Cassie. With all the drugs and rendezvous, I got sick. HIV. I guess I shouldn't be surprised. It's under control. I don't have full-blown AIDS or anything. But I don't know how much time I have. I want to see you.

See me. No. That requires me to be in the same room with her, to acknowledge she exists. I made my way through life since I was eighteen without her just fine. I graduated college, acquired a job, even rented my first apartment and now own my own home. I don't need her.

This isn't about me. It's about *her*. *She* needs *me*. This is some attempt to get something. She must be desperate for money. There's no other explanation. For what, though? If she wants money, fine. I'll give her a thousand dollars and send her on her way. I can afford that. She doesn't deserve it, but it's not like me to turn away anyone in need, even it if *is* my mother.

Is Sasha aware my mom is using her address? How does she know where Sasha even lives? Once I turned eighteen and cut myself off from my mom, the whole family realized I wasn't some teenage girl causing drama for the sake of drama. She became a ghost to everyone. Mom *was* a drug addict. She *did* leave me for hours on end by myself. Everyone thought she worked so hard and never invited anyone over because she wanted to spend time with me. The truth was she didn't want anyone coming to our one-bedroom apartment that housed a mattress, a table, and a bean bag chair she picked up at a rummage sale.

My phone number is below. Please, call me. I've considered stopping by your house, but I don't want to barge in like that. Please don't text — call. I want to hear your voice, and, more than ever, see your face. I've heard you're quite successful now and a beautiful woman, and, I hope, a forgiving one.

Pfft. *A forgiving one.* What gives her the right to even suggest I forgive her? Yes, I *am* forgiving, but under the appropriate circumstances. This is not one of them.

A normal daughter would cry tears of joy after her long-lost mother wrote a letter begging for a new beginning. She'd pick up the phone and call her, excited to reconnect with her after all these years. She would be so grateful to God that her mom wants to be a part of her life again.

I'm none of these things. I'm not sobbing. My eyes are dry and tearless. My hand is, for once, far away from my cell phone. I'm not grateful to anyone this letter found its way into my mailbox. Rather than weeping and jumping off my chair in bliss, cement fills my stomach, and I'm trembling.

Damn her! I ball up the paper and toss it across the room, slamming my arms on the table. That's not good enough. I stand up, march over to the corner the paper landed, pick it up, and rip it to pieces. There's only one thing I'm sure of.

I'm not a normal daughter.

Chapter Five

"Now this man has come in and because he's related to my boss, I'll probably lose my job." I'm spilling my guts to my Dating for Decades group, which I don't normally do. Usually, I listen and offer advice, or judge quietly in my head. I need to get this off my chest, though, and to a party other than Shannon, who knows me much too well. And I'm not ready to discuss the letter from my mother, so I'll share this in its place.

"Is he attractive?" Cheyenne interjects from the left side of me.

"Yes, but that's not the point." What do his looks have to do with anything?

"It's exactly the point."

"What?" No. The point is this boy – yes, *boy* – is related to my *boss*, so, I think, he is more than likely to overstep me and make me look bad to his uncle. He's new to the game and power-hungry. I was that way once. Hell, I still am, except now I'm aging as well.

"She's right." Luna gives her unsolicited opinion. "You're not freaking out about this because you think he may take your job. You're afraid of hooking up with him and jeopardizing your career because of it."

I raise a finger at her as she takes a potato chip out of the bag sitting on her lap. "First off, I'm *not* freaking out. Second, I'm genuinely concerned about my job. This guy's a kid. I'm not hooking up with *anyone*." Although now I'm picturing him naked, and I'm impressed. A smooth chest with rock hard abs, a rounded ass I can hold onto, and legs like a soccer player. I've spent the night with my fair share of men, but never someone so young. I'll admit the idea does intrigue me.

Luna drinks her bottled water and rolls her eyes at me. "I give it a month before you're dating this guy." She speaks at a rapid pace and always with such a knowing attitude.

"Two weeks," Cheyenne pipes in, holding her fingers like a peace sign. She waves her hand at the group like she's Chuck Woolery.

Everyone places their bets and for the first time in a long time, I'm offended. My life is a game of roulette and I'm the ball whipping around the wheel, the crowd cheering and hoping I land on their number. In this case, the number of days or weeks until I succumb to sheer horniness. *This* is what my life has become.

"Wait. You're all guessing on how long until I sleep with this guy? Do you think I should be running some sort of a sex addict group instead?" I don't *only* have sex. The men I date take me out to dinner and movies. Most times we go dutch. Sometimes, I treat.

All the women look at each other and then burst out laughing. "Not at all Cassie," Noelle assures me, only slightly bringing ease. If anyone can bring reason to this group, she can. She's the oldest of us all, having turned forty-five two weeks ago, and as a veterinary technician, she helps pet owners feel comfortable when she's assisting their animals. Her kindness is something the group needs. "You started this group because *you* wanted us to be able to work through any issues stopping us from committing to long-term relationships. We've all discovered some reason why we're holding ourselves back. This is your pattern."

Pattern? I never realized I had a pattern. No, I don't. I don't have a fear of commitment or a desire to put notches on my belt. None of these guys have piqued my interest enough to maintain something longer than a month, and, even if they did, I'm much too busy with work to be involved in a romance. Besides, I don't plan on getting married, so is there even a point to calling someone my boyfriend? That sounds so high school, anyway.

Cheyenne's voice scratches like nails on a chalkboard when she tries to explain. She's a sweet girl, but too cocky after her one Introduction to Psychology class. *You're not a psychologist!* "You meet a guy and pretend you're not interested, play a little cat and mouse. Just when he's about to give up, you give in. You date him, or whatever it is *you* call it, for a few weeks, and then the minute he starts to show signs of wanting a commitment, you break it off and move on."

"Who? Who've I done that with?"

They all begin rattling off names, including Monica who tends to stay quiet most meetings. They think they know me so well, but if they were involved with any of the men they mentioned, they would understand why I broke it off. I don't *want* to get married. Marriages don't last and also produce children, which I *also* do not want. I was subjected to my half-ass mother the first eighteen years of my life, and I'll be damned if I put somebody else in the position to hate me as much as I hate her. And I don't need a man to define who I am.

"You're all wrong." I point my finger at every single woman in the room. "Each and every one of you is *wrong*." Whew. That felt good. "I don't move on the minute a man starts to show commitment and trust. I simply don't have time in my life for a full-time relationship and I don't want anyone getting attached. I've hurt no one in my process."

"Then why do you even run this group anymore?" Monica throws her hands in the air. She has plenty to say tonight, that's for sure. She scratches her head, and curls her nose up. "Your goal for us seems to have shifted from let's find out why we can't commit and make a change, to let's all sit around and chat and keep going as we are." She rises from her chair and slides her hands into her back pockets. "I'm thinking about leaving the group."

"What?" We all respond in unison as she turns and moves to the refreshment table. "You can't ditch us." I won't have it. If there is one thing we *all* are committed to, it's Dating for Decades.

Monica spins around and high-tails it back to her chair, plopping down and slamming her hands to her knees. "You never talk to us, Cassie. We share all of our ups and downs and you're never short of an opinion. We always listen to you. You *never* lend an ear to us. We're supposed to be a team here, a safe circle to discuss anything and support each other. We want to help you. I'm just ..." She closes her eyes as she pinches the bridge of her nose. "I'm just tired of this."

"She's right, Cassie." Cheyenne leans back in her chair and crosses her arms. "You're not modeling the same behavior as us. To ask us to take your words into consideration and ignore ours is counter-productive."

I couldn't be any different from the women in this group. Our personalities are as different as night and day. Well, maybe they're the oil and I'm the vinegar. We can mesh together for a short time, but eventually we separate and our differences are apparent. Cheyenne takes one psychology class at the local college and suddenly she's an expert. Under normal circumstances, these women and I would never be in the same room together. Still, even if we're not committed to any man in our lives, we're committed to each other in a way. I should value the fact that they want to help me but I really don't think I need any. I'm irritated at this jackass who came into my job with full intention to take over the first chance he's given, I'm sure.

"You're right. I'm sorry." At this point, I'll agree with them. They may be onto something, but I'm not buying into it quite yet. I'm not some woman broken by my past, my nonexistent relationship with my mother affecting my ability to maintain a long-term connection with someone. I'm not a made-for-TV movie. None of us are, so we should stop pretending in the final twenty minutes of the program a miraculous change will occur. "Let's move on. Does anyone else want to share?"

I want to push the focus off me, and if I'm lucky, Monica will forget her consideration to leave. I brought this group together, and I don't want anything to tear it apart. Every Thursday these women are here for me, and me for them, no matter what.

A knock on the door interrupts Noelle before she begins to speak. A rare find around here, a man of medium height with unmanaged dark hair enters the room. His flannel shirt and ripped jeans turn me off right away. This isn't a rodeo. "Can I help you find something?" Every once in a while a stray stumbles into our meeting room. We direct him to the AA meeting down the hall.

He looks down on a sheet of paper. "Is this the Dating for Decades group?"

All heads turn to him. "Yes," I answer. "Are you looking for someone?" A man has never stepped foot into our territory on purpose.

"Actually, I want to join. How do I go about doing that?"

"You don't, Sir. This group is for women only." I turn back to the members and cross my legs, fold my hands, and set them on my lap.

"Sir?" He walks through the doorway toward me. "Please don't call me Sir. I can't be much older than you. Should I refer to you as Ma'am?"

I stiffen and my face flushes with anger. Ma'am is for spineless women wearing cardigans, their hair tossed into a bun as though they've given up completely on themselves. "Point taken. Seriously, though, we can't help you. This is a women's only group."

"Sorry, ladies." He scans the room and finds his way back to me. "Is there some sort of bylaw that states this, or do you make the rules and can change them should someone happen to want to join, like a man?"

Who the hell does this guy think he is? He comes in here trying to challenge me and make me look bad in front of my group. "Actually, *I* formed the group and *I* intended it to be for women."

"Because men don't need groups like this?"

"That's not what I said."

"It's what you implied."

Ugh. The group is focused on me, and waiting for a response. Am I a jerk for not letting him in? No, there aren't any written bylaws or anything like that, but the online description for the group is clear: a support group for women over 35 unable to retain a long-term commitment and, thus, have been dating for decades.

"Look," I lean in so no one else hears me. "I run this group, and I don't think that the women would be comfortable with a man listening to their, um, *experiences* with men."

"I'm a spectacular listener."

"Good for you. Go find a men's group."

"This is the only one I found."

He isn't budging. If we had security, I would be on the phone with them already.

"Please leave."

"Keith."

"I didn't ask your name." I make eye contact with Monica and raise my eyebrows. She responds with a small smile. I can't tell if she agrees with me or not.

"Well, I'm telling you. And your name is?"

My name is irrelevant.

"Cassie!" Luna shouts. "Her name is Cassie."

I snap my head over at her and she lowers her eyes.

"I think you should take a vote," Keith says.

"You don't have a say. Please leave before I'm forced call the police."

I'm not backing down from him. Men are not welcome in this group, whether he thinks they should be or not. I already dealt with one man moving in on my territory today and I'm not about to deal with another.

"Fine. But, we're not done here." He reaches in his back pocket and hands me a card. "This is my business card. Give me a call if you change your mind."

He's an electrician and appears to own his own company. "I won't."

He shrugs and leaves.

"Now, where were we?" I continue with the meeting, taking one last glance at Keith before the door shuts behind him.

Two men waving their manliness around within a week on my territory. This is my court, and I control the balls on it.

Chapter Six

I'm so glad a new week is upon me. Last Thursday's meeting didn't go too well. Keith left me rattled, and I called the meeting to a close shortly after he left. A man has never tried to join, or even set foot in our meetings, in the three years I've been running the group. The letter from my mother certainly didn't help either. Toss in Lucas, and I'm caught in a blender of emotion, each rotation cutting me deeper.

Work is a welcome distraction as long as it's me in my office. There are some days in life when speaking to people is the last thing you want to do and today is one of those. With all that's going on, my mind is boggled and every single thing is irritating me. I want to shake this feeling, and when I finally am about to, Lucas knocks on my door. I don't want to deal with him today. Or ever. I invite him in, pushing my annoyances deep to the pit of my stomach, which is already overflowing with anger and confusion.

When he enters, I catch myself scanning him from head to toe. I dislike him so much, but I can't recall the last time I met a man this pretty. When I do date, I go for smart, funny, and good-looking men in their mid-thirties to mid-forties. I've never looked twice at someone this young. But Lucas, well, he's got that movie star quality, picture perfect for a magazine cover. My physical attraction seems to win out on my disgust for him on a daily basis.

"What can I help you with, Lucas?"

I offer him a seat, but he remains standing. His hands are resting in front of him, his dark dress pants and teal polo shirt accentuating his body. If I focus enough, I can make out the outline of his pecs. *No. Stop.* I can accept he's attractive, but I need to acknowledge it and move on.

"I want to share a few of my ideas on the Pilot Project. I know Terrence put me as the lead on it, but I also know how much time you've already put into it. I want to run some of my ideas past you and get your input."

I'm both shocked and flattered. I've been very vocal about the fact I don't want this project taken away from me, but Terrence has been equally vocal that my opinion on the situation doesn't matter. I doubt anything Lucas says will impress me, but I can at least listen to him. Lend an ear, as my group mates so blatantly said I never do.

"What's on your mind?"

"Okay." He sits down, sitting up straight and a smile spread across his face. "I've been thinking about this a lot. You were trying to reorganize the data with this server migration. After reviewing this from a dozen different angles, I think we need to consider more server space. We can definitely reorganize the network file shares, but in the long run, we need more space."

"Basically, you want to spend thousands of dollars?"

"Look at it like an investment. Either we do it now while we're working on this cleanup, or you have to do this all over again in a year."

I'm staring back at Lucas, certain my eyes are as big as his grin. "I can't believe this. I can't ask Terrence for more money. And where is this space coming from? We already have servers on site and another in Madison. Where do you anticipate getting more space?"

"I heard through the rumor mill that one of the building occupants is leaving after their lease is up. We can rent their space and put the new stuff there."

"And who is your source?"

He smirks. "I overheard it in the janitor's closet when I was eating lunch."

Very funny. I'm sure he eats lunch at the fancy restaurants his uncle does, not shoved into a crawl space like a high school outcast. But, he may be onto something here. I don't want to revisit this entire project in twelve months, or even in three years. This could be a great opportunity. "It will take an awful lot of time."

"It's been more than three months already, and you haven't even started the migration. The whole process could have been done by now."

Whoa, slow down, buddy. How's he going to come in here and insult me? What gives him the right? Yes, maybe there is a *little* truth to his statement, but I'm stunned at the blatant disregard for my feelings. I've been with this company much longer than him, although *I'm* not related to my boss. Still, this gives him no right to come in and suggest I've done *nothing* these past months. Pages of notes fill my desk, and I've spent hours researching different consultants to contact to assist in the migration, not to mention the other responsibilities collecting on my desk. I can't boast much of a social life, but I don't live and breathe this job 24/7. Maybe 16/7.

"And now there's a firm deadline." He continues with his obvious statement in an attempt to make me feel even more incompetent. I won't let him succeed.

I want him to stop talking. Just. Stop. Talking. How can I get him out of my office without physically shoving him? That's what I want to do. I picture myself getting up from my desk, pushing him out the door, and slamming it in his face. "I'm well aware of the deadline, Lucas, thank you."

"What do you think?"

"What do I think?" I tap my fingers on my desk. "What do I think? I think it's too time-consuming. I think it costs too much money. And I think this is a project I've devoted a lot of time to and plan to follow through. Why don't you think about it some more and get back to me?"

He widens his eyes and curls his lips down. "Oh. Well, actually, I came to you for your opinion, but either way, I think I'm going to present this to Terrence."

"Don't do that!" I spit out. He can't tell Terrence his idea yet. *I* should've come up with this. *I* should have determined that space would be an issue again in the future and thought of this. He needs to give him some bad ideas first, and then present this. If Lucas goes to him with this right out of the gate, I'll look incompetent. He already thinks I am since he had to call Lucas in on this in the first place. "I mean, Terrence is so busy so without a solid plan locked down, I think your best option is to wait."

"But I do have a firm plan. I don't think I should sit on this. We wasted enough time on our asses."

By "we," he means me, and there's no way to sugar coat that. Energy shoots up from my feet and through my body, and I'm ready to explode. The lava is bubbling at the top of my head and any second I'll bubble over. Although, when Lucas stands there, looking at me, and I mean really at me, and not making his way up and down my profile as most men do, it's hard to be upset with him. If he weren't so young *and* related to my boss ....

"Cassie, I know it's difficult having me come in here. I'm not trying to uproot you in any way. Terrence told me some of your ideas, and they're great."

I'm flattered, and I shouldn't be. I know they're good ideas. I'm successful at my job. I'm just a little behind right now.

"But, they aren't as good as this one."

And strike. He had to go and ruin the small moment I was having actually liking him. My mouth falls open, and for once in my life, I can't speak any words. I want nothing more than to ream him out, make him feel bad for his choice of words and for insulting me, but I know he's right. I'm pissed I didn't come up with the idea. It seems so easy now. Why didn't I realize any of this? I'm kicking myself in the ass for being so blind to the obvious. Have all my years in this business and spending so much time in meetings tossed the logical side of me away? Am I so focused on learning the latest and greatest and being equal to my counterparts that I overlook the keep it simple, stupid format?

I don't refute him, accepting my inadequacy at the moment. It may take some time, but I'll prove my place at this company, even though I've done it once before. If there is anything Cassie Noble can do, it's prove other people wrong.

Chapter Seven

My first class arrives, and the knots in my stomach are making more knots. I shouldn't be so apprehensive. Technology is my life. I know most operating systems inside and out, and something as simple as Facebook should be an easy thing to teach. However, as I enter the room and am faced with a group of elderly people, I catch my breath, tempted to turn around and leave. Teaching someone only ten years older than me how to use the computer is difficult, now I have to explain the ins and outs of Facebook to people in their seventies and eighties? I sigh as I set my laptop up on the rolling cart in front. I should be at yoga. I switched my sessions to Sundays, but as I stand in front of these people I yearn for the peace of my sun salutations.

Computers trace the perimeter of the room, which is perfect because the class can still see the big screen behind me while they work. I set up a new email address before I came so I can create a profile from scratch. I have a Facebook account, but don't use it. Ever. I signed up a few years after it started and haven't been on it since that week. MySpace was still hot when I joined. My profile picture is me in my late twenties. I don't look much like that anymore. My hair is starting to gray and the lines by my lips are prominent. That's fine. I don't want to be twenty-seven anymore. I'd much rather be an established business woman with a few strands of silver than a twenty-something still trying to fight my way up the corporate ladder while having way too much to drink and ending up on a strange man's couch in the morning.

I'm all set up and waiting for the participants to arrive. I count eight women and two men. I'm not too surprised. Facebook is more of a woman's thing anyway. Men are on Facebook, but they aren't as interactive. I hope they can catch on.

After only a few hours of sleep last night and my workout this morning, I'm relying on my coffee to get me through class. I stopped off at the gas station and bought the largest size possible. Twenty ounces of black coffee ought to keep my eyes open. If that doesn't work, I'll have a few Red Bulls for lunch.

The women situate themselves away from the men, all chatting about grandkids and backaches. The lady who appears the eldest takes her time sitting down, her rounded back touching the back of the chair at its most curved point.

My mom isn't as old as any of these women, but I can't help but imagine what she looks like now. Does she massage her hips while she walks, wear her hair in a ponytail in an attempt to look younger? Did the drugs thin her out so much she could break if I touch her? Or did the opposite happen and she turned to food and is now obese?

I push the thoughts out of my head. I don't want to satisfy her by even giving her the time of day in my mind. I can't win, though. I drink my coffee and my mom is replaced by Keith.

Keith.

My eyes find their way to the two men who have joined the class. I notice a wedding ring on one finger. The other is bare. The two don't talk to each other, even with being the only men in the class. They sit next to each other and stare at their computers, waiting for me to begin. Would Keith be this silent? Would he come to the group and keep his mouth shut? I don't see the appeal for him to join us other than to pick up women, and we are *not* a singles club. Dating for Decades isn't a mixer. I'm not convinced he's right for the group, though. I don't *want* to turn anyone away, but he goes against everything the group stands for. Doesn't he?

A lady to the left clears her throat, drawing my attention to the clock. Class starts in a few minutes. Before I begin, I walk around the room to each computer and check their Internet is working and Facebook is up on the screen. Each person is ready to set up an account and log in. Good. We can start.

Once at the center of the room, I tap my hands on the table. I wait while everyone situates themselves and finally focuses on me. "Hi, everyone. My name is Cassie and welcome to Facebook 101. I'll be teaching this class for the next couple Saturdays. I'll help you set up an account, create a profile picture, and add friends. Most importantly, I want to teach you about security on the site, and online in general."

Everyone stares at me. They don't look the least bit interested, but I assume they must have some curiosity or they wouldn't have signed up for the class. Unless for them, it's a Saturday out of the retirement home and a way to spend some time. Hopefully, someone retains the information. I don't want to waste my time here. I could be in a downward dog or Warrior Three right now instead of standing in front of a group of people who don't give a shit about what I have to say.

"I would like to go around the room and have everyone introduce themselves. You may all know each other, but I don't know any of you. I put card stock next to your computer, along with a marker, so please write your name there as well. Then I'll be able to identify you each class." I'm bad at remembering names and these cards should help.

I wait as everyone writes their names down and then go around the room and introduce themselves.

"I'm Edward. You can call me Eddie." His voice booms across the room. "My wife Roberta dragged me here." He points across the computers to a woman with vibrant red hair. Remind me when my hair goes totally gray to dye it something natural. She's cute, though, even if she is in her eighties and trying her best to pull off Lucille Ball.

"Frank." The chubby man folds his hands and rests them on top his belly. He doesn't offer any more information than his name. I have my bets on him not learning a thing in this class.

"I'm Lucille. She's Melinda." The short woman starts pointing at all the name tags as she runs through the names. "Lissy, Sharon, those two are both Patricia and both go by their full name, and Dominique. Can we get on with the class?"

I contain my smile at Lucille's obvious leadership role in this group and her anxiousness for me to teach her. I'm torn between if she really wants to be here and is excited, or wants to just get the class over with so she can get back to a Bridge game.

I begin with a brief history of Facebook and Frank is already in the corner falling asleep. I won't wake him. If he doesn't want to learn, I'm not going to force him, especially in a class he didn't pay for, and I'm not getting a check for, either.

"The first thing we need to do is set up an account. It's very simple. You can see there's a button that says "Create an account." All you do is click on that and follow the directions." Ten people (well, nine because someone is asleep) stare at me. Do they not know how to click a button? "Who here needs me to help?"

Every person raises his or her hand. Every. Person. If I have to go around to help everyone, I won't cover a third of what I want to go over today. But if we don't get through the first step, we can't move onto the second.

"Okay. I'll go through one by one to help you create your account. Sound good?"

No one budges so I move away from the front of the room and help the first person. About twenty minutes pass, and I only have about twenty-five left of class, when I arrive at the last person. Lucille. She's so adorable with her snow white hair pressed in a bun on top of her head. She's aged well, and dare I say, the cardigan she's wearing is actually kind of cute. Does this mean I've officially crossed over the hill? "What brings you to this class, Lucille? Why do you want to learn about Facebook? To keep in touch with your grandkids?"

"Pfft. My grandkids. Whatever happened to picking up a phone to call your granny? All these electronics. They've got their TV and video games in their isomethings and computers that sit on their laps. It's disgusting, I tell you."

Should I defend my field or laugh at her obvious denial of the 21st-century? People are so scared of technology when really it's a wonderful thing. People can communicate with loved ones on the other side of the world and see their faces. You can go shopping in your bathroom and have the item the next day. You can even have your groceries delivered. I wish people stopped avoiding the way of the future.

"Well, I still use the phone." My grandmother passed when I was very young, before my mother relied entirely on drugs to get her through the day. She was feisty like Lucille. As I watch her click around the computer, I wonder about her and how she would react to the technology.

"Not one of those cordless ones either, you know, the kind you could take anywhere in the house." She's getting upset at even the thought of a cordless phone?

"I have a good old-fashioned phone. With a cord." I don't, but for the sake of argument, I agree with her.

"Good. That's the way it should be."

"Now tell me again why you're here?"

"Men."

"Excuse me?" I catch a laugh in my throat. Did I hear her correctly?

"My husband passed away two years ago. My daughter and grandkids tell me it's time for me to get out there, whatever the hell that means."

"Facebook isn't a dating site," I tell her. Yes, a lot of creeps are on there, and this is one of those safety issues. But I would expect to discuss those with a class of middle-schoolers, not a grandmother.

"I know. I'm on that Match-a-whatever site, and my daughter said I can Facebook stalk the men I like to be sure they aren't some serial killer, gold digger, or only out for sex."

Now I'm forcing back the laughter. "Lucille, I'm not sure you can find out all that information on Facebook."

"Maybe not, but I can see if the picture matches the one on the dating site, so I don't think I'm meeting Clint Eastwood and someone really ugly shows up."

"You got me there."

This morning started off with me upset over my mom and Keith and Lucas, but Lucille has come in now and turned this day upside-down. I love her outlook and her attitude and maybe teaching this class isn't such a bad idea. I could use someone like Lucille in my life, if only for a few months. She's older, experienced, and I'm pretty sure the only drug she's high on is life, possibly living proof that not all mothers are like mine.

Chapter Eight

I wish these hands could stay on me forever. The way his hands knead into my feet and scale up my legs bring a feeling of euphoria I need so desperately right now. "This is amazing," I say to Shannon who is sitting next to me receiving the same incredible treatment on her feet. I can't wait to see the deep red polish I picked out on my toes, but I wouldn't complain if this never ended. I've spent the entire week on my feet, running between my office and Terrence's while trying to maintain my composure around his nephew. He presented his idea to Terrence, and of course, Terrence thinks it's incredible. He might as well have told him he invented an app that can find the best parking space before you arrive at the store. It's not like he did *that*. Give me a break.

"So, this guy comes into your group and you kick him out?"

I filled Shannon in on Keith and his attempt to join Dating for Decades. I wish we'd talked sooner, but her in-laws were visiting and then they took a vacation over the Fourth of July. This is the first time in over a month we've been able to sit down in the same place and talk longer than a few minutes.

"Yes, and I don't think it's uncalled for. I created the group. I get to choose who is allowed in." That's part of the advantage of being the leader, right? I'm not wrong, right?

"Basically, you're in second grade and have a no boys allowed sign hanging from your tree house?"

If she weren't my best friend, I'd punch her in the nose, comparing me to an eight-year-old. Am I *really* being that petty? I don't think I am. I notice these types of things. I'm well aware of what battles to fight. "This is a group of *women*. Some talk about ..." I glance at the man massaging my feet and whisper the next word "Sex. I don't want this guy getting off on their stories." There are too many perverts in this world and none of us have ever met Keith before that night.

"Wait? Is this like in the episode of Taxicab Confessions in there? I should cancel my satellite and get late-night HBO right in your support group?"

The man stops rubbing my feet and starts polishing my nails. The wet lacquer slides across the nail. It's cold and relaxing.

"No. Honestly, Shannon. I don't think the women would be comfortable, though."

"These women, or you?"

"Please. I don't have any encounters to discuss anyway. It's been almost *six* months. I'm in quite a dry spell."

A group of girls laugh loudly across the room. I'm sure one of them said something funny, but for some reason, I can't help but feel as though they're laughing at my lack of sex over the past months. I'm sure their twenty-year-old bodies get plenty of it, and at thirty-nine I can't complain, but I miss it when I don't have it.

"Girl, please. Have a baby and then we'll talk dry spells."

"Are things okay between you and Ben?" I've sensed something for a while now, but she's never made a remark like that before. It may be more serious than I thought.

"I guess. He'd rather watch sports than get down and dirty with me, though."

"But you have the boys. Don't they get in the way of things?" Another reason not to have kids. If I want to chase my man around the house naked at the drop of a dime, or jump in the shower and have crazy sex there, I want to be able to.

"We have a lock on our bedroom door. And they're in bed by ten at the latest. Instead of sitting and watching TV for another hour and a half, he could join me in the bedroom. Maybe I'm not attractive anymore." Shannon not attractive? You've got to be kidding me. Her hair flows perfectly on her head and her freckles are the cutest thing I've ever seen. Back in high school, all the guys wanted to date her. She bypassed them all and chased Ben until he finally asked her out.

"I doubt that. Maybe work is really busy for him. He could just be tired."

"Well, if he can stay up and watch the game, he can stay up and have sex with me."

The guy painting her toes glances up and back at her feet. I'm sure we're embarrassing him. Shannon isn't bothered by things like this. She can talk about her sex life, her period, her kid's puke, and she doesn't care. Her not having a filter comes as a positive *and* a negative sometimes. I lack discreetness at times as well, but I'm tame compared to my best friend.

"Have you ever tried putting the moves on him? Maybe strip down in front of the television?"

"Yep."

"Nothing?"

"Nothing."

Wow. I find it hard to believe her husband wouldn't jump her bones if she stood there naked, ready, willing, and able. No wonder she feels rejected. I would, too.

"I'm sorry, hon."

She covers her eyes with her pointer and index fingers. "It's fine. I'm not the woman I used to be." Her voice squeaks as her lips curve downward into a frown. She's fighting back the tears.

"You're right. You're not. You're a gorgeous, hardworking mother who puts aside *everything* for her family. That's a far cry from the party girl I went to high school with."

"Maybe he wants that party girl back."

"Ben?" I'm not sure we're talking about the same person. "He can barely lift himself off the couch some days. I doubt he wants to go out and party. He'd never make it past ten."

She takes her hands off her eyes and starts giggling. "You've got that right."

Most days when I visit Shannon and Ben is home, he's lying on the couch with his hand down his pants like Al Bundy. A beer settles in his other hand while he yells at the television. Don't get me wrong — he's a good dad, and I always thought a decent husband. He works hard and deserves to relax. I didn't realize trouble lurked beneath the surface of their marriage.

"Maybe you need to talk to him."

"Ben talk? As in have a conversation about our relationship?" Her laugh makes me laugh uncomfortably. "The last time we had a conversation like that was probably when we got married. He isn't a feelings kind of guy."

What constitutes a feelings kind of guy? How hard is it to give a hug or a kiss every once in a while? I'm not one to commit, according to my group, but if I *were* in a committed relationship, I sure would do what I could to keep the relationship going.

"Okay, enough about me. What about this guy trying to join

your group? Is he cute?"

"I don't know." I do know. And I already know where she's going with this. The same place she always goes — trying to make me date someone and get married.

"He *is*," she teases. "Is he so cute you want to go out on a date with him?"

"What? I think we're a little bit more mature than this."

"Then admit it."

"Admit what? That he's cute? Fine. He's cute. But he's still not welcome."

"What about the guy you work with?"

"Lucas?" I spit out, realizing I basically shouted it across the room. "No, no, and more no."

The man finishes polishing my nails, and we both waddle to the drying area to avoid damaging our lacquer. "You're attracted to him."

"What? I am not." Thinking someone is good looking and being attracted to that person are two very different things. I pick through the magazines at the table and decide on *People*.

"Cassie, you're interested in a lot of men. That's fine. Give one of them a chance. Maybe you'll fall for one."

"Absolutely not." I want to switch the subject, but the only other topic on my plate is my mother. I don't want to go into that. Not here, not with Shannon already upset about her relationship with Ben. If I bring up my mother, I know she'll try and defend her and get upset with me when I refuse to see things her way.

"At least admit they're both cute."

I close the magazine and fold it up as though I'm going to swat a fly with it. "Fine. They are both cute. Lucas is young, vibrant, and knows what he wants. Keith is handsome, owns his own business, and wants to hang out with a bunch of women. There. That's how their dating card reads. Happy?"

"For now." She grabs a magazine of her own to read. "I still think you're crazy."

"I think *you're* crazy. I'm not letting a man into the group, and if I did, I certainly wouldn't date him."

"Is that against the rules?"

"No, because that rule doesn't exist. Since men aren't allowed, it's unnecessary. It would be dumb, though, I couldn't even imagine."

She flips open the magazine and stuffs her face in a page. "Oh, but I sure can."

Chapter Nine

It's the perfect day for an event like this. Seventy-five degrees and not a cloud in sight. Tents are spread out in the parking lot, and once I lay my eyes on the snow cone truck, I know I'll be making a beeline for that later. The smell of barbecue fills the air surrounding the tent where the food will be served. I'm a tad annoyed the bouncy house is right next to where we will be eating, but the kids sure do enjoy it.

Every year our firm holds a back to school event. We gather donations and materials to fill backpacks and buy clothes for the less fortunate children in the area. The firm has been doing it for many years — well before I even started working here — and it's always a huge success.

Everyone can sponsor a child or make a donation. I give money so I can do it for many kids instead of only one. I set aside two hundred dollars each year for this event. I'm always glad to give money when I can.

I'm good at helping to be sure everything runs smoothly. Multiple games are set up for the kids as well as crafts. I've assigned volunteers to each area and by the time the event officially begins at eleven, the kids are swarming the area like they're bees and it's their hive.

Lucas has already beat me to the main tent, and Julian and a few of the interns have joined him. They're setting up for the pepper eating contest. I don't mind a pepper here and there but I can't imagine eating as many as I can in one minute. I'd like to be able to keep all of my senses. And even though the weather is perfect outside, I can't imagine sweating buckets while eating peppers. The men of the group sure seem excited.

"So which one of you is participating?" I wonder who the brave one will be.

Julian and Lucas both raise their hands. "I fully intend to drive anybody into the ground." Lucas makes a hand gesture as though he is pushing the competition into the ground.

I can't say I'm surprised at Lucas's comment. I wouldn't expect anything less. He seems kind of like the man's man who will do anything he can to prove he's as manly as they come.

"Are you planning on competing?" Julian sets down a plate of the peppers.

"I don't think so. I like peppers in my Chinese food, but eating nothing *but* peppers? No, thank you." My mouth is burning just looking at them.

"Are you afraid or something?" Lucas' words slice through me.

First, he thinks he can come in and take my job from me. Now he questions my abilities at something as dumb as a pepper-eating contest. All he wants is to win and throw it in my face. I glare at him but don't respond. I can't let him know he's pissing me off.

"It's okay if you don't compete," Julian says to me. He's pouring water in glasses and setting them next to each competitor's spot. I always thought milk was what you were supposed to drink when you had something hot like that. I may know computers, but I guess I don't know food.

"Are you guys challenging me?"

"No, no." Lucas waves his hand at me. "I'm not trying to make you feel threatened."

"I hardly feel threatened," I say as I cross my arms and jut my hip out. How dare he even suggest that.

"She could've fooled me. Right, Julian?"

Now I can't hold back how mad I am. I wanted to give Lucas the benefit of the doubt and possibly even befriend him. He wants me to compete. He thinks he can kick my butt. He really thinks that if we do this, he's going to win.

"Fine." I cave. "Set me a place. I'm in." I hope I don't regret this. A burning mouth when it's nearing eighty degrees, sweating profusely in my work clothes, and maybe some canker sores after this is all done. No. No regrets at all.

"You're doing this?" Kimmy comes racing up to me. "I think you're nuts. I would never do that."

"That's what separates the girls from the women, Kimmy." Julian clicks his teeth and pretends to shoot guns.

"*That's* what separates us?" I ask. Not the almost twenty year age difference or the level or expertise or the fact that MASH is a TV show for me and for her it's a grade school game where you determine your future on a piece of paper and whether or not you'll live in a mansion, apartment, shack, or house? Sure. *That's* what separates us.

"Cool it, Cass."

"*Don't* call me Cass," I dart my eyes at Lucas, evil shooting out of them. I hate that nickname. The kids in middle school would say, "Cass, cass you're such an ass." I cried so many times in the bathroom. That's why in high school I took it to a whole new level, changed my style to include skirts and heels, splashed on an appropriate amount of makeup, and even involved myself in some activities. I became pretty darn popular. No one even knew my mom was a drug addict, and I slept at random guys apartments half the time.

"Sorry." He puts his hands up in surrender. "Seriously, though, are you sure you want to do this?"

"Why wouldn't I? What's so hard about it?"

"It's not that it's hard. It's just really, *really*, hot."

"I can handle plenty of hot things." I wink at him and immediately wish I could take it back. Why am I flirting with him?

He steals a drink from one of the glasses. "Anyway, if you don't do things like this often, it's more difficult."

"Do you participate in pepper-eating contests often?"

"Not peppers, specifically. But hot dogs, pies, barbecue sauces. It's kind of what I do."

He shrugs as though this is a normal daily activity for someone to do. I can imagine him in college at frat parties, drunk off his ass and downing twenty hot dogs in a minute. He's so young, maybe he still does these things on the weekend.

"Well, eating hot peppers isn't rocket science. I think I can figure this out." I shove my finger in his face. "And kick your butt in the process."

Kimmy and Julian 's heads bounce between us like they're at a tennis match. We're probably giving them vertigo.

"Fine. We'll see. Meet you back here in fifteen." Lucas shoos my finger out of his face, and he and Julian march off.

I grab onto the back of the folding chair in front of me and shove it under the table. "Damnit!"

"Are you okay?" Kimmy offers her support. Why does Lucas get to me so much? Why does he feel the need to challenge me all the time?

"Yeah, yeah. I'm fine." I rake my fingers through my hair. I should put it back. "Can you get me a rubber band?"

"Sure thing, Boss."

At least someone still views me as a superior. The way Julian has latched onto Lucas I wonder if he even remembers he reports to me, not Lucas. I'll admit, Lucas is easy to like — for most people. When he's trying to prove you wrong all the time, he's not all peaches and cream. I blow my hair out of my face and leave the tent. I can find the rubber band on my own and walk off my frustration in the meantime.

Fifteen minutes later, I'm seated next to Lucas, a pair of latex gloves on my plate. "What are these for?" I pick them up.

"Oh, you're so cute," Lucas says as he taps my knee.

"What?"

"Cassie, these are peppers. *Hot* peppers. They can burn your skin, too."

He shakes his head as I say "Oh," and look down in embarrassment. What was I thinking? What did I sign up for? I accept my stupidity as I slide on the gloves. The announcer, Danielle from Human Resources, explains the rules, and I already feel the beads of sweat on the back of my neck.

I'm ready. I think. I can't back out. No. If I back out now, Lucas wins and I'll never hear the end of it. I can't put up with weeks of teasing from him. I'm doing this.

I pick up the first pepper as soon as Danielle announces we can begin. It's not so bad. In fact, it's not spicy at all. I take a few bites and chew it up and it's down. This is a snap. I glance over at Lucas' plate and he's already on his third pepper and I haven't even started the second. No time like the present. I take a bite. This one has a bit of a kick to it, but it's not too bad. It's tolerable. Okay, onto number three. I wince at the first bite. That was a tad rough. I slow my chewing and force it down.

Lucas is ahead of me by two peppers. He smiles at me and I smirk back at him. Just because he's ahead doesn't mean he's going to win.

Number three. I take a bite and as soon as I swallow it, I start to cough.

"Are you okay?" Lucas asks.

"Yeah. Don't talk to me. You're the competition." I won't accept his pity.

"Whatever you say, Cass."

Now I'm fuming. I *just* told him not to use that nickname. I take the next pepper and snap into it without a second thought. Before I can even begin chewing, the sweat dribbles from my forehead and down my cheek. Wow. This one is *hot*. Can I even get it down? Lucas is only one ahead of me now. I have to do this. I force it down, but not before I vomit a little bit in my mouth. If I puke, I'm out. I do the worst and most disgusting thing ever. I swallow it.

Three people have already quit and now me and Lucas are all that is left. Half the crowd is shouting his name while the other half is shouting mine. I can't let my fans down. I wish I could see who they are. Between the heat and the sweat, my eyes are practically sewn shut.

"The last one is pretty hot. Want to call a truce?"

I stare at him. I could and then move on and not force my body into this, but I've come too far. "Never."

I take the last pepper and bite into it with purpose. Lucas follows my lead and we stare each other down as we chew. Sweat pours down both our faces, and we can't stop squinting our eyes. We both swallow at the same exact time.

"Ladies and gentlemen, we have a tie!"

Lucas stands up and it takes me a minute. I'm miserable and my stomach is torturing me. I manage to stand and he takes my hand and lifts our arms in the air in victory. "Damn, girl, you sure held your own."

A smile breaks through as he squeezes my hand. I turn my head and he's looking right at me. His eyes are watering from the peppers, but through the puddle of water, a sparkle shines through.

"I'm tough as nails."

Except when I'm not.

Chapter Ten

A long night's sleep is what was needed after burning my mouth and throat on the peppers. I think I'll stay away from anything with pepper, even black pepper, for quite a while. The back to school event was a success, but I'm glad to be back into my routine. Straying from my day-to-day gets me into a bit of a tizzy sometimes. I welcome structure.

I'm at my desk peeking around some of the files. My end goal is to find the best solution to our problem without buying more server space. Lucas has a good idea, but I want the credit for this. Or even *partial* credit, maybe seventy percent me, and thirty percent him. I've given so many years to this company. Lucas can't beat me to the punch. This project is *mine*.

Three cups of coffee later and my hair a ratted mess from racing my fingers through it in frustration, Lucas knocks on my door. I wave him in. *Great. What the hell does he want?* He can't gloat about yesterday. We tied. No one won.

"Good morning! And it's a great one, isn't it?" He hops into the room.

Even with the florescent lights his skin is perfection and the most beautiful shade of brown. When he smiles, the right side twists up and the tip of his tongue pops through between his teeth. I hate him.

"I guess. What can I help you with?"

"Did someone get up on the wrong side of the bed this morning?"

"What does that even mean? I've never understood that saying. So I get out of bed on the right instead of left. It doesn't change my mood."

He ignores me, and he's right to because I'm not very happy to see him right now. I don't like being interrupted when I'm trying to think. Especially if I'm trying to work in order to upstage *him*.

"Terrence and I went out for drinks last night to discuss the Pilot Project."

My body weakens and my heart drops. "Oh? Was this a business meeting I wasn't aware of?" I click through my calendar. "I don't see a meeting request."

He waves his hands at me. "It was very last minute. We stayed to help clean up after the back to school event, and I suggested drinks."

I stand up, attempting to tower over him, but he's still taller than me, even though I'm in heels. "I'm a part of this project, too. Why didn't you call me?" My voice is shaking, rolling in like thunder.

"I checked your calendar. You had a pedicure the first time I wanted to do this and yesterday you left pretty soon after the contest."

I love I can access my boss' calendar if I need to, but the fact Lucas can see mine really bothers me. He doesn't need to know what I'm doing and with whom. "My friend needed some time with me the other day, and you could have mentioned this to me any of the eight hours of every day I see you."

"There's no need to explain yourself."

"Well, I think *you* should explain. I'm part of this, too, and should be involved in every step. You did this on purpose."

"I swear, I didn't." He pulls at his collar. A sure tell. He knew very well what he was doing.

"What happened during this meeting?" I'll bypass his sneaky method of this secret meeting, but I need every single detail.

"I presented my idea to Terrence —"

"You what? I thought I told you not to do that."

"I did anyway. Sue me. This project needs to get moving. He loved it. We start next week."

Next week? How does this reflect on me? I've been working on coming up with a solution for months; Lucas is here a mere month and he not only has a solution already, but we start implementing it in seven days. "Okay. What can I do?" My involvement is necessary.

"I can handle all the technical stuff."

I close my mouth and inhale deeply, sure he can see the steam rising from my head. Of course he'll handle the technical stuff because *I* am not technical at all. What a jackass. I want to be involved in that. I'm sure, though, that he already went over all of this with Terrence. All during his *private* meeting. It makes sense that Terrence's *nephew* is lead on the project. "Great," I respond through gritted teeth.

"We need an electrician to run the wires. Can you handle that?"

"You need me to call an electrician?"

He stares at me. "Is that a problem?"

Am I a 1950s housewife? I'm supposed to call the electrician like a good wife does. What else can I do for you, dear husband? This guy really corks me. Unfortunately, if I want to stay up-to-date and have a say at all in this project, I need to do this. "Fine."

"Thanks! Let me know as soon as you have it lined up." He taps his fingers on my desk and a weird sensation works through my body as I take note of their size. I lick my lips, my frustration turning to curiosity. He shuts the door behind him, pulling me out of my trance.

Lucas leaves the room and once the goosebumps erase from my skin, the anger finds its way back in. An electrician. Like I have nothing better to do than spend my time searching for an electrician.

I sit back at my desk, open Google, and type "Electricians in Milwaukee, WI." A map pops up with a few listings. The first one has a rating of four out of five stars, but only six reviews. The second has a few reviews, but no rating. The third is one we've used in the past, and I'd prefer not to do business with again. I click to see more and a larger map appears on the right with a bunch of listings on the left. I scroll past most until one catches my eye. KLM Electric. Isn't that the name of Keith's business?

I have his business card in my purse. Sure enough, that's him. He has a four and a half star rating. I read through the reviews.

Fast and resourceful.

Trustworthy.

Reasonably priced.

Knowledgeable, on time, and a pleasure to work with.

Should I call this guy? I'm sure he wouldn't mind if I tossed some work his way. The reviews are great, and if I went with him, we could get moving on the project instead of sitting around another month while I gather quotes. Will he even remember who I am?

I crease the business card as I contemplate this. Ugh. Why is this a struggle? Fine. *Fine.* I'll call.

He picks up on the second ring. "Keith here."

His voice is deeper than I remember. "Keith? Hi. I'm not sure if you remember me. This is Cassie."

"Oh! From the *ladies only* group."

I deserve that. "Yeah, about that —"

"It's fine. I understand, I guess. What can I do for you?"

"Well, I'm in need of an electrician. Do you think you could help me out?"

"What kind of project?"

"At my work. We're going to be building server space, and I need someone to come in and run the electrical. I don't know how long it will take, but I need you to start in a few weeks." The previous tenants should be out in a few days, giving us some time to clean up and tear down what we need to before he comes in.

"Do you want me to come out and give you a quote?"

I probably should, but I want to get the project moving and done with, and maybe then Lucas will be out of my hair. I think the reviews speak for themselves and he's in good standing with the Better Business Bureau. "No, it's fine. I'll pay you what you bill."

"What if I bill five hundred thousand dollars?"

"I know you won't do that. You'll charge me what's fair."

"Do you know what's fair?"

"What?" I can't wait to hear what this guy thinks is fair.

"You letting me join your group. Just because I'm a man doesn't mean I don't need a support group."

How is he still on this? He came to us over a month ago. We haven't seen him since. "I thought you let that go. You never came back."

"Was I supposed to? You kicked me out. It seems to me I'm not welcome."

I never want to come across as an unwelcoming person. He has to consider the circumstances, though. And he caught me at a really bad time. Lucas, my mom, it all was blowing up in my face. *He* was not what I needed at that moment.

"I never said that. I think you'd be better off in a group with only men, though."

"Men don't know anything. I need a woman's insight."

He knows what he's talking about there. Of course, bringing a man into the group would also help with *us* gaining a man's opinion on things. Maybe it's *not* a bad idea. I don't know, though. He'd be working with me *and* part of the group. My personal and professional life don't cross unlike my boss and his nephew.

"I'll think about it."

I hang up the phone, a little irked at him. I could have just as easily called somebody else, but I called *him*. His points are valid. I'm sure the group will not be upset if I agree to let Keith in, but I'm still not sure how I feel about it.

Now it's my turn to stop in at Lucas's office. I haven't been in there yet. I know he's on the same side as his uncle, so he probably has an awesome view of the lake as well. Of course, I get the small office. Put the big man in the big office.

I peek in through the window slot next to his door. He's on the phone and looks a little agitated. So I guess he's not always sunshine and rainbows. People who are happy all the time frustrate me. I'm sure they aren't and are only putting on a front. No one is happy 100% of the time. It's like those Facebook statuses I hear about. Shannon tells me that people on there are constantly writing the super happy status updates when everyone knows that's not the truth. Another reason why I avoid that place.

I knock before turning the knob and walking in. He puts his finger up to his lips to tell me he'll be with me in a minute. It's then I take note of how thick and soft they look.

"I'm sorry, but that's just not acceptable." Lucas shakes his head as he says goodbye and hangs up the phone. "Well, you've finally entered into my territory. Is it as bad as you imagined? Or did you hope for something worse?"

"I'm not sure what I expected." He has the window, and the desk, but there are boxes throughout the whole room not leaving him a lot of space. "I guess I thought you have something similar to your uncle's."

"You mean Terrence, remember?"

"Ah, yes. I forget you don't want me to refer to him as your uncle while at work."

"I only want to be able to prove myself, and I can. Anyway, what brings you in here?"

"May I have a seat?"

"So you plan on staying awhile?" He smiles at me. Does he want me to stay?

"My feet are starting to hurt." I wanted these shoes so badly and had to go down a half size to get them. A mistake on my part but they look spectacular.

"That's why I never wear my heels."

Quite a funny guy, that Lucas. "Anyway, I called an electrician, and he'll be able to start in a few weeks like you want."

He folds his hands and puts them on his desk. "That was fast. You're not bringing in a couple of electricians to give a quote?"

I cross my legs and I notice his eyes move with them. "It's someone I know." I won't tell him that I use the term loosely because I only met him once. Should I have called multiple companies? Probably. But, I don't have time to waste on this. And I consider myself a pretty good judge of character. Even though I don't think he's right for the group, I have a good feeling about Keith and his work abilities.

"Okay, if you're comfortable using someone that you know personally, I have no problem with that."

He shouldn't have a problem with it. He works for his uncle! Besides, he's the one who told me to pick the electrician, so he really doesn't have a say in the matter. If I don't have a say in the technical portion of anything, then he doesn't have a say in the job I'm assigned.

"So, I'll need you to supervise this guy as well. Does he have a name?"

"Yes, it's Keith. And that's fine. He's a grown-up, so I don't think he'll need much supervision." Yes, an adult, which Lucas barely is. All I need to make sure of is that Keith does his job. I don't know anything about being an electrician, so I'll need to trust he knows what he's doing.

"Look," he leans in toward me. "I know you're upset about me coming in here and at a management level."

I let out a small "Pfft" by mistake. I swear it slipped out.

"Please trust Terrence in his decision. I may be right out of college, but I grew up on computers. This is my generation."

I think I feel older now than I did when I found those chin hairs, which, by the way, I've been plucking at least once a week. As far as my grays, thank God for hair dye.

"Please."

His eyes are locked on mine. Wow. They're quite amazing. I noticed them before, but not like this. They're small, but distinct, and dark. His lashes extend lengths most women pay lots of money for. He's pulling me in. I can't be attracted to him. No. He's cute, but he's a *boy*. Twenty-two at best. He's ... oh my God ... *seventeen* years younger than me. Seventeen! I own jeans older than him.

"Fine."

I'll trust him, but those gorgeous eyes better not screw me.

Well, maybe.

Chapter
Eleven

The rest of the week with Lucas is tolerable. I avoid him when possible, but run into him an awful lot. We even occupy the lunch room together one day. Most of the half hour we spend in silence but exchange a few words. By the end of the week, he even makes me smile a few times.

I'm relieved Saturday finally arrives and I'm teaching my class. As much as these old fogies don't understand technology, they at least look to me for direction and don't try and correct me in my own class.

We spend the beginning of the class getting everyone set up with their account. Even the man who fell asleep during the first class pays attention. Now we can dive into the ins and outs of Facebook.

"The fun part is next," I say with forced enthusiasm. I don't consider this fun at all, though I'm not a frequent visitor, so maybe that's to blame. "We get to add your friends. The best way to start is to search for your family. Type in the name of your spouse or a sibling, maybe your son or daughter. If your grandchildren are old enough, you can look them up, too." Users are supposed to be at least thirteen to use the site. I'm sure much younger than that do, but considering some of the things Shannon tells me are on social media, eighteen may be a better requirement.

I scan the room and not one person is typing. "Do you see the bar with the magnifying glass in it? Type a name in there."

The light bulb goes off in their heads and they begin pecking at their keyboards. Not having grown up in the computer age, I'm sure none of them have ever taken a keyboarding class. I can type almost eighty-five words per minute and that's without even looking at my computer while I'm doing it. Waiting for these people to type in a few characters is enough to drive me crazy.

I step slowly around the room as I observe the names they type. A few are hovering their mouse around the ones with multiple names. They're definitely confused.

"You can tell if you've found the person you're looking for based on their profile picture and where they are located. If you want to add that person, click the Add Friend button. They will receive a notification you want to be friends and will either accept or reject it." I need to interject a warning here. "Sometimes your family members *will* reject you." Much like in real life. Better they find this out now. "This is most often between teenagers and their parents. Their parents often want to be friends, but who wants their parents spying on them online?" Had social media been a thing when I was a teen, I probably would have welcomed my mom snooping. At least that way I knew she cared.

Lucille is typing and typing, but she isn't clicking to add anyone. "Don't you want to look for your daughter or grandkids? They're the ones who wanted you on here."

"Ah, phooey. I'm on. That's all they need to know. They're in my business enough. They don't need to be seeing what I'm doing on here, too."

I like her spunk and attitude. I hope I have her attitude when I'm her age. Who am I kidding? Of course, I will.

"Okay, who can we search for, then?"

"Billy Brown, Class of 1949. We separated in 1938, after the first grade. His family moved away and I have no idea where he disappeared to."

"Wow. Someone you knew in first grade?" I'm thirty-nine and can barely remember anyone's first name from my grade school years, much less their last name. "Brown is such a common last name. I'm not sure if we'll find him."

"Honey, he may not even be alive. But you bet I'm looking."

"Should we add a few friends at least? Sometimes you have mutual friends. So if you find someone you went to school with back then, that person may be friends with him."

"Okay, but I'm doubtful. I'm sure most people my age are either dead or banished to a nursing home by their kids."

What a depressing statement, though she doesn't seem bothered by it at all. If my mom cared enough to be around when I was a kid, maybe we'd have a decent relationship now. If that were the case, I doubt I would want her in a nursing home. Now, I don't give a damn where she is. That stupid letter sticks in my mind, the way she loops the letters of my name together and the hearts to dot her i's as though that's enough to pique my interest to see her again.

"Tell you what." I push my thoughts of *her* away. "I don't go on here much at all, but why don't you add me?" I reach past her and type in my full name. My profile pops up, my younger-self looking back at me. I click the Add Friend button. "As soon as I get on here again, I'll accept it. And just add your daughter and grandkids. That'll make them happy."

She yanks the mouse away, her fragile fingers swiping cold against mine. "Fine. But if they start sending me those game requests I hear them talking about all the time, I'm dumping them."

"Fair enough." Another reason to avoid that place. Everyone I meet who frequents that place plays a dozen games. I have better things to do with my time. "Is there anyone else you want to look for?"

"Nah. That's good enough for now." She snorts. "I can't believe I'm even doing this. My husband is probably turning over in his grave. He hated computers."

"Were you married long?"

"Fifty years." She shakes her head and places her hand on her forehead. "He was a wonderful man. I loved him with all my heart and soul. He didn't leave suddenly. He had an illness for many years."

Should I ask for more information? Does she want me to inquire? Small talk was never a strength of mine.

"He suffered from Alzheimer's," she says reading my uncertainty. "What a horrible shame. By the time he left, he had no idea who I was." Her fragile hands are shaking now and she wipes a tear. "It took a long time to come to terms with that, but I'm sure he knows who I am now." She pulls her head back, her eyes meeting the ceiling, showing me her faith, something I lost years ago.

"How did you know he was the one you were going to spend your life with?"

"If I'm being honest with you, Billy Brown probably would've been the man I married had he not moved away. Once he left, I vowed to find someone with as much compassion and liveliness as Billy. And I did. Stan loved me and our family with every ounce of his heart until he forgot who we were."

"You don't need to continue," I tell her as I see her struggling with her words.

"No, no. It's okay, sweetheart. It's very healing to talk about Stan. You asked how I knew he was the one I should spend the rest of my life with. That's easy. He listened."

"He listened?"

"Yes, he listened. When I needed to talk about something or vent, he always listened to me, regardless of how busy he was or how dumb the subject matter. He always took the time. I think that's rare and hard to find. No one wants to listen to someone complain about the clouds in the sky or the dust settling on the mantel. But Stan did. He wanted to hear my ups and downs and wins and losses. If it was in my heart, he wanted to know."

Shannon is the closest I've met to someone matching that description. I haven't met a man who wanted to hear everything about my life, and, honestly, I've yet to come across someone I want to know all that stuff about either.

"Is there a man in your life you can tell me about?"

"I doubt it. I haven't been married, nor will I ever be. And even if marriage did interest me, I'm not even close to putting on a wedding gown."

"Such a shame, dear. When I was your age, I was already married and had my children."

"I'm not planning on having any children either so that doesn't worry me. No biological clocks ticking here."

She stares at me, truly horrified. "I don't understand the women of your generation."

"What do you mean by that?" I'm interested in her theory of "my" generation. Each generation complains about the one after it, as though theirs reins king.

"All these women today want to be independent and think getting married puts some sort of chain on them. It's a partnership, not an imprisonment."

"True. However, on the flip side of things, why does a woman's life journey seem to revolve around finding a man to take care of her?"

She takes her hand off the mouse and places her hands in her lap. "Now, Dear, I never said your life had to revolve around your husband. But don't you want to find someone to connect with, to share your heart with, and have as much time as possible with that person?"

I understand what she's saying. I really do. Yes, living decades with someone I love would be wonderful, but I'm not forcing myself to connect with anyone. When it happens, it happens. I'd rather spend forty years single and happy than even one married and miserable.

"Plenty of my friends are married and even have kids, but it's not for me. My focus is on my career." Not to mention I've only ever seen one solid relationship in my life, Shannon and Ben's, and now they're one counseling session away from proving that untrue.

"My job was raising my kids and tending to my husband. I didn't need to go out and make money. I made a home."

"Things have changed."

"I wouldn't say for the better." She checks the clock on the computer. "Class is almost over, so I'll keep searching next week."

Fifteen minutes remain of class. My views on marriage obviously offend her. Still, I adore her. I hope she finds Billy Brown and true happiness.

At least one of us should.

Chapter Twelve

I roll my hand across my stomach in hopes the massaging settles my gurgles inside. Tonight is Keith's first meeting and I'm officially introducing him as a member. After class on Saturday, I meditated and considered all my options. I'm being stubborn, allowing my competition with Lucas to shade my view on everything else. I called Keith and hired him for the job and invited him to the group. I'm nervous but feel good about my decision.

I'm relieved I have nothing to share tonight because I'm not so sure I want to divulge too much of my personal life with him. We'll be working together, and I'll see him every day. This may be awkward and uncomfortable. Oh, hell, why did I agree to this? What on Earth was I thinking? Then Lucas' smug face with perfect eyes and lashes I would die for enters my mind and I remember. *To take my job back.*

I prep the snacks and refreshments, including the water which I've infused with cucumber and mint along with a pot of coffee. I may need the full pot myself tonight. Next to the coffee I've placed a variety of cookies. I sure could use them right now, but I'm not going to eat away my stress. My mom did drugs to deal with her life. Had she realized she just had to take responsibility for herself and me and sought out the help of her family, maybe we both would have been better off. I learned the hard way, though, about addiction. Within months after separating myself from my mother I gained thirty pounds living off a diet of sweets. Shannon kicked me in the ass and helped me lose the pounds. I owe her so much.

Cheyenne arrives first and grabs four cookies. That girl could eat every cookie there and not gain a pound. I work hard to keep my extra weight off and applaud her for being able to eat like she does. Luna arrives next and tells me she came right from dinner and she's stuffed but grabs some water. A few others show up after her and take their seats.

"Are we going to start?" Cheyenne asks after about ten minutes of chatting about her new college courses. She's working toward an associates degree in Psychology. I've asked multiple times what she plans on doing with it. Right now she's a checker at the local Piggly

Wiggly. She doesn't have a specific path in mind, but she certainly enjoys spreading her knowledge of human growth and development. She's in her second year of what will be a four-year process since she works full-time. I'll admit, I admire her dedication. Working full-time and going to school isn't easy, whether taking one class or five.

I ring the little handheld bell to call the meeting to order. "We have a new member coming tonight, and I'm waiting for him." Typically I don't like to begin a meeting until everyone is present, but I can give everyone the details while we wait.

"Him?"

"Yes. Him." I figured that was the most subtle way to bring it up. "You remember Keith from a few weeks ago?"

"The hottie?" Cheyenne bites her cookie and moans as though she's sinking her teeth into him.

"What am I?" Keith startles us upon his sudden entrance. I'm sure he overheard Cheyenne gawking over him. Here I am concerned about him listening to *our* sexual encounters, and they're basically cat calling him. They should be disgusted with themselves.

"I'm glad you made it, Keith. Please, grab some cookies, coffee, or water, and have a seat."

He heads over to the refreshment table and all eyes follow him. He's not dressed like a cowboy tonight. Instead, he's in fitness shorts and a black T-shirt. I wonder if he came from the gym. His arms are sure proof he goes to one. We wait as he pours himself a glass of water and he sits down. Next to me.

"Thanks for letting me join." He emphasizes the word "letting" as though it's some big honor I bestowed upon him. Is he being sarcastic, or genuinely nice? I can't tell anymore.

"How did you convince her to let you in?" Cheyenne scoots her chair a little closer. "Cassie seemed very against the idea."

"I wasn't *very* against it." I wasn't *that* bad about it, was I? I still don't think denying membership to a man is so unreasonable. "I had ... reservations."

Keith places his hands between his legs, holding onto his water. "She needs some work done at her office and called me. This was one of my conditions of taking the job."

"You bribed her? Cassie *can't* be bribed." Luna jumps in, giggling in disbelief.

"Oh?" The ice clinks in his glass as he drinks it. "Well it appears she can be, and she was. Was I your first, Cassie?" He smiles at me, raising his brow, a deep line creasing through his cheek.

"Hardly." Luna laughs. I glare at her. "Sorry."

"Anyway, welcome to the group. Do you want to start today and tell us why you're here?" Everyone has a reason they joined and I'm very interested to hear his.

"We just jump right in, don't we?"

"Well, if you don't want to share with us, then why *are* you here?" This is how I start with every new member. If he's going to be part of the group, I'll treat him like part of the group. No special circumstances, no beating around the bush.

He cocks his head and slides his tongue along his lips. "Okay, then. You've got me." He sets his glass on the floor. "There's not too much to say." He crosses his leg and grips his knee. "I've had a few long-term relationships, even been engaged once, but I really haven't found someone I can settle down with."

"But if you were engaged, weren't you planning on settling down with her?" Monica offers up what everyone else is thinking.

"Yes, but things didn't work out and now I'm going on pointless dates since I can't seem to meet anyone worth taking on a second date."

"And what makes someone worthy of a second date with you?" I'm curious of his criteria to take someone out again.

"Whoa." Keith throws his hand in the air like a stop sign. "Is she always this crass?" He points to me as he questions the group.

"What? I'm not crass. I'm straight-forward. There's a difference."

"Is there?"

For once I can't say anything. I've gone through life proud I can speak my mind and not sugar coat things. Shannon and I are always honest with each other and that's perfect for our relationship. Maybe, though, not everyone can handle such honesty. Or perhaps Keith doesn't really understand the concept of sarcasm.

"Enough about me. Tell us why these dates don't work out." I don't want to sit here and listen to everyone judging me, even quietly in their heads.

The circle of women wait for his reply, their eyes fixated on him like he's a cult leader and they his followers. I mean, he's handsome, sure, with his light brown hair, strong jawline, and angled smile. But what else does he have to offer?

"Who knows?" He shrugs and that smile that captivated his audience only moments before transforms into a frown. "I can't seem to stay interested."

Okay, so it's *him*, not them.

"I'm searching for someone I can debate with. I want to share my ups and downs and argue with her. I want that person that when something exciting happens, she's the first person I can't wait to call. I want my best friend. I haven't been able to find her yet."

"So, wait." Luna can't understand Keith's reasoning. "You *want* to fight with your significant other?"

"I didn't say that. I want to have debates, great conversations, fascinating discussions. I'm tired of all these couples sitting at dinner on their phones. Talk to each other. Have a conversation. People are so engrossed in their technology these days they forget to be *people, to date*."

Everyone turns to me. "What?"

"Cassie never puts her phone down." Cheyenne moves closer to Keith again. "She lives on that thing."

I'm glad I kept it in my purse tonight. Most times I have it on my lap, but for some reason, I forgot to take it out. "Okay, enough about technology. You said you were engaged. What happened there?" I've never gotten close to that, even in the vicinity of it, which is fine because I don't want an engagement, wedding, *or* marriage. I'm not against meeting someone special and falling in love. Eventually. The possibility sounds appealing, I can at least admit to that.

"Her job. She moved to New York to pursue a career in the publishing industry. I didn't want to follow. The big city isn't for me."

"A job? Who moves for a *job*?" Cheyenne bites her cookie and pieces fall to the ground. Guess I'll be sweeping later, too. "No way. I like what I do, but there's no way I would let my job control me."

"She always wanted to move there. When we first got together she told me. I guess I never thought she would go."

"I'm sorry, Keith." Luna is leaning against her knees with her hands under her chin, batting her eyes. Gross.

I clear my throat in an attempt to distract Luna from her daze.

"Are you out on the scene now?"

"No. Not dating anyone right now." He winks at me. "How about you?"

"None of us are attached right now."

Luna is quick to jump in and state her relationship status. I roll my eyes at her. I may date a lot of guys, but she really throws herself out there.

"Okay, everyone, now that we've all met Keith, does anyone else want to share?"

I listen to Cheyenne and Luna both share stories of recent dates. Keith listens and offers up some advice. They hang on his every word. I'm quite annoyed, actually. Usually, I'm the one they look to. I'm the one in control. This is new territory for me and I don't like it.

When the meeting ends, I start cleaning up the refreshments as Luna and Cheyenne huddle around the new member of our group. They're acting as though they haven't seen an attractive man in years.

"I thought the meeting went well." He joins me at the refreshment table and starts picking up cups after his groupies drift away.

"I think so, too." I stack the leftover napkins on top of the plates. I put my bag somewhere so I can take the remaining supplies home. "There's no need to help me. I've got this." I like cleaning up after the meetings. Everyone leaves and it's only me and the quiet. Once in awhile I hear the laughter of the people leaving other meetings in the building as they head home. But I sometimes clean up, sit down on one of the folding chairs, and read something on my Kindle app. I think it's the only time I can truly clear my mind besides yoga.

"No, it's fine. I'll help. I want to."

This is new. Even if I wanted the women in the group to help, no one has ever even offered. Once the meeting wraps up, they rush home or to other plans. I suppose I'll make him feel more welcome if I agree. "Well, thank you very much." I hand him a bag to put the trash in. The company may be nice.

"How long have you been running the group?"

"A couple of years."

He opens the bag so I can toss in a few cups. "Well, if you can commit to anything in life, I guess that's it."

"Very funny." I stick my tongue out and pull it back in realizing one, it's juvenile for someone almost in her forties, and two, I'm flirting. I swear flirting is ingrained in my personality. "I enjoy it. It helps to talk with other people."

"As opposed to staring at a computer screen?"

"Even funnier. You're quite the comedian." I snatch the bag from him and twist it shut. "My job happens to be *in* technology. I *need* to be on the computer."

"*All* the time?"

"It's not all the time." Although it probably is. I don't think that's a bad thing, though, even if other people think it is.

"Thanks for letting me join the group. I really appreciate it."

He joins me as I walk over to the larger trash can by the door and toss the bag in. "Don't you have any lady friends you could discuss your woes with?"

"Don't you have any other lady friends besides this group?"

"My friend Shannon. That's pretty much it. I'm sort of close with my cousin, but she just got married."

"Is that why you started the group?"

"I started it when all of my friends were marrying themselves off or being coupled and having babies. I'll admit I felt a little left out, even though I never want to be married. It doesn't mean I don't want to be in a relationship." Why am I sharing all this information with him? He *is* easy to talk to, but I'm usually not so forthcoming. He's like a human vacuum, and he's pulling all the dirt out of me. Before the end of the night, I'll probably have told him the color of my underwear.

"I get what you mean. A lot of the men I know are married as well. I'm forty-two and single. Most single men my age are that way because they're divorced. Most I know have kids too."

"Kids. I don't intend to have any of those." I shake my hand, waving off any curse that comes with the word kids. Even though I'm on birth control, it's a real fear. The best way to scare me is to show me a positive pregnancy test and have it be mine. I know if it happened, I probably would feel different and become an all-star soccer mom. But, if I can avoid a jam-packed schedule of school activities and feeding an additional mouth, I will.

"My best friend has two boys and they're quite a handful.

They're great when they're somebody else's." I've sat with them a few times when Shannon ran an errand or two and I barely thought I would make it through the hour. People say it's different when they're your own, but I don't want to test that theory.

He moves closer to me and touches my arm, making me suddenly aware of my heartbeat. "I can appreciate that. My brother has a set of twins. They're eight and think they're going on seventeen."

I inhale him at that moment, the rich aroma of his cologne tickling my nose. Even coming from the gym he smells amazing, and I'm transported to the lake with the sweet and salty scent. I open my eyes once I realize I closed them.

"Are you okay?"

Shit. My smell session didn't go unnoticed. "Yeah. I'm fine." I take a glance around the room and I think we cleaned everything up. "Thanks for coming." I put an end to this weird silence that lingered between us.

"Like I said before, thanks for letting me. And thank you very much for the job. Work has been a little bit slow."

I got the impression from his reviews online he keeps pretty busy, so this is a bit of a shock to hear. "I hope you're good."

"Oh, I *am*." He knocks his elbow into mine.

Is he flirting with me? I don't think that would be so bad. But while we've never had a man in the group, I'm constituting a rule: no dating within the group, just like at work. It can only mean trouble.

Chapter Thirteen

Keith arrives at my office two weeks later on a Monday morning right on time. He seems a little out of place in my office wearing his blue jeans and T-shirt that has his company name written on it. Everyone here fancies up in their suits or skirts, even in the IT department, so he sticks out. Though next to Lucas, he's the only one in the department who makes me turn my head. Everyone here is super young, with the exception of me and Terrence. I'm surrounded by children practically straight out of college. It'll be nice to work with another person who has a little bit more experience in life.

"I hope you had a good weekend, Keith." I greet him with a handshake. He's been to two meetings now and everyone seems to like him. He's okay, I guess. I can tolerate him just fine. I'm still getting used to a masculine presence in the group. The other women fawn over him like he's the answer to all their problems. I'll admit he's nice to listen to, but I don't want him pushing me away as leader of the group.

"It was okay. I'm doing some work around the house, so I was able to get that done. You?"

"Nothing exciting. Same old, same old." And that's certainly the truth. I worked, but that's a normal night for me. My emails never seem to stop, and there's always some fire I have to help put out. People can complain all they want about turning off cell phones and putting down the tablets, but the truth is, I work almost all the time. I need mine. Shannon jokes that it's an extension of my body, but really it is.

"If you want to point me in the right direction, I can get started." He crosses his arms and his muscles round even more. Is he flexing and doing this on purpose, or are they like this in their natural state?

I take the plans Lucas drew up from my desk. I unroll them on my desktop and Keith stands next to me. I didn't expect him to smell this good. Even the cotton from his shirt relaxes me. He's got my attention.

"Here's what we're looking to do. You'll have to reroute the wires from here," I reach across him and brush his arm. "To here. Is that something you can easily do?"

"Definitely." He scratches the top of his nose and points to where I'm pointing. I don't know if it's an accident that his fingertip touches mine. "Although I think it may be a better option if I start here." He moves my finger to the left a little bit and I tingle in places I shouldn't be while at work.

"Start where?" Lucas enters my office, his hands in his pockets as though this is *his* office. Smug.

"Lucas, I'd like you to meet Keith. He'll be handling the electrical portion of our project." I cross-point to each of them.

The two shake hands and I swear one of them grunts. I'm not sure which one. "Hi, Lucas. I was just telling Cassie that I think we should move this over here."

"You're the electrician." Lucas doesn't look at Keith. He only shrugs and turns to me like he's not even in the room. "Hey Cassie, since you missed out on our meeting the other week, I thought maybe you would want to go out tonight for drinks and discuss this further?"

"Is there anything left to talk about? Since we're going ahead with everything, I'm pretty sure we're all set."

"There are some other projects I want to discuss with you. I thought instead of going straight to Terrence, you and I could go over them first. I know how upset you were when he and I made the decision to move ahead with this without your input."

Oh, so *now* he's considering my opinion. I pick at my shirt pulling off lint that really isn't there. Keith doesn't need to know how things work around here. He's here to do his job, not get dirt on how incompetent Lucas wants to make me look. "Is this something we can discuss in your office?"

Lucas looks between me and Keith again and nods his head like a secret code exists between them. "Why don't you just come out with me tonight? I feel bad about last week. I'll buy."

I don't have anything going on tonight unless watching *Dancing with the Stars* counts. I look forward to my Monday nights in front of my TV on my iPad watching celebrities dance. Lucas is staring at me, waiting for a decision, and his hypnotizing eyes plead with me. What if it leads somewhere other than work? When we're here I can be professional and his age is forefront on my mind. Take us out of this building and he's some guy I'm with at a bar or restaurant. I can't miss out again, though. "Fine."

"Don't make it sound like it's the worst possible way to spend your evening."

Keith chuckles in the background. I guess I could have been a little less forceful with my answer. "Sorry. I didn't mean for it to sound that way."

"How about you meet me at The Spot around six?"

We're done here at five, but I'm sure I'll have enough to keep me busy until then. That gives Keith a little extra time to work as well. "That's sounds great."

"Okay! I'm looking forward to it. Keith, nice to meet you and I'll let you get back to it." He gives a small wave and leaves the room. Good. I can get back to discussing the plans with Keith.

"Sounds like you have yourself a date tonight." Keith sits down and taps his fingers on the chair.

"What? This is not a date. We're simply having a meeting to discuss projects that need to be done." I'm glad, too. I don't want him upstaging me every chance he gets. Maybe we can even come up with some ideas to present to Terrence together. Become a power team. But then we have to work together, not against one another. This can be a great opportunity if I use it correctly.

He shakes his head. "Nope." He accentuates the P with a popping sound. "That Lucas guy is into you."

"I highly doubt it. And even if he is, he's *way* too young for me." I'm *not* a cougar. I'm into guys my own age. Mature men who own their own homes and can buy a car and their own alcohol. Sure. Lucas *can* buy his own drinks, but barely. "Didn't you come here to work?" I pull my lips together to avoid a smile.

"Hey, I'm only calling it like I see it. I wouldn't be surprised if he's the next person you talk about in our meeting."

Whoa. This is territory he doesn't have permission to hone in on yet. We've known each other all of a few weeks and he's trying to judge me? The smile I almost cracked is now tucked far away. "Do me a favor. Let's keep the meetings and work separate from each other. I don't want to co-mingle the two."

He slips the paper from my desk and rolls it back up, tucking it under his arm. "Like you don't want to mix business with pleasure like you are tonight?"

"Please leave my office and start working." I don't have to sit and listen to this. He doesn't know my work ethic or beliefs. And I don't need to defend myself to him, either.

"Are you always this bossy?" He asks as he stands up, sliding his hands into his pockets with a big grin.

"I'm *not* bossy." Sure, I may be a manager, but being a manager doesn't automatically make me bossy.

"Oh, yes, I remember now. Women refer to that as being leaders now, right? You don't like to be called that anymore."

I can't believe this guy. So not only is he sarcastic and kind of a jerk, but he's also sexist. He's giving me a deal on the work, but that doesn't give him the right to talk to me that way. "Where do you get your news? Twitter?" I doubt he even knows what Twitter is with his small town attitude. "Anyway, here's an entry card into the server room. You'll need this to get in and out. If you walk out of my office and make a left, you can take the stairs to the basement."

"You're banishing me to the basement?"

"That's where the server room is." And good riddance. Then I don't have to deal with his chauvinism.

He takes the key from my hand. "Okay, then. I'm sure I won't see you down there. I don't think you're someone who would find her way to the basement."

"Trust me, I've been down there plenty of times. I've spent days down there. Be here when there's an outage of some sort." I don't know why I'm letting him get to me and finding it necessary to defend myself.

"Have fun on your date tonight."

As he leaves the room, I shout, "It's not a date!"

At least I don't think it is.

Chapter Fourteen

I'm out the door a few minutes before six, and Lucas is already there. He's sitting at the bar with a drink in his hand and, surprisingly, not talking to anybody. The way he is at work I assumed he would be more sociable and chatting with at least the bartender, if not women who probably flock to him. I've imagined him as the frat guy always surrounded by a group of sorority sisters. He's the life of the party, kicking butt at beer pong, the crowd shouting his name. Never did I consider he'd be the lone patron at the bar.

I tap him on the shoulder and he turns his head to me. "I actually thought that I would beat you here."

"I didn't have a doubt in my mind that I would be here first. I'm always on time."

I slide onto the barstool. "Me, too. Most days I'm early. It's not even six yet."

"A woman who is early? You don't need all that extra time to work on your hair and makeup?"

What is it with men today? Do I have a sign around my neck that states I enjoy being talked to like this? "That's a pretty sexist comment."

"I didn't mean to offend you." He grabs a beverage napkin and places it in front of me. "For what it's worth, I think you look pretty fine."

Fine. I forgot about our age difference for like a minute. That's a term I would never use. "Thank you." I won't decline the compliment. Those are hard to come by these days.

"Besides, I should admit that I snuck out early."

"Which you were able to do because you're the boss' pet."

"I'm *hardly* Terrence's pet. Just because we're related doesn't mean he'll treat me any differently than he treats you."

I order a gin and tonic while I formulate my response. "Actually, that's exactly what it means. Of course he'll treat you differently.

He'll listen to your ideas more than he'll listen to mine, and he'll consider all of your ideas first. I'm sure you'll never run into any issues with him."

"My uncle happens to adore you."

"Your uncle? So you're referring to him as your uncle now?"

"I guess I can. We're not at work."

"But technically this is a work function between you and me."

"Is it?" He takes a drink and smiles at me when he sets it down on the counter.

I take my drink from the bartender and hold it in my hand, the glass cold against my skin. Damn if Keith wasn't right. Lucas thinks this is a date. "Yes. This is a work meeting. That's it. Nothing more." Let's get that out of the way.

Lucas cocks his head and rests his head on his hand. "You don't like me very much, do you?"

My drink slides down my throat wrong, and I begin coughing. I pat my chest as I try to regain control.

"Are you okay?" He slaps my back like I'm a baby, forcing me to put my hands up to ask him to stop.

"Yeah, I'm fine." I ask the bartender for a glass of water and that soothes my now scratchy throat. "I'm surprised by your question, that's all."

"Really? I think your dislike for me is pretty obvious."

"I don't dislike you, Lucas." Do I? He's interrogating me, his magical eyes winning me over minute by minute, his smooth skin begging for me to touch it. I want to hate him. I want to *strangle* him. But the woman in me wants to rip his clothes off and touch every inch of what's underneath. Damnit, why am I so attracted to him? His gorgeous face combined with his rippling body and sharp brain make him hard to resist physically. So *do* I dislike him? Because he wants to take my job, yes. Otherwise, I want every part of him.

"Come on, now." He crosses his arms and leans back on his stool. "The second I waltzed into your office you had my head on a stick. Why?"

I'm warming up to him, slowly, but my desire to see him fail isn't something I want to discuss. I switch from my water back to my drink, finish it off, and order another.

"Slow down. We've only just gotten here. You may want to

moderate yourself when it comes to your drinks."

"You have no idea what I can handle." This young kid hasn't seen anything in life, raised in a well-off family and earning scholarships to big schools and jobs landing in his lap. Try living without knowing who your father is, a drug-addict mother, and then after freeing yourself from it all, spiraling into a life of overeating. I overcame it, and that's why I'm a survivor.

"Is that a challenge?"

I really didn't mean for it to sound that way. "Lucas, you're like, what, twenty-two years old?"

"Just turned last week."

"You're a baby."

"Last time I checked I feed myself, rent my own apartment, have a full-time job, and am built like a man."

Even though a young man lies beneath those clothes, I don't doubt he's built like a man in every sense of the word. But he's seventeen years younger than me. That is wrong on so many levels. "It doesn't change the fact that we work together. So let's enjoy our drinks together and discuss work like we intended."

"I never intended to talk about work. This isn't a job interview." His demeanor changes to that of a professional recruiter. "Where do you see yourself in five years? What goals have you set out to accomplish? What is your greatest strength? What is your greatest weakness?" He teases me in a deep, serious tone. "Really, Cassie, there's not much to discuss. The pilot project was the main project, which I have now taken over, and now you're focusing on your smaller projects while I put my energy into this one."

He's one-hundred percent correct. There really is nothing for us to discuss. "I guess I'll finish my drink then and get out of here."

"Why? Why don't you stay and we can get to know each other? You don't have anything going on."

"How do you know that?"

"Well, for one you agreed to meet me here so that tells me you don't have anywhere else to be. Just stay and have a few drinks. No strings attached."

I don't get out very often unless it's with Shannon, and that's so hard to accomplish half the time with all of her kid's activities. And ever since my cousin got engaged, she kind of fell off the face of the earth. Now that she's married, I never see her. I don't hang out with anyone from my Dating for Decades group, so unless I do want to go home and watch *Dancing with the Stars* by myself, I guess this really is all I have to do. Although I'm not totally against lying on my couch and watching TV. At least I can open up my iPad and get some work done.

"Come on, Cassie. Just do it."

"Peer pressure and a Nike slogan. I guess you sold me."

"Great. Let's get you a refill."

"Should we grab a table?" My butt is getting sore from sitting on the barstool.

"No. Let's stay here. I like the bar."

We're so close to one another I can practically feel his breath on my neck. I curve my body to the right so I distance myself a little. "Fine." I loop my feet around the bars on the bottom of the stool. He scoots his stool over. I have to say something. "I'm okay with sticking around for a while, but enough with the flirting, though, okay?"

"Flirting? I'm not flirting." He puts his hand to his chest and raises his voice. "If I were flirting," he leans in, "you'd know."

He whispers the words and I know right then and there he's telling me something. I'll ignore it. If I don't show interest, maybe he'll stop. "So, what would you like to talk about?"

"It's not like I have a list to pull out of my pocket."

"You were the one who wanted me to get a refill. You direct the conversation." He seems like the kind who wants to take charge. I'll let him do so right now.

"Okay." He scratches his chin as he thinks up a topic. "Tell me how you got started at the company."

I cross my legs and there he goes looking at them again. "Well, I started at the help desk like *most* tech people." I don't think he even pays attention to the fact that I've emphasized the word most. He should have started off at the help desk as well. But, that's neither here nor there at this point. "I worked my way up the ladder. I built a relationship with your uncle, and proved myself to him many times over."

"He speaks very highly of you."

"Does he speak of me often?" I can't think of any circumstance why Terrence would even need to discuss me with anybody in his family.

"When I spoke with him about coming on, he raved about you. He really did struggle with giving me the main portion of the pilot project."

My eyes leave his and I focus on my glass. Knowing Terrence didn't hand the job to him without any thought has me rethinking my stance on Lucas. Could it be he's not a bad guy? I may have allowed my anger mask my image of him. I know he didn't have some master plan from years ago to come and take my job. Things worked out in his favor he ended up here. Should I hold his success against him?

"He knows how important it is to you, and that you would do a great job with it. But I think he has the impression you're overworked."

"Overworked? How do you mean?" I'm refocused on him, shocked over what I'm hearing. I think I do a pretty damn good job of holding myself together and meeting deadlines. This project got the best of me, and it has never happened before. I'm professional, ethical, and focused. You don't get where I am today by being the opposite. I can't imagine a time I could have come across as burned out, or close to it anyway.

"You work all the time. My uncle is the Chief Technology Officer and he doesn't even work as much as you do. Let me guess. If you were at home right now, instead of out with a handsome guy like me, you'd be sitting at home, with your laptop, and working."

I look down at my drink. And then I take one. And then another one.

"Ha! I totally got it right didn't I? You're a workaholic. They have groups for that you know."

I'm not about to admit that I already belong to a group for women thirty and over who haven't been in a committed relationship and don't think they ever will be. Although I suppose now it's just people and not just women since Keith came along "Enough about me. You seem to have a very high opinion of yourself. Tell me something that you're bad at. What *can't* Lucas do?"

"I would say I'm not able to get you to go out on a date with me, but, it seems we're already here, whether you think so or not. There's not a lot that I'm *not* able to do. I truly believe that if you put your mind to something, you can make it happen."

"So, there's absolutely, positively, nothing you *can't* do?"

Of all the things to stump him on, this is not one that makes me happy. How arrogant does he have to be? I can think of a thousand things I can't do, but you bet your ass that I'd give them all a shot.

"I've got it!" He takes a swig of his drink and pounds it back on the table. "I can't birth a child."

And he takes the easy way out. "That's cheating."

"How is that cheating? You asked me to name something I can't do. I physically cannot birth a child. That's an honest answer."

"You know what I meant."

"I may know what you meant, but that's not what you asked me."

"What on earth does that mean?"

"That means you asked me to name something I cannot do. What you should have asked me was to name something I'm unable to do in relation to work. Or to name something I've tried that I've been unable to accomplish."

"You're telling me that I need to be that specific with you in order to get an answer?"

"It's more fun that way." He clicks his teeth and taps my knee. I surprisingly don't pull it away. "How about another drink?"

Technicalities. He's getting away with this on a technicality. That's so incredibly frustrating. Lucas irritates me to no end. But there's something about this guy. While his remarks are a tad annoying, he kind of lightens up the mood. I'm laughing and actually enjoying myself. I can't believe it, but I let him order me another drink.

A couple of drinks later, and we're adding dinner to our little outing. We both order a cheeseburger and fries to share. To *share*. I hope that Lucas realizes what type of a commitment that is for me. I don't share my fries.

"Well, your uncle tells me you just graduated. Where did you graduate from?"

"University of Wisconsin – Milwaukee. I was able to attend mostly on scholarships. My parents made me start applying as early as I could, and they managed to pay for most of my tuition. The rest of the time I worked odd jobs and fixed computers around the dorms to make some extra cash. It came in handy because I was able to get a car and find a place to rent."

"Impressive. Is your degree in networking?"

He takes a bite of his fry. "Programming, actually. It just seemed to interest me more at the time. But I can't really see spending all my time living in a basement while I code things. I really think I want to take the same path you're on."

So this is it. This confirms he wants my job. I've now lost my appetite, thoughts of my being fired swirling in my brain.

"I don't want your job."

"Can you read my mind?" I never thought I had a *bad* poker face. I'm not the best at lying, but I don't suck at it.

"My uncle got me this job because I need to stay close to home right now. My dad is sick, and I'm helping take care of him."

"I had no idea. Is that Terrence's brother?"

"No. My mom's. My plan is to move out-of-state, but not until..."

"You don't have to say it. That's pretty commendable. Especially at your age."

"I may be small in number, but I'm pretty damned grown up. I've got my head on straight, money in the bank, and I'm smart."

And horny, I want to add. But this doesn't seem like the appropriate time. Taking care of a parent is something I have never done nor want to do. I wonder if my mother is curious why I haven't replied to her. I shake the thought away. Why do I care? Just because I'm here with a twenty-two-year-old man who has a close family and loves his dad enough to take care of him when he's sick doesn't mean I should feel any shred of guilt about my mother. *She* is the one who is covered in guilt and shame. Not me.

"Look, let's get out of here. Let's do something fun." He takes my plate and shoves it aside as he motions for the check. "I'm sick of chatting. I honestly could talk for hours. Let's blow off some steam."

There are only two ways I blow off steam — yoga and sex. I wonder what he has in mind, and if it'll get me in trouble because if there's one thing I *don't* want, it's to do something I'll regret.

Chapter Fifteen

I slide my arm through the vest and fasten it in the front, careful when I detach the phaser from the clip, as though it's a real gun. When Lucas mentioned relieving stress, laser tag was the last thing I had in mind. The flashing is playing with my mind, and I'm worried vertigo may set in. I practice my pranayama breaths as I wait for the rest of the participants to prep.

"Is this your first time?" Lucas holds up his phaser and practices aiming it. I'm really going to suck at this.

There are so many things that go through my mind with that question. No, I've never done something like this and I never intended to in my life. I'm pretty sure I've passed that stage in my life to participate in things like this. Being stealth in the dark while trying not to get shot is not really my idea of a good time. I'd much prefer to be sharing a glass of wine over my TV show. I didn't want to admit my obsession with *Dancing with the Stars*, but that may have been a better option.

"It's okay if you've never done this, Cassie. I'll walk you through it."

The two other people who are joining us in our game keep putting on their gear but look over at me, and I'm sure they're judging me. The young couple, so madly in love, trying to impress each other. The woman is tall, sun-kissed hair falling in curls over her shoulder. The man looks like he's straight out of a heavy metal band. But they're young, agile, and easily entertained.

Why couldn't Lucas's friend own a coffee shop or a bookstore or anything other than something that involves running around like a teenager? I'd even a settle for a comic book store and force myself to read the latest Superman comic.

"No, I've done this before." I brush off his doubt in me quickly to avoid showing my depressing poker face. "It's been a while, that's all." As in thirty-nine years.

"Probably since college, right? So almost twenty years?"

I point my gun at him and pretend to shoot. "You better watch yourself, boy. Never ask a woman her age and *definitely* never comment on it if you want to survive."

Valley Girl and Bret Michaels giggle and the girl whispers something to the boy. This behavior annoys me. We're standing three feet from them. Whispering is very impolite.

Lucas takes a hold of the gun and moves it out of his way so he can approach me. "We're on the same team. Don't worry, amateur, I'll protect you." His lips meet my cheek, and I slightly bow my head when he pulls away. Now I'm certain he's flirting with me and even I have to admit it's not the worst thing in the world.

"Well, let's meet our opponents." I reach my hand out to the woman. "I'm Cassie and this is Lucas."

"I'm Renee and this is my boyfriend Marty."

"Oh! Like Marty McFly!" *Back to the Future* is one of my favorite movie franchises. Michael J. Fox was always one of my crushes from *Family Ties* to his movies. I once wished my boyfriend in high school was *Teen Wolf*. Lucas, Renee, and Marty all stare at me as if I'm speaking another language. "Sorry, before your time." Am I really this old? I want to start this game already.

"Isn't there supposed to be a third team?" Marty, who looks nothing like Michael J. Fox with his blonde hair pulled back into a ponytail and a mustache he's trying so hard to grow above his lip, asks Lucas.

"Yeah, but it's a slow night and my buddy who runs the place doesn't really care if it's two on two."

Techno music begins to play through the speakers in the room. This is what I have to listen to for the entire event? I'm really starting to regret what I signed up for. This is loud and obnoxious.

"Okay, players, this is your Game Master." A deep voice takes over the room. "You will enter the arena through the door on your left. Please find your base. Blue team you are base one. Red team you are base two. You will collect points by shooting at each other and trying to destroy each other's base. The game will last fifteen minutes and you will hear an announcement when the game is over. You will then find the exit, which will bring you back to this room. Remember, there is no running in the arena, do not climb on anything or you will be disqualified, no physical contact, no lying down, and no foul language. This *is* a family facility. You're here to have fun. Just remember that."

I didn't realize that this game had so many rules. I imagined us running around and shooting each other. I hope I don't have to be too strategic because I don't know how well I can do that in the dark.

The person on the loudspeaker begins speaking again. "You'll hear a buzzer, which will allow you to open the door and proceed to your base."

The buzzer sounds and I follow Lucas to our base, which is base one. We huddle in the corner, and I can hear him breathing. It's not as dark as I anticipated, and I can still make out his face.

"What are we waiting for?" I whisper.

Another buzzer sounds and I jump, almost knocking Lucas over. "Sorry."

"It's okay. You go left and I'll go right." He not only has to direct me at work, but he has to direct me here, too. "Cassie, what are you doing? I can already see the red flashing lights coming towards us. Go, go, go!"

Adrenaline shoots through my body, and my heart is pumping overtime. I dart out of the covered area and quickly close the gap between my steps when I realize I'm running. *No running.* That was the first rule. The music is blaring, and I can't hear Lucas or any of my opponents. I'm being hunted by Marty McFly and his girlfriend and quite honestly, with a flashing vest, there's not really anywhere to hide. I slide against a wall and crouch down. I can wait here until I see the red lights coming toward me. Then I can shoot and keep shooting until I'm out of sight. I think it's a good strategy.

I'm waiting for what feels like hours, but I'm sure was only less than two minutes, when I hear footsteps. Someone's coming my way, but I can't see any lights flashing. Which way are they coming from? "Lucas?" I say in a loud whisper. "Lucas? Is that you? I'm over here."

I begin to stand and as the muscle tenses in my leg I realize crouching was probably not a good idea. When I'm finally in an upright position, I stretch my body and my bones crack. I get my phaser to be safe. The beating of my heart thumps so hard I can feel it between my ears. I force a swallow, as hard as it is.

"Gotcha!"

I scream as a flash of red lights appear in front of me and shoots me in the front of my vest. I aim my gun and nothing happens. "I can't shoot! I can't shoot!" I pound on the gun and try again. "What's going on? Why isn't this working?"

"Cassie," I hear Lucas running up behind me. "You can't shoot for ten seconds. Hide!"

I panic and bolt to the right, away from whomever shot me. I'm running and I realize this is against the rules, but I need to hide like Lucas said. I'm using my hand to maneuver around the arena and as I turn a corner I smack right into somebody and fall on my ass.

"Are you okay?" It's Lucas. He reaches his hand out and pulls me up, though my worn out body takes a second to find its balance again.

"Yeah. Are you?"

"I'm fine. You weigh like a hundred and twenty pounds. I didn't even budge."

I'm flattered that he thinks I'm only a hundred and twenty pounds, but a little more than slightly embarrassed about how I freaked out and knocked right into him. "I'm sorry about that. I kind of panicked when I got hit."

"Remember that I said I would protect you?"

"Yes."

"Wait here." Lucas steps in front of me and aims his gun at the opponent coming toward us. He shoots everywhere he can, in the shoulder, on the front, on their phaser. Both Marty and Renee are frozen. Lucas grabs my hand and we quickly make our way to their base. "Shoot the base! Keep shooting!"

I take his direction and pull the trigger. I shoot until the lights go out. Lucas wraps his arm around my waist and yanks me so I'm against his body. "I'm pretty sure we've won."

I think so too, and I can't believe it, but I think I'm having the time of my life, and I don't want the evening to end.

•••

My head hurts. *Really* hurts. Like I feel like it's going to crack open and my eyes are going to pop out hurts. I drank *way* too much last night. The sun blinds me and I cover my eyes as fast as I can to avoid it. "I don't want to get up..."

"Well, tough luck. You have to."

I widen my eyes to Lucas standing next to the bed in boxer shorts, his perfect six-pack bulging out, among other things, and he's handing me a cup of steaming, hot coffee. "Lucas?"

"That's me. In the flesh. I bet you're suffering from quite the headache."

"Yeah..." I manage to sit up and take the coffee from him. This roast is amazing. Dark, fresh, perfection. The second the coffee splashes into my mouth, my headache starts disappearing. "What happened last night?"

His eyes pop. "You don't remember?" He rubs the top of his head. "Damn, I wish you could."

"We ... " and I *do* remember. I wasn't *that* drunk. After laser tag, we came back to his place for a few drinks. We laughed and played Never Have I Ever until there were hands everywhere, lips on every inch of our bodies, touching, clothes ripping off, the passion so strong I could barely breathe. I hoped it was all a dream. "Damn it. I broke my rule."

"What rule?"

I sip my coffee and don't make eye contact. "To never get involved with a coworker." And such a young one, at that.

"I'm glad you broke it. Last night was totally worth it. I don't think I'll ever forget it. This was my first time with such an ... experienced woman."

"Did you just call me old?" I slam my hand onto the covers and my coffee spills onto the sheets. "Sorry."

"That's fine, and no, I didn't call you old. I called you experienced. Two entirely different things. Girls my age, they're not as ... "

I shake my head and wave my finger at him as I drink more coffee. "I don't want to hear it. Never talk about other women, especially with the woman currently in your bed."

"Sorry. Again."

Who is this guy? The Lucas I left the bar with was much more forward and confident. He wouldn't apologize and he'd be downright cocky about his sexual encounters. "I do remember. And yes, it was pretty damned amazing."

I can't remember the last time I had sex like that. And multiple times. Lucas is built in all the right places and is gentle and patient. No. No. No! He's my co-worker, and this can't happen again. I'm a sex addict, aren't I? My mom was addicted to drugs and got HIV and ... oh no. "We used a condom, right?"

"Of course. I'm young, but I'm *not* stupid."

I breathe a sigh of relief. I don't want to end up like my mother.

Ugh, my mother. I can't believe I'm sitting here in this gorgeous man's bed, and I'm thinking about my shitty excuse of a mother. This is probably something she would do. I lay my head back on the pillow, gripping my coffee so it doesn't spill again. I haven't thought about her and that letter in quite awhile. Maybe I *should* face her. I can yell at her and tell her all the horrible ways she made me feel. It may be therapeutic.

"Are you okay, Cassie? You haven't said anything in a few minutes." Lucas sits down next to me on the bed.

"I'm fine." I sit back up and shake off the thoughts of my mother that are invading my brain at such an inopportune time. "What time is it?"

"Almost seven-thirty."

"Seven-thirty! I need to be to work before eight to let Keith in." I hand him my mug. "There's not enough time to go home and change." My eyes dart around the room. "Where the hell are the rest of my clothes?" At least I'm in underwear and a bra right now. I lift the sheets enough to confirm I'm in my cotton white panties. And not the bikini cut. The high cut. The grandma cut. Of course.

Lucas points out the bedroom door. "In the kitchen. On the table. Where it all started."

Oh, yes. I told him I always dreamed of someone tossing the items off a table and screwing me on it. And he did just that. And then again on the couch, and then we made gentle love in the bedroom. Man, he could have gone all night, but by the time 1:00 AM rolled around , this old lady needed some sleep.

I hop out of bed paying no mind to my ratty underwear giving my butt plenty of coverage. My blouse is on the counter, my skirt on the back of the kitchen chair, my shoes ... aha! Placed ever so nicely on the stove. I slide the heels on and realize I don't have my car. It's still at the office.

"Do you need a ride?"

"Are you kidding me? We can't show up there together. I'll take the bus. It's not that far." What do I do here? A kiss goodbye? No. This isn't a relationship. We're not a thing. One time. This won't happen again. "Okay. Bye." My hand struggles to wave, and finally, one escapes.

The bus ride seems to take forever, and I swear everyone aboard is eyeing me up and down in my walk of shame. I tug my skirt closer to my knees, a patch of dirtiness dusting my body. I could practically be Lucas' mother. His *mother*. Every person within judgment range knows this, I'm certain. I've made a horrible, disgusting, satisfying mistake. Gosh, I needed to get laid in the worst way, but I should've known better. I'm the adult here.

I rush off the bus as soon as it arrives a block from my building. I didn't realize how quickly I can run in heels. I catch myself from falling outside the office when I misjudge the level of the sidewalk. I swing open the door and race to the elevator.

I catch my breath during the ride up to my floor, thankful I'm the only one in the elevator. The bell dings and the door opens. The gap is barely large enough for me to fit, but I sneak through and bump into Terrence.

"Oh, Terrence, I'm so sorry." My purse falls onto the floor and I quickly reach down and grab it.

"Why are you in such a rush?"

"I woke up a little bit late this morning and the contractor is supposed to be here by eight." I point toward my office.

Terrence thumbs in my office's direction. "Keith? He's already here. He's been here for a half hour. I like that guy. He seems like a good worker."

Is he already here? I told him not to arrive until eight. How early did he arrive? "I'm sorry he got here so early. I hope you weren't disturbed."

"Not at all. He was outside the building and we walked in together. He's an interesting guy, has a lot to say."

You've got that right, I think to myself. I hope he didn't say too much and mention the group to my boss. That's a part of my life I try to keep separate from here. It's not that I'm embarrassed. I mean, I founded the group, but my love life is no concern to my boss.

"Cassie, if I'm not mistaken, those are the same clothes you wore yesterday aren't they?"

Crap. Not like he has any way of knowing I spent the night with his nephew, but this is completely unprofessional. Is this outfit that out there that he would even notice? Men don't notice those things. It's not in their DNA to pinpoint a change in hairstyle, a new outfit, or that their significant other is even speaking to them. Selective eyesight *and* hearing. "This old skirt and blouse? No. It's new. Well not new, because I've had them for a while. By new I mean that I didn't wear it yesterday. I wore something else yesterday, and I'm wearing something different today. In that respect, it's new." *Stop rambling, Cassie. You're making it worse.*

He shoves his hands in his pockets. "Whatever you say. I should get back to work."

I sigh in relief when he walks away. That was a close one. I practically race to my office and Keith is seated at my desk, hovering over the server room plans.

"You're early."

"You're late."

"Touché." I hang my purse on my coat hanger. "But, if you're planning on arriving before eight in the future, please call or text me."

"That sounds a great idea. Why didn't I think of that? Wait!" He snaps his fingers. "You never gave me your contact information. You have mine, but I don't have yours. And isn't that the same outfit you were wearing yesterday?"

The one day I wear the same outfit as the previous, every man suddenly develops a photographic memory. "No."

He eyes me up and down. "I'm pretty sure that's the same outfit. I guess drinks went a little bit better than expected?"

"Excuse me? That's none of your business. Drinks were fine, for your information. We met, drank, and went to our respective houses. Now I'm here today in a brand-new outfit."

He smiles smugly at me, and while I hope I fooled him, I'm not so sure.

"Knock, knock." Lucas raps his hand on the door and invites himself in. *He sure got her quick. When I left he was still in his boxers.* "I wanted to check in and make sure everything is on schedule."

Sure. That's what he wanted. It's getting to be a big, old party in my office. "Everything is perfect. Thank you."

"Sounds great. It's a beautiful day, isn't it?" He's staring straight at me. I don't know if he could make this more obvious than he already is. For a young man who seems so grown-up, he really isn't well-versed on being discreet.

Keith stands up from my desk and knocks on the table. "For some more than others." He breezes past me and hangs in the doorway for a moment. "We'll check in later."

He leaves the room, leaving me with an awkwardly happy Lucas and my realization that Lucas may be expecting a little bit more than only one night.

Chapter Sixteen

Fine. I'll take everyone's advice and take the night off. September has been welcomed with deadlines. The class is going well, and I'm even warming up to Keith in the group, but despite my yoga once a week, I'm feeling a little burned out. Admitting such a thing is a big step for me, but I refuse to confess this to anyone but myself. One evening off from work email and anything surrounding the office may do me some good.

The perfect evening for me is soft music playing in the background, a glass of wine, and my laptop. I have enough self-control to play around on the computer without finding work as a distraction. I think since I'm teaching a class centered around Facebook, maybe it's time I make a visit to the website myself.

I don't even remember my password since it's been so long since I've been on the site. I click the *Forgot Password* link and work through the steps to select a new one. I love creating new ones and do so every month for all of my logins. Most people are intimidated by the rules: a capital, special character, punctuation, and a mix of letters and numbers. I enjoy the challenge.

Once my password is reset, the screen welcomes me back after my long hiatus. The big empty box asks for a status update, but no one cares what I've been up to. I leave it blank. How many friends do I even have on here? I glance over at my "Friends" box and see a lonely seven. *Seven.* That's probably pretty accurate, anyway. A red bubble appears on top of the Friend Request icon. Seventy-six friend requests. Next to it I'm alerted to 459 notifications. I can't stand seeing these unanswered so I click on the button and select Clear All. Most are game notifications from Sasha, anyway. I'm not wasting my time going through all of this.

I select the friend requests, and most of them are people I've worked with in the past or people I went to high school with. I don't know why I would want to be friends with any of them. I wasn't the most popular kid in my class, but I wasn't an outcast either. I had a decent number of friends, but I was so different in high school and college, that Shannon is the only one I want to remain close with. I choose to ignore most of them, only approving a few. Then I see it.

Claire Noble wants to be friends with me. My mother. On Facebook. Requesting to be friends with me.

How am I supposed to react to this? As if the letter wasn't enough, she's now stalking me on here. I can't see when she sent the request. I wonder if it was before or after she sent the letter. I can't accept it. There's no way. That doesn't mean I'm not curious.

I click on her profile picture, which is a photo of a lotus. It takes me to her page, her cover photo an array of flowers. I'm surprised it's not a field of marijuana. I know she said she's clean, but I'm not so sure I believe her.

The first thing I click on is her photos. I need to see what she looks like now. It's been such a long time. The last time I saw her, she was withering away, very underweight with bloodshot eyes and thin hair.

Not anymore.

I'm a little shocked, and confused, to see photos of a beaming, healthy woman. Her hair is fuller now, though completely gray. Her eyes still appear tired, and she has wrinkles. But what else should I expect from a woman almost sixty years old? Many of the pictures are taken at different landmarks. It looks as though she's been to Las Vegas, Washington DC, New York, and even Italy! Where on earth did she get the money for any of this? Is she *selling* drugs now? Has she gone from taking them to thinking she's clean because she's only selling them? My mother, the Drug Lord.

I continue scrolling and stop at a photo of her standing with a gentleman who looks to be about her age with his arm around her. She's holding a bouquet of flowers. Did my mom get married? When? Why? She didn't believe in marriage much like I don't. We never even had a home. We stayed with whatever boyfriend she had at the time. Now she's married? Is she now some sort of a June Cleaver? That's an interesting combo — fifties housewife *and* a drug dealer.

I slam my laptop closed, the pictures making me feel sick to my stomach. But I have to see more. I open it back up and click off of the pictures and onto her friend list. I don't recognize any of the names, but there are quite a few. Over one hundred, in fact. I notice a button that says mutual and there's a one next to it. Who on earth would we be mutual friends with? I click the button.

My cousin, Sasha.

How long have they been friends on here? Why hasn't Sasha said anything to me about it? My mom said she used my cousin's return address, but could it be she actually lives with her? No. She's married now. But why isn't her last name changed? I can't even process this. I need to talk to Sasha about this.

•••

I enter into a dewy morning mist of freesia, lilies, and peonies. As much as I love my job, I'm a little jealous Sasha gets to spend her days surrounded by these amazing aromas and wonderful displays. The shop isn't busy this morning, and she's at her counter cutting stems and creating arrangements. I ran to the office and let Keith in and then headed right back out to Sasha's Scents & Stems. I slept on it last night, as much as I could anyway, and I kept coming to the same conclusion. I need answers.

"That arrangement is gorgeous," I compliment her on the vase full of hydrangeas, irises and moss green carnations. If I ever took the plunge, I think I would want something like that. Simple, contrasting, and blended nicely all at once. Sasha sure does amazing work.

"Cassie!" She sets her cutter down and meets me on the other side of the counter, embracing me. "How are you? It's so nice to see you!"

I return the hug, a light one with not a lot of emotion. I'm not sure how I feel about her right now. I'm partly mad she hid my mother from me, but I'm a little relieved at the same time. Besides, I have no idea how long she's known my mom has been around, so I may be jumping to conclusions. I don't want to pass any judgment until I have a few answers. "How's married life treating you?" That's what people normally ask, right?

"I love it! Garrett and I had such a marvelous time on the honeymoon, and I think we're ready to get to work on babies!" She jumps up and down, but I can't return the sentiment.

"Already?" She's so young. They've barely lived life and they want to add tiny human beings to the mix? Don't people usually give it at least through a full year of marriage before taking on such responsibility?

"Well, I can't very well wait until I'm in my thirties. I have a biological clock and it's certainly ticking!"

I bow my head down. I don't want kids, but I don't need another reminder of how old I am. Trust me, I know. And in less than a year, that number enters me into another decade.

"Oh... that was insensitive of me to say." She lifts her hand up to her mouth, then drops it to her heart. "Forgive me?"

"Yeah, it's fine. I know I'm almost forty."

"That seems *so* far away." She takes my hands and leads me around to the other side of the counter. I try my best not to squeeze her fingers and break them. Enough about my age.

"Tell me what brings you here. I hope you don't mind I work while you talk." She picks up baby's breath and places it in the vase. "Why aren't *you* at work?"

"My boss is pretty flexible. I have about an hour before I need to be back." Sasha doesn't leave the shop too much since she owns it. She has a few employees, but she runs it alone most of the time. I wish I was as successful as she is at this age. It took me until my thirties to get where she is already in her twenties.

"Well let's get chatting then. We don't have a ton of time!"

I grab a stool and sit down, placing my hands on my lap. I'm not sure why my heart is racing. I'm not afraid to ask her this. I want the answer and I want it now. "Have you been on Facebook lately?"

"Yes! I moved up a level in FarmVille!"

I'm assuming she wants a congratulations so I offer one. "Anyway, I haven't been on for quite a long time. I'm teaching a class at the library showing seniors how to use it."

"That sounds incredibly boring! You must teach them the games if they're going to have any fun on there."

"I'll make note of that." No, I won't. Teaching them how to use the site is difficult enough before throwing in the rules of a computer game. "I went on the other day and found some interesting information."

"Ooooh, an old boyfriend? A friend from grade school? A *crush?*" Times like these I'm so glad to be past this stage in my life. I don't want to gossip nor do I like it. Her voice is full of excitement like I'm about to give her the juiciest piece of information. Little does she know, she *is* the detail and the reason I am here.

"No. Not even close."

"What then? Who? Tell me!"

Sasha loves anything that may be even close to considered a scandal. I'm surprised she kept my mom a secret in the first place. Normally she would blab information like this everywhere. *Did you hear about Aunt Claire? Can you believe Cassie's mom has come around? I wonder how Cassie is handling this.* I can hear her already as she gets her nails done giving anyone within earshot the details. "My mom."

She stops arranging the flowers and sets her cutter back down, her beaming smile dropping into a long frown. "Oh."

"Oh?" Apparently she *was* hiding it from me. "How long have you two been friends on there? How long have you been in contact with her?" Now my heart rate speeds up and my hands are shaking.

She shrugs. "Maybe six months."

"Six months?" I jump off the stool and begin to pace the room. "You've been talking with her for half of a year and you didn't think to tell me?"

"I didn't know how to. I invited her to the wedding — "

"You *what?* And what would you have done had she shown up?" Of all the nasty things to do I can't believe she would even *think* it a good idea to put the two of us in a room together.

"Calm down, Cassie. She didn't come because she was afraid of how you would react."

"You think? It would *not* have been good. And what, does she get some sort of a medal for turning down the invitation? I can't believe you even would do that to me."

"With all due respect, *I* was the one getting married. It's not your decision who gets invited."

I glare at her and all I really want to do is punch her square in the face. This is my most reflective action toward anyone when they piss me off. I think it often, though I would never act on it. Violence isn't something I condone nor take part of, but it doesn't mean I don't ever have the urge to punch someone. "Do you even know what kind of a mother she was to me?"

"I do, and she's changed. She's clean now. My mom — "

"*Your* mom is talking to her again?"

"Kind of. She's working toward forgiveness." She picks at the petals of a flower and holds a stem between her fingers. She refuses to look at me, instead giving all of her attention to the daylily. The bright and open petals taunt me, trying to push their happy tone onto me in this situation. A few more changes to the arrangement and Sasha finally meets my eyes. "You should, too."

I lean against the counter and get in her face. I'm so close I can see her eye twitching. "Don't you tell me what to do. There is no way in *hell* I'm forgiving my mother. She robbed me of my childhood. For what? For a high?" Spit collects at the corners of my mouth. I suck in the saliva and back off, sitting back down in my chair.

"She's sick, you know." Her voice deflates in a state of concern, offering up the information as though it's something she's privy to and I'm not.

"Yes, I know, and I really don't care." I don't know if that's true or not, but it's the only emotion I'm capable of feeling right now.

"Wow. That's harsh. She really *is* clean, and she did it for you."

I highly doubt that. I'm sure if she had done it for me she would have contacted me months ago. Maybe invited me to *her* wedding. "I don't buy it."

"Well, don't then. But she did. And she's been scared to contact you. Why don't you two come to my place for dinner? It's a good common ground for you to talk."

"I doubt that's going to happen."

"Come on, Cassie. You don't have to stay long. Stay for dinner and leave if you're uncomfortable. It would mean a lot to her."

"Since when do I care about her feelings? She never cared about mine."

"That's not true."

"You have *no* idea."

She picks a rose from the fridge and hands it to me. "It's very freeing to forgive. Please. Come."

I prick my hand as I seize the rose from her. "I'll think about it." A small spot of blood forms on my palm, and I realize I've been bleeding on the inside this whole time, all these years. It was only a matter of time before it showed on the outside.

Chapter Seventeen

"I met this woman through a mutual friend." Keith scans the room for no one in particular. "She seemed nice. I took her to a fancy restaurant downtown. Not too fancy, like suit and tie and evening gown, but we still brought out our Sunday best. Dinner — amazing. We had appetizers, an entree, dessert, wine after. And she ate. I can't stand when I take a woman out and she picks at her food. She wasn't shy and cleaned her plate. I picked up the bill and suggested we take a stroll on the Riverwalk."

I haven't been on the Riverwalk for years. It winds along the Milwaukee River and offers a delicate breeze and delightful views of sailboats. A very romantic suggestion, and one I should keep in my back pocket. I'm trying my best to listen to Keith's story. Sharing is such an important part of our group and while I don't participate too often, I listen to the others and try to pick out key elements of the story we can expand upon. I'm lukewarm about Keith's date, not sure how I feel about listening to the other side of the spectrum. I'm not used to this.

"We're walking along fine, enjoying our conversation. At least I think we are." I straighten myself in my chair and widen my eyes in an effort to retain my focus. "We're laughing and telling jokes, sharing our thoughts on the presidential candidates, or lack of competent ones, at least. Then, as if out of nowhere, she tells me she's not attracted to me so it won't work and asks me to take her home."

Welcome to a woman's world is the first thing I think, but then I see the confusion in his eyes and I know he's hurt by this woman's words. He has a little scruff on his face, and I'm not hating this look. I love his image is so rough but clearly inside he's in pain. Okay, I don't like to see anyone in pain, but let's say the softer side does make him attractive.

"What were her exact words?" Luna asks.

"I'm not attracted to you. I don't think this will work."

"Wow. Just like that?" Cheyenne snaps her fingers.

"Just. Like. That."

"Well, I think you're hot," she compliments him.

"Cheyenne!" I can't believe she said that to him. I'm sure he's embarrassed and a tad humiliated someone in the group would act like that. And someone in her thirties, at that. Grown women don't need to be so loud about their attraction. We're not in high school with secret crushes and giggling whenever said crush passes by. And "hot" may be an accurate term, but "handsome" is a more mature use of the word.

"It's fine. You're not so bad yourself." He winks at her and for some reason, this upsets me.

"Does anyone else want to share?" I cut off this flirting between the two. I'm not having it in my group. No one answers, all looking at me like deer in headlights. "We can cut the meeting short if everyone is done."

"Are *you* okay, Cassie?" Keith asks out of the blue. He reaches his hand out and places his hand on mine, and I'm warmed by his touch. "You're a little distant tonight."

"I am?" I pull my hand out from under his and tuck my hair behind my ears. "No. Everything is fine. Nothing to report."

"No recent dates have gone bad ... or *really* good?"

He's talking about Lucas. I know he is.

"Oooh, who did you go out with?" Noelle crosses her legs and grips the side of her chair. She never says much during the meetings, but I guess my lack of discussion has piqued her interest.

It's not just Lucas, either. It's my mom. I have so much swirling in my head right now I don't know what bothers me more. On one hand, I had a fantastic night with a man much too young for me. He's hands-off because of his age *and* because he's related to my boss. And I don't *want* it to go anywhere. But, after months of being stuck in park, I'm ready to be driving again. I still have needs! On the other hand, I want to lock myself up in my house and shield myself from my mother, afraid maybe I'll run into her on the street. The situations are two extremes, and I don't want to deal with either of them.

"No one."

"Cassie, it's been awhile since you've shared and something is obviously bothering you. We're here for you." Monica soothes me with her motherly voice. She's kind of like the school nurse, counselor, and music teacher in the group. She'll bandage you if you're hurt, she'll offer an ear when needed, and she'll never pass up the chance to belt out "Soft Kitty."

She's right. As much as I hate other people being right, that she is. This group is my safe place. They want to hear what I have to say, otherwise, they wouldn't even be here. "I guess I can go."

"Yippee!" Cheyenne claps as though she's a child I told could stay up five minutes later.

I ignore Cheyenne's reaction as I decide how to approach this. Keith isn't dumb, but I still want to mask this if I can. "I went out with an old friend the other day."

"From where? You don't talk about many friends besides Shannon." Noelle points this out and I feel trapped already.

"Someone I worked with years back. Like a decade ago." Okay, I'll go with a half truth. "We ran into each other at the store and chatted for a while and thought we'd get together to catch up."

"So what happened?" Keith raises his voice in a curious tone.

What happened? I slept with my boss' nephew. That's what happened. I wish I could say that. If Keith weren't here, I probably would. I could be completely honest and gather the opinions of everyone in the group. Keith has only been to a few meetings and while I enjoy him being here, I now see the negative side. I can't allow my two worlds to collide. I must tread lightly. "We talked for hours, even played laser tag."

"*You* played laser tag?" Cheyenne can't believe it and either can I.

"I know, right? I felt so ... so *young*. Like I could take on the world. I'm apprehensive about my fortieth birthday. My bones are cracking and my hair is graying. For the first time in a long time, I acted like I was in my twenties again. After the game, we went back to his place, and before I knew it, I was waking up in his bedroom."

"Did you have a good time?" Luna asks.

"Yes, I did. It was amazing in so many ways, but I can't see him again. It's not a good idea."

"Why not?" Keith leans forward and rests his elbows on his knees, and his chin on his hands.

"It's not. It never is. My relationships are barely relationships. They last no longer than a month if that. This guy seems really into me, and I want to spare his feelings."

"That's awfully nice of you. You know for sure he's interested?" Keith acts as though someone being interested in me is out of the question.

"Well, I guess not for sure. He's super nice, though, and I'll admit, great in bed. He brought me coffee in the morning. We talked for a really long time."

"And you can't see this going anywhere?" Cheyenne gets up and grabs a bottled water. "He sounds pretty dreamy to me."

He *is* dreamy, if I were twenty years younger. My adolescent self would have dated him for a few months, slept with him numerous times, and broke things off when the next guy came along. I don't mind casual relationships. That's all I do. A romantic relationship with someone so young and a coworker, though, are two touchy areas. Combining them is a recipe for disaster.

"I don't want to start a relationship I know won't go anywhere."

"How do you know it won't go anywhere unless you try?"

Keith makes an excellent point, but as attracted to Lucas as I am, that doesn't change the fact that he's Terrence's nephew. And I don't want a relationship. The closer you hold someone to you, the more it tears you up when they leave. Shannon is the only person in my life I really depend on and know isn't going anywhere. She's been there most of my life. Her, I trust with my life. Anyone else I wouldn't trust holding my purse.

"That's neither here nor there, anyway I've got bigger things on my plate right now."

"Like what?" Cheyenne takes her seat slowly as though she's watching a movie unfold.

"It's nothing I want to get into here. You wouldn't be interested."

"Try us." Keith urges me. "We might be able to help."

Maybe he's right. I'm so upset about my mother and this invasion she's put into my life. I can't sleep and anytime she crosses my mind I want to punch something. The people in this group have been through their own share of tragedies. Maybe they can shed some light. I can give them a cliff notes version.

"A very long story short, my mom had some issues when I was young and the minute I turned eighteen, I cut off contact with her. It's been many years, and now she wants to get in contact with me. She is been talking with my cousin, and my cousin wants me to have dinner with her and my mom so we can work out our differences."

"I think you should do it." Keith doesn't hesitate.

"That's easier said than done."

"And that's a cliche if I ever heard one."

Keith is right. It *is* cliche, but it's true. I don't want them to tell me to go see her. That's exactly what Shannon would say and the precise reason I haven't gone to her about it. She would drag me to see my mom, to make amends, and I don't want to do that. A mother is supposed to be there for her daughter, and she was anything but. How can she expect me to forgive her? "I'm not so sure I'm ready."

"You're almost forty years old," Luna says to the group. "Grow up already, grow a pair, and go see your mom."

"Grow a pair? No offense, but I really can't do that."

"Stop stalling," Cheyenne says. "You know very well what she means. If this were any of us, you would tell us the same exact thing."

"Not to mention, your relationship with your mom is probably what is holding you back from maintaining a long-term relationship."

I don't doubt Keith is correct. I'm well aware why I don't want to commit. Forgiving my mother may bring some sort of relief in my life, but how can someone accept abandonment? Every time I look at her I'll remember her with the sunken in eyes and the slurred speech, the zombie-like posture when I asked her to help me with homework. I'll never see her as a woman, a mom. She'll always be the drug addict. They don't know because I won't share this information, but they don't have to. That detail is too shameful. "I don't think I can do it."

"Well, you'll never know if you're ready unless you try." Keith stands and moves to the refreshment table.

Everyone is looking at me for direction. I guess that's it, then. Go see my mom. That's what they all think I should do. I think they're crazy. "Let's call it a meeting for tonight." I want to get home, take my bra off, pop open my laptop, and do some work. It's the only way I know how to unwind.

I meet Keith at the table and he already has a plate of potato chips. "Dinner?"

"Yeah. I wrapped things up at the office at around six and then hit the gym. I didn't have time to eat before I came here. Want some?"

He shoves the plate of chips at me and I want nothing more than to inhale their saltiness and calories. Where is this coming from? All these changes are causing me to want to revert back to my old ways, back when food was the answer. I'm still attending yoga, though I've missed a few classes since I moved to Sundays. I need to center myself again. I need to find peace.

"No, thanks." It takes all my willpower to deny myself the binge. I'm proud of myself, though. I can't seem to control anything in my life anymore, and at least this is the start of finding my way back to the right path.

Although I'm not so sure I know what that path is anymore.

Chapter Eighteen

I feel like I'm cheating on my regular yoga studio, but I needed something new today. I've heard a lot about this hot yoga and am excited to try it. I sweat during my normal class so I can only imagine the pool of sweat that will be underneath me when I finish today.

The studio is more intimate than I'm used to. Only fifteen people fit in a class, and I like we have a little bit more room to spread out. I'm sure the person next to me doesn't want to be able to smell me by the time this is done, and I sure don't want to smell them. I lay my purple mat so it fits in the designated area under the solar panel. This studio is different than the other hot yoga studios. When I researched online which studio to try, this one jumped out at me because they use infrared heating panels instead of just hiking up the heat in the room. This should allow me to still be able to breathe. And yoga is all about the breath.

Two women take the spots to the left of me, both adorably cute in their Capri yoga pants and form-fitting tanks. Not sure what to expect today, I bypassed my pants and chose shorts and a somewhat loose tank, a sports bra underneath. I sit down on my mat crisscross applesauce and start to regret my decision. While I consider myself in shape, there's no way to stop the inevitable cottage cheese legs that I've been graced with. I rearrange my legs in hopes the dimples aren't noticeable to those around me.

The space to the right of me remains empty. I consider moving my mat over so there's a space between me and the two cute girls, but if I make the switch now, it will be obvious as to why I'm doing so. I'll stick it out.

Relaxing music plays through the speakers as I begin stretching. I like to be able to straighten my legs as much as I can during the balance sequences so stretching can only help. I'm certainly losing my flexibility. I doubt I'm as limber as the rest of the young people in this class.

The class begins, and I'm relieved to see the instructor can't be too far from me in age. Though her dark hair is pulled back, silver strands are streaked throughout. She's short, but as she moves us through the sun salutations, her body lengthens in ways I only hope mine is. I imagine I look as graceful as she does when she raises her leg in the air and swoops it through next to her hands. I'm sure I'm anything but, my leg bending and having to hop forward for my foot to reach my hand. I'm warm and sweating by the time class is over, but as I lie in Shavasana and the instructor sprays us with lavender, I'm in a state of relaxation I've needed so badly over the past few weeks. What took me so long to do this?

Once she dismisses us, I approach her. "Emma? My name is Cassie. I'm new to your class."

"Hi, Cassie. Thanks for joining us. I hope you enjoyed it." She's catching her breath. Instruction while participating can't be easy, but I love she does so. I've attended numerous workout classes and the instructor never joins in. If I'm working, I want my teacher to as well. "Is there a pose I can assist with or do you have any questions? I like to be hands-on and focus where you need me to."

I'm a fan of this approach and she's sold me on buying a membership to the studio. I can hop between my other class and this one. "That's wonderful. This is my first time trying hot yoga. I really enjoyed it."

"You didn't find it too hot, did you?"

"Not at all. I was a tad worried, but this is so comfortable. I think I'll be here every day in the winter."

Emma's laugh echoes through the room, and the two girls who were next to me glance back and wave to her. "That's Josie and Ellen. They've been coming since the studio opened. They are very nice and can help you whenever you need it."

I take note of their names, though I doubt I will remember them. "I use yoga to alleviate stress. I love the slow flow, but I'm curious if there are other options that may be more —"

"Uplifting?" She beams as she interrupts.

"I suppose that could be a good way to describe it. While the relaxation is welcome, I want to be more energized."

"Our hot happy hour starts in thirty minutes. You're welcome to stay for that session if you want. It's a forty-five minutes class."

I don't know if I have the energy to take a back to back class, even with a half hour break. "Let me roll up my mat and think about it. I need to grab some water, whether or not I take the class."

She nods. "Sounds great! Let me know if you need anything. I'll be around the studio. Samantha teaches the happy hour."

Who knew yoga had a happy hour? Did they serve wine as well? That would be perfect, like one of those videos I've seen online with women doing a downward dog to a wine glass with a straw.

I head back to my mat and crouch down to roll it up. Crap. The last time I did that getting up wasn't so easy. I tighten my grip as I roll the mat forward and velcro the strap. A small puff of air later, I'm upright with my mat swung around my shoulder. Happy hour sounds fun, but I think I'll go home and do some work instead.

I exit the studio into the main area. The little shop also sells tank tops, t-shirts, yoga mats, and meditation journals. I don't need to spend money on any of that. I head for the door and stop in my tracks when I see Keith entering.

"Cassie?" He asks as though *me* being here is the weird thing.

I slide my fingers down the strap of my yoga bag and adjust my tank top with my right hand. Suddenly self-conscious about my perspiration, I allow my hand to rest on the back of my neck as I greet him. "Keith, hi. I didn't quite expect to run into you here."

He waves at someone behind me and I glance back and witness the two girls from class waving and smiling at him. Now I'm trying to remember their names. Was it Josie and Ellen? No. I think Josie and Helen. That sounds right.

"Ditto."

"What are you doing here?"

"I should ask you the same thing. I come here every other day."

He's a *regular*? Of all the men I can imagine doing yoga, Keith is the last one I would expect. I could see Lucas doing it before Keith. Now I can't take my eyes off of his arms. I'm sure a lot of his strength comes from advanced poses. I've been practicing for many years and have built up a lot of my strength this way. Yoga can be relaxing and healing, but it is a very good way to build muscle as well. Keith certainly proves that.

"Oh. This is my first time here. I'm actually going to sign up for a membership."

A smile overtakes his face and it brings me ease. It's not like he owns the place, but since I at first denied membership into Dating for Decades, I wouldn't blame him if he didn't want me here. Yoga is a very personal thing and he may not want me in his space.

"That's great! Maybe we can take a few classes together."

"Yeah. Maybe." I'm not sure where this is going, but I think I like it. Are we, in a way, *bonding*? Have we found a commonality we can enjoy *together*?

"Do you want to stick around for the next session?"

I didn't before, but I do now. I think I want to attend a few more classes on my own, though, before I make a fool out of myself in front of him. I don't know how good he is. Judging by the fact that he said he has been attending sessions here for many years, I can only imagine he's pretty advanced. I'm definitely not a beginner at yoga, but adding in the heat is a bit of a change. "I would love to, but I have some work to do."

"Are you ever *not* working?" He cocks his head and looks at me with concern.

I realize I still have my hand on the back of my neck and remove it promptly, unsure of where I should place it now that it's loose. I cross it over my body and take a hold of the strap with the other hand. "I know it seems that way to a lot of people, but I really do love my work. People find it crazy that I like to work after hours, but it's something I like to do. I get a lot accomplished."

"As long as you're happy. That's all that really matters."

That's what people say all the time. As long as you're happy. How does one find true happiness, though? We go through life with our ups and downs and some days we're happy and some days we're not. What constitutes accepting life as it is and being able to shout to the world, "I am ridiculously happy and no one can take that away from me?" Does anyone really have the answer to that? I'm satisfied. I love my job and I make decent money. Shannon is the best friend anyone could ever hope for. I'm not too happy about these chin hairs that have made an appearance, and what seemed like a slow crawl up the hill is now a sprint. I want to slow down before I tumble over. I'll be forty years old soon and not sure if I can even answer if I'm happy.

"That's the truth." Not sure what else I can really say. I don't want to get into a philosophical conversation in the middle of the yoga studio. Or ever, for that matter.

"Have you thought at all about what we discussed in the group?"

I purse my lips and squint my eyes. Lucas? Did we even discuss the topic enough for him to be asking this? I don't think anybody really gave me any advice. Not that I need any. What's done is done and he and I are not moving forward.

"I'm talking about your mother." Keith specifies as he catches on to my confusion. "Do you think you're going to go see her?"

Wow. I try to swallow, but it seems impossible at the moment. This wasn't a topic I was expecting to discuss right here in the open. "I don't know." My answer is short and I eye the door, wanting to make a run for it. I could knock him out of the way and be out of here so fast he wouldn't even have a chance to say goodbye.

"I can't pretend to know what you're going through. I think there's more going on than you're allowing us to hear about, something that happened between you two that is making this a much more difficult decision, and I can appreciate that. For what it's worth, she is reaching out to you. After all these years, it could be possible she's found peace with herself or is trying, and she needs to make amends with you. Aren't you the least bit curious?"

"I don't know, I really don't know. Maybe one percent of me thinks she's realized all her mistakes, and even though she can't give me back my childhood, she can try her best to give her all while she's still here on this Earth. But the rest of me, the rest of me that has been through hell and been through so much pain I feel numb sometimes, that part of me doesn't believe a word of it. There's a hidden agenda, something she wants or needs that has nothing to do with being a mother." I can feel my face turning different shades of red and Keith reaches out and places his hand on my shoulder.

"It's okay, Cassie. It's okay to doubt her and it's okay to be experiencing these emotions. I'm here for you if you need me."

The only other person who's ever said those words to me was Shannon. My eyes feel heavy as they fill with tears, tears that I push back so hard I'm afraid they'll come pouring out of my ears. He's staring back at me, those dreamy eyes offering me the comfort I'm so desperately in need of. I want to forget everybody is in this room and wrap my arms around him in an embrace that never ends. I want to thank him for those words and press my lips to his, unable to breathe but not caring because this, *this* is what I needed in my life for all these years. I've misjudged him.

Maybe I will stay for the class after all. Keith and I can place our mats next to each other and who knows what may happen. I open my mouth to thank him and tell him I'll stay when he clears his throat and adds, "The group. The group is here for you."

Of course. Not him. *The group.*

Chapter Nineteen

I can't believe I'm doing this. Something about what Keith said stuck with me and here I am at Sasha's house, ready to enter into the boxing ring. If this goes anywhere close to how I think it may, a UFC ring may be a better description.

I arrive at Sasha's at five-thirty. Dinner is at six, and I want to arrive before my mother. I want home-field advantage. If I'm already there laughing and drinking and enjoying myself, I may deal with this better. She'll be the one intruding, not me.

I stand in front of the door, holding a bottle of Coca-Cola. I skipped the wine, considering my mom is a recovering addict. I know she didn't have an addiction to alcohol, but I don't want to tempt any further dependencies. Not that I care. However, as I glance down at the bottle, complete with its red label, I can't help but think of how people talk about how there was cocaine in the product. I know there isn't, but right now I appreciate the irony.

I knock on the door, swearing at Keith in my head for causing me to question my stubborn attitude. Had I never ran into him at yoga, I probably wouldn't be here right now. I could be at home on my laptop engrossed in a project. Instead, I'm preparing for an evening of either uncomfortable silence or a roomful of flying accusations. I'm going in with no expectations. Unless the night turning into complete shit can be considered expectation.

The door swings open and Sasha is beaming. It's clear she's leaving a fun conversation, and based on her red cheeks, I'm pretty certain she's been drinking as well. "Why hello there, Cassie!" She yanks the soda out of my arms and pulls me inside. "Welcome to my humble abode. I'm so glad you could make it. And I'm sure your mom is as well."

She takes my jacket and directs me to the living room. Upon entry, my mother stands up from the couch, straightening her pants and blouse.

She's exactly like I saw her in the pictures on Facebook. Her hair reminds me of a raincloud, a mix of whites and grays that sweep across her cheeks. Her hair is so long and all one length. As she moves it out of her face her wrinkles become apparent and the bags under her eyes look as though she hasn't slept in years, which is probably true. A mound of clouds hovers over me and lightning strikes inside as I try to control the beating of my heart back to a normal pace. My stomach twirls in circles, and I wish someone could stop the room from spinning. Every piece of my heart is being ripped apart and put back together, confused by this woman standing before me. This isn't the woman who didn't care about me as a child. She doesn't appear frail and damaged. Or lost and depressed. She's aged, but she's *happy*.

What is wrong with this woman? How can she possibly be like this? She's face-to-face with the girl, now a *woman,* she abandoned more times than I can count. She's in the same room with her own flesh and blood she chose to refuse her love to and caused years of pain to as a result. I don't know what to say, so I respond in the only way I know how. "Excuse me." I race past my mother and into the bathroom where I empty my stomach into the toilet.

This was far from a good idea. From the minute the meeting was suggested I didn't want to do it. Damn Keith for convincing me to come. I allowed his honey eyes and Zen Buddha aura to infiltrate my fortress and I let my guard down. I thought, sure, I can be the bigger person and try to come to terms with my past, and here I am with my head in the toilet. She can't know she got to me. She can't.

"Are you okay, Cassie?" Sasha slightly opens the door, and I turn my head away from her.

"I'm not going to throw up again if that's what you mean." My voice is shaking as well as the rest of my body. It's been years since I've thrown up, and I don't want to do it again anytime soon. "Am I okay otherwise? That remains to be seen."

"Can I come in?"

I grab some toilet paper and wipe my mouth and then flush the toilet. Cinnamon air freshener is on the back of the tank so I grab that and spray quickly. "Sure. Come in."

I sit down on the floor against the bathtub and she sits on the toilet seat cover. I'm little grossed out considering I just threw up in there, even if she did put the cover down. "Of all the things that could have happened tonight, I didn't expect this to be one of them. And the second you walked in, too. I'm sorry."

"I honestly didn't know what would happen." I sweep her apology under the rug. Even though I agreed to this, the entire thing was still her idea, thus, her fault. "I thought I would be here before her." This doesn't mean I *wouldn't* have thrown up. But, at least I would've had more time to prepare. My mom practically threw herself on top of me the minute I arrived.

She stands and leans against the counter. "I really hope you plan to stay. Your mom is very concerned about you."

"Because I threw up? Anytime I felt sick as a kid, she never took care of me. She gave me some Tylenol and told me to lay down and sleep it out. Why is today any different?"

"I don't know, Cassie, it just is." She's eyeing me up and down waiting for a response she'll never get. "I have a toothbrush that hasn't been opened in the drawer." She slides open the drawer and grabs one for me. "Why don't you freshen up and come join us at the dinner table? If you don't feel like eating, that's fine."

"Thanks for the permission."

"Come on, Cassie."

I suppose I'm not coming into this with an open mind at all. I'm still upset she's been talking with my mom, but I don't need to treat *her* like this. I want to blame her for all of this, make her the reason I'm falling to pieces in the bathroom, but as she stands here, checking up on me and looking at me with those concerned eyes, I know she only is trying to do what she thinks is best for me. Imagine that, my little cousin taking care of me. She's a sweetheart and when someone wears their heart on their sleeve, it doesn't give you permission to break it. She wants me to love my mom like she loves hers. I won't, but I don't need to put this on her. *I* still made the decision to come.

"I'm sorry. I don't mean to take this out on you. I'll be right there."

"Great." She leans in and gives me an awkward hug. "Thank you."

I wait for moment after she closes the door before I brush my teeth. Much better. I look at the person staring back at me in the mirror. "You can do this, Cassie. Sit down, eat, chat for an hour, and leave. This is so simple." I close my eyes, take a deep breath and exhale. Time to face reality.

When I return to the little reunion Sasha has set up, both she and my mom are already seated at the table. My mom is seated on one side, and Sasha on the other. This puts me is smack dab in the middle. I take my seat and while I'm not making eye contact with her, I can feel my mom watching my every move. "Where's Garrett tonight?" I ask Sasha, avoiding any opportunity to say something to my mother or look in her direction.

"He went out with his friends. He thought this should be a family thing."

I want to ask why my mother is there then because she certainly isn't my family, but I know this means a lot to Sasha and I told myself in the bathroom I would give this a shot.

"You look amazing." My mother tries to break the ice. I don't respond. Is she waiting for me to accept the compliment, or offer her one in return? Sure, she looks great. She doesn't look doped up or like she hasn't eaten for days. I don't recognize her and I don't want to.

"Cassie?"

I turn to Sasha. "What?"

"Why don't you tell your mom thank you?"

I'm not a three-year-old learning her manners who needs direction. Is this how the entire evening is going to go? My mom will say something, I won't respond, so Sasha will play the mediator. The only thing I have in common with my mother is we share the same bloodline. Even if we did have something we mutually enjoyed, I wouldn't want to discuss it with her. We haven't even begun eating and I'm ready to get out of here. "Thank you." I turn back to Sasha. "Are you happy?" Sasha frowns and a tinge of regret forms in my belly. "I apologize. I'm a little bit uncomfortable."

I'm sure we all are, which is why no one confirms or denies my statement. I think Sasha expected this to turn out like a great family reunion. My mother and I would see each other and we'd embrace and cry and list all our apologies after years of separation. We'd tell stories about our lives and share our hopes and dreams for the future, one that included us together. That's the thing about Sasha. She's a dreamer, and she believes dreams come true. I stopped believing in fairy tales long before I became an adult.

Sasha has prepared a meal of spaghetti and meatballs. I slap some pasta on my plate along with some sauce and sprinkle on a ton of Parmesan cheese, because, come on, that's the best part. I whirl my fork and spiral some on and take a quick bite. Luckily, I don't feel like hurling. I think I actually may be a little hungry. I should get a lot of food in my belly because I plan on drinking tonight.

"What are you doing now? I haven't heard from you since before you started college." My mom starts right into the conversation, as though we sat down after a day of work and we're shooting the shit. Old buds, great friends. One fat lie.

I try to figure out a way to get through this. Maybe if I pretend I'm on a job interview this will be easier. If I answer her questions and don't go into too much detail, I can make it through this. "I'm an IT Manager at a law firm downtown."

She nods, and I can't tell if this is because she is impressed, disappointed, or only acknowledging my answer. I don't offer any further words while she eats a bite of her food. When I think maybe she's decided not to speak anymore, she asks another question. "How did you pay for college, if you don't mind my asking?"

I kind of do mind her asking, but Sasha is keyed in on me, watching my every reaction, and pleading with her eyes for me not to blow up. I don't like this interrogation. I haven't a clue how to make this conversation work, but this isn't it. My success is no thanks to her. This shouldn't be a shock. "Financial aid and everything is already paid off. I've learned to take care of myself. I learned that a very young age." I don't look right at her. I can't look into those aged eyes without seething at the mouth.

"Hm." In my peripheral vision, she nods her head again. Her and her damn nodding. My stomach growls at me, but it's not out of hunger. The bubbles in my belly are stuck in my abdomen and I could really use a Gas-X right about now. I can't eat another bite as I anticipate her response. Finally, she says, "I got married recently."

Is this supposed to impress me? What am I supposed to say? *For years, you slept with every man you possibly could and didn't even stay with anyone long enough to know who my father is, and I'm supposed to be happy you're married now? Now that you're almost in your sixties?* "I saw the pictures on Facebook."

She drops her fork on her plate, startling both me and Sasha. "So you *did* get my request?"

Oh, the joys of Facebook. Everyone's favorite app to spend time on and their favorite one to hate. "Yes, I did, recently. I haven't been on there in ages. I checked it recently." This is more explanation than she needs.

"Why didn't you accept it?"

Why is Facebook the true determination of friendship? No one is actually dating until they are "Facebook Official." It's the one place people seek out validation. Who has the most friends? Do we have mutual friends? Why won't you send me additional lives in

Candy Crush? *This* is part of the reason I stay away. "I haven't gotten around to it yet." Nor will I ever. She's lucky I'm not giving her the answer I want. I'm trying my best to keep our hostess in mind and not be rude, but my mother is testing my ability to do so.

"His name is David. He used to sell insurance, but he's retired now. I was his secretary."

Talk about cliché. And *she* has a job? "So you found a *legitimate* way to make a living?"

"That's not really fair, Cassie." When my mother says this, every muscle in my body tenses. I'm stiff from head to toe, but at the same time, my entire body shakes, goosebumps raising with every hair.

"Are you *really* going to talk to me about what's *fair*?" I push my plate aside. I shake my head in apology at Sasha. I can't do this. I can't pretend to be here and enjoying my mom's company. There's a fire in my body and her remarks are only fanning the flames. I'm ready to toss out fireballs. "What's fair about forgetting to pick me up because you're off with your flavor of the week? What's fair about not being able to help me with my school projects because you're high off your rocker? What's fair about being a teenage girl and not having my mother around to teach me about my period and boys and being a good person? You tell me, what's fair about *that*?"

She swallows so hard I can hear it across the table. "I was scared, Cassie. I took the wrong paths in life. So many of them. I wish I could change that."

I slide my chair out and stand up. "Well, you can't. I'm sorry, but this is too little too late. I don't ever want to see you again." I flick my head over toward Sasha. "Thank you for a lovely meal."

"Why don't you stay and we can talk this out?" Sasha pleads.

She put a lot of work into this, and she really wanted it to work out, but this isn't *her* estranged mother sitting at the table. It's *mine.* "No offense, Sasha, but I can't stand to be here another minute."

"You're being very rude." My mother stands and tosses her napkin on the table, pointing her finger at me.

She can't scold *me.* I'm not her child anymore. I'm a grown woman who worked her ass off to get where she is today, and I did it without anyone's help. I did it *on my own,* and she has no right to come in here and try to win me back as a daughter. The fire is burning at my fingertips, and I'm opening and closing my fists. I want to throw something. Anything. Without a second thought, I dig my hand into the pasta, the now cold and slimy noodles slipping through my fingers, and whip a handful at her. My mother gasps as the pasta hits her on the neck and slides down her shirt.

"I really don't care." I stand up proudly and march out the door.

Chapter Twenty

The disastrous dinner with my mom was easily managed with a bottle of wine. Now, I need to shift my focus to finishing the Pilot Project. The November deadline is only weeks away, and Keith has been working diligently to complete his portion.

Keith has been working all day and it's nearing dinner time. Terrence and Lucas left early for a family event, which is fine by me. I'm trying my best to avoid Lucas altogether, or at least not be alone with him. He hasn't mentioned our night together, but I still catch him checking me out during meetings. That's in the past and it has to remain there.

Keith knocks before coming into my office. "Hey, Cassie."

"Hey." I shut my laptop so I can give him my full attention. "How's it going?"

"Good." He steps closer to my desk, his hands in his pockets. I'm recalling him in his tank top from yoga class. I should go again on Sunday. Maybe not his class, but if I run into him again after I can get another glance of his arms. "I want to finish today if I can."

"I can't believe how quickly you've done this. How much more time do you need?"

"About an hour and a half. Two hours, tops."

I glance at the clock on the wall. It's only five-thirty. I can stick around until seven or seven-thirty. No big deal. "Do you want to work some overtime and finish up today?"

"Are you trying to get rid of me?" He winks as he sits across from me.

Once he finishes his portion, Lucas takes over, and I'm completely out of the project. And then I only see Keith on Thursdays at the meetings. I don't know why I'm sad about this, but I am. But I can push this project out of my mind and put my all into the other things I'm working on. I can shine in those areas. Prove myself again. "Of course not. But if you're so close to finishing, why not get it done?"

"If you're cool with that, so am I."

"It's a deal."

Keith doesn't wait and heads down to the basement to work. I open my laptop back up, the light stir of the processor fan the only thing I hear. Most of the staff has left already so the floor is quiet. I enjoy quiet.

Not sure where to start, I remember reviews are coming up, so I can utilize my time best by making notes on that. This will give me a solid head start before I write up the full performance report for each worker.

Rain has started falling outside. It's mid-October and while I'm thankful there isn't any snow yet, I'm sick of the wind. The rain I could take or leave. The pellets pound against my window, the small one I actually have, and the wind rattles the frame. I didn't think it was supposed to be this windy today.

Okay, I'm distracting myself with the weather. Time to get to work. I open the program I use for reviews. Julian is up first. What to say, what to say. He's young, like Lucas. He can take a difficult situation and turn it around. He brings fun to the office, something I consider important. He's also smart and ethical, like Keith. He's knowledgeable in his area of expertise and works until he gets it done, not allowing himself to get sidetracked.

Why am I comparing Julian to Lucas and Keith? And why have those two even entered my mind while working on this review? The rain has picked up and the noise is distracting me. I open my Spotify app and start a nineties playlist. The extra noise should do me some good. As much as I *do* love the quiet, too much silence can be dangerous.

I finish up Julian's review and move onto Kimmy. What to say about her? She's a sweet girl but tends to follow. I want her to lead. Maybe I haven't given her the opportunity to shine. Of course, shouldn't she want to do that on her own? All my life I wanted to rise above my crappy existence and make myself someone I would admire. I'm not trying to sound cocky, I'm not. I spent my childhood and teen years pushing my face to the books, getting straight A's, and hiding who I was all at the same time. Don't people with perfect upbringings want the same? I think everyone should strive to be better than they are today, always improving on themselves.

This may be what attracts me to Lucas. He's easy on the eyes, but he's working toward a future. He's doing what needs to be done to be successful. A confident man with perfect skin and an athletic body. He's desirable in every aspect of the word.

I shiver the thoughts of his hard body off me. *That's enough, Cassie. He's young. He's still inexperienced. He's still learning.*

But Keith isn't. He's *my* age. He's seasoned. A *man*. I'll admit I wonder what his hands would feel like wrapped around my body. A sensual embrace. A few days scruff brushing against my cheek. I shake my head and clear my throat as I refocus onto Kimmy's review. I shouldn't be thinking about this.

Yet I am. I can't concentrate. Damn it. I blame both of them, I really do. If Lucas weren't so gentle and romantic ... and much too young. If Keith didn't attend my meetings, if he didn't get on my nerves so much. Maybe together they could be the perfect man. I could commit to them both. Would they approve of a three-way relationship? We can be one big couple. Together, but separate. I know a lot of men dream of two women, but what are the chances *I* could date two men?

I'm being ridiculous. I've lived the past twenty years stern in my position never to marry or even *be* in a long-term relationship. Why am I stuck on these two? Why are they hitting all the right buttons? Why do I care so much? The calendar keeps moving, and I keep staying the same. I can't see there being much of a point of pursuing any sort of relationship, even a casual one since it never can go anywhere anyway. I just set myself up or somebody else for disaster.

I switch to the eighties station and it's in the middle of "Don't Wanna Fall in Love" by Jane Child. She certainly has a point. Love, no matter if it's maternal, friendly, or sexual, can certainly cut like a knife. I'm sure I've hurt Lucas, ignoring him every chance I get after our night together, and he's probably not the only one. I'm poison.

Enough is enough. *Focus, Cassie!* Onto Trevor. He's the middle ground for the group. He doesn't suck up too much but enough to get brownie points from me. I whip through his review, the easiest of the three to write about.

Keith interrupts my flow when he waltzes through my door. I've been working on reviews now for almost two hours. "Hey. You must be about done."

"I am. Completely. Want to take a look?" He gestured toward the door.

"Yes!" I respond a little too eager. "Let me turn off my laptop." I do so and follow him to the basement where he shows me his work.

"Wow. I'm thoroughly impressed. This is so ... *clean*. I don't think I've ever known someone to do such a neat job."

He slides his hands into his jeans pockets. "I'll take that as a job well done."

"Definitely. Worth every penny."

I wish all my contractors did this great of a job. I wonder if there is anything else I can hire him for. "I aim to please."

"Okay, well, this is it. I guess you'll bill me?"

Our eyes don't lose connection. He's partially smiling, but I sense pain in the part that is not. I tried so hard to keep him out of the support group, and once he maneuvered his way in, I'll admit, he's grown on me. Even though we'll see each other every Thursday, we won't see each other every day. Why is that difficult to process? Why does this seem like the end?

"Yeah. I'll get it in the mail next week."

We're two teenagers with our hands in our pockets kicking the ground waiting for one to ask the other out. I haven't felt this socially awkward since my eighth-grade dance. "So, I'll see you at the group, I'm sure. Unless ..."

"Unless what?"

I don't know. What do I even want to ask him? Out on a date? To go back to my place for a fun evening? For a packet of stamps? I trail off without a response prepared. What sort of a maniac am I? "Nothing," I whisper. "I guess I'll see you out."

"Sure."

I turn and start to walk toward the door, saddened by the end of this relationship. Me, heavyhearted at the end of this arrangement. *Me*. This feeling, it's perplexing and new and different. In this seemingly simple moment, I'm trying to stop myself from falling apart.

"Cassie, wait."

I stop my exit and hope overcomes me. "What?" I turn and he's already moved ahead and is only a step away from me.

"I know you were talking about Lucas during group."

"What? No ... I ... " *This* is what he stops me for? Not to confess his attraction to me and to kiss me under these fluorescent lights in the basement? He wants to discuss *Lucas*?

"Cassie ... I've seen the way he looks at you, and you went out with him that time. Do you have feelings for him?"

"Feelings?"

"Yes. Feelings. Emotions. Do you want to be with him?"

"No." Wow. I realize I didn't even have to think about it. But why does he care? He hasn't shown any interest in me outside of the group or work. How does this even concern him? "I don't. We had a good ... time together. That was it."

"What about me?"

"What about you?" This takes me by surprise. *Does* he care? Does he think about me when I'm not around? Does he close his eyes and see my face? Does he want to touch me as badly as I want to touch him?

"Have you ever thought about me? You know, outside of the group or here?"

Oh. My. God. Is this going where I think it is going? No. He's playing me for a fool. He's so stuck on how things are with Lucas. He's digging for information. "What does it matter? You and Cheyenne seem to be getting a bit chummy together." It makes me sick thinking about them flirting with one another, but it's true. Those two are enjoying each other's company in the group.

"After your tale of Lucas, I got a little jealous. I'm never jealous. I didn't know how to deal with it, so when Cheyenne flirted with me, I flirted back."

Well, it worked. "Juvenile."

He smiles and leans against one of the server racks. What do we do now? What do I say?

"I went to see my mom." Why did *that* pop into my head? Here we are on a path and I totally stick a fork in the road. He doesn't want to hear about this.

"Oh?" He straightens himself up. "How did that go?"

Now I have to go into it. Great. This is the last thing I want to talk about. "Not too well."

"I'm sorry, Cassie." He reaches out to me and rests his hand on my shoulder. It's heavy, much like the burden I'm putting on him to discuss something so personal and non-interesting to him.

"It's not your fault." I shrug and his hand falls off my shoulder. "I figured this was how it was going to go."

"I feel bad for pushing you."

I cross my arms and hug myself. "You didn't push me. I made the decision on my own." I back up against a rack and slide down to the floor, wrapping my arms around my knees. Keith joins me. "I'm just so mad at her." I'm shaking my head and I can't seem to stop. I'll probably give myself whiplash. "I'm so mad." I drop my head on his shoulder, my eyes popping open wide when I realize what I've done. But he doesn't push me off, so I stay where I am.

Keith shifts forward enough to slide his arm behind me. He pulls me closer to him and I can feel his heart beating. When he reaches his hand across and touches the back of my neck with it, I remind myself to breathe.

"It's okay to be mad. It's okay to have those emotions. No one can tell you what you're feeling is wrong."

I turn my head and our faces are inches from each other. As he looks at me, I'm holding back the tears that want to pour out of my eyes. I don't know why I want to cry. Am I sad about my mom? Am I shocked at what he's telling me? Am I confused at this sensation that seems to have taken over my heart?

I don't know if he leans into me or if I reach up to him, but our lips collide at a force powerful enough to create another Big Bang. His hands are moving up and down my back, and I come to a kneeling position as we continue to kiss, forcing him to the ground. He's on the hard floor and I'm lying on top of him, my lips moving from his lips to his neck to his cheek, back to his lips. Every moment of this is perfect. Each kiss fills my heart more, and I still want to cry. Am I ... happy?

"What's wrong?" Keith asks as I halt our session.

I climb off of him and struggle to find my balance as I stand. I wipe my mouth, eliminating any trace of him on my lips. "This isn't a good idea."

He sits up and forms an O with his lips, "Okay. Why not? I thought we had something between us. I thought we both wanted this."

I tug at the hem of my shirt and ball it into my fist. "I ... I don't know what I want. This is a really bad time for me." Timing. I'll blame it on that.

"Oh." He drops his gaze to the floor and then picks it back up. "Okay, then." He hops up from the seated position and wipes down his pants. "Well, it's been great working with you and I'll see you on Thursday I guess."

Really? This is how he's ending it? He's not upset or bothered by the fact that I shot him down? We were *just* kissing, right? I didn't imagine that. This isn't the response I would expect from somebody in a situation such as this. "Yeah. I guess I'll see you Thursday. I have to let you out though because I'll need to collect your entry card to the building." Now *this* is awkward.

"Sure thing." He unclips his card and hands it to me. "Lead the way, Ms. Noble."

And with those five words, he's broken my confidence, and I'm pretty sure, my heart.

Chapter Twenty-One

People tend to think Shannon and I are crazy. We do this every year, and I swear every year we get more creative. I lay down newspaper over my entire kitchen table and put the pumpkins on them. I cut open the tops, and we each dig our hands into the pumpkin scraping out as many seeds as we can, our hands covered in slime.

"I'm glad we're doing this today." Shannon shakes her hands and seeds fall onto the newspaper.

"Me, too. I've had a bit of a rough week."

"What do you mean? You haven't said a word to me about anything."

It's true. I haven't. After the failed dinner with my mom, I tried to push her out of my mind. It's been proving impossible. I'm keeping all these feelings locked up inside of me, and I need to talk to someone other than myself. My discussion with Keith led to a much-fantasized kiss coming true and ended with me proving why I don't get too emotionally involved with anyone. Maybe my mom was onto something with her short-term relationships with men, sans the drugs.

"I'm sorry. I don't even know where to start."

"That good, huh?"

I hold my hands in the air as though I'm operating on the pumpkin. "Well, I slept with my boss' nephew, who is seventeen years younger than me. I kissed Keith, who did work for my company and is in my Dating for Decades group. Oh! And I also saw my mom."

I move over to the sink and wash my hands as I leave Shannon at the table trying to pick her mouth off the floor.

"Wait. This is a lot of information to take in. One thing at a time. You slept with someone seventeen years younger than you?"

"Sure did. It's not like he was seventeen. He is seventeen years *younger*."

"So that makes him what, twenty-two?"

"You're great at math, Shannon." I dry my hands off and meet her back at the table.

"Don't be so sassy. And then you kissed this other guy?"

"Yep." I pick up the carving knife and begin to cut.

"I can't get my husband to have sex with me more than twice a month, and you're getting busy with two men?"

"Don't get too excited. I don't plan on sleeping with Lucas again, and I'm not pursuing anything with Keith. As far as I'm concerned, Lucas is hands off and forbidden. And he's too young. Let's get real." I round the knife and make a perfect circle. I pop out the piece and start another one. "And Keith, well, whatever. We kissed and I told him it was a bad idea and he didn't really care. So I don't either."

Shannon rests her hands on the back of the chair. "So you have no feelings for either of these men?"

"First off, Lucas is barely a man. As much as I want his head buried between my legs every time I see him, we work together."

"Whoa! Too much information."

I stick my tongue out at her. "Well, you asked." I finish the other circle and pop it out. "And Keith, well, I just don't want to go there. I don't think it will end well, so it's better to end that before it starts."

Shannon's silence speaks louder than any words she could ever say. She knows me well enough to leave the situation alone. "Are you carving what I think you're carving?"

I back up from my creation in progress and observe what I've done so far. "What do you think? I think I can carve a pretty nice penis. A small keepsake, perhaps."

"That's far from small."

I shrug and a laugh escapes me, and soon I'm holding onto my belly because I'm laughing so hard it hurts. "This is such a corny tradition."

"I like it. How many other people do you know carve dirty pumpkins every year? I don't even remember how we started doing this, but I love it."

"Just be glad that I'm not married or have any kids so you have a place to put your pumpkin. Something tells me that Ben or your kids would have an issue with this."

Shannon plays a fake violin. Back in college, Ben would've

loved something like this. I can understand, though, with the kids. Shannon would have a lot of explaining to do.

"Okay, back to your tough week. You really don't think I'm going to ignore the fact that you said you saw your mom."

I hoped my love life was enough to discuss, but of course she wants to hear the details. "Well, it turns out that she's been in contact with Sasha and a little bit with Sasha's mom. Sasha really wanted me to have dinner with them, so I went the other night."

Shannon has begun carving out her pumpkin. She's focused on her detail, cutting the skin at a snail's pace. "I'm proud of you for going."

I don't doubt she is. Shannon knows my past — every single detail. She's the only one who does. Even those in my family don't know everything. They know my mom was a drug addict, and they know she was a shitty mom, but they don't know about the conditions we used to live in or how my mom often stole food for us. I don't want them to know. I was ashamed then and I'm ashamed now.

"It didn't go so well. The night ended with me throwing spaghetti at her."

She stops carving what I can only imagine are nipple tassels, and sits down at the table. "You what?"

"Yes, you heard me correctly. I tossed pasta at her. It landed right on her shoulders and went down her shirt."

"I can't believe you would be so immature."

"I'm not proud of it."

"You're sure acting like it." She drops her knife on the table. "You've been given a chance to reconcile with her and this is what you do?"

This conversation is moving into uncomfortable territory. I don't sit at the table with her, and instead, pull a stool out from underneath the breakfast bar and sit down. "I knew I shouldn't have gone, but Keith convinced me to go."

Her lips practically disappear as anger grows on her face. "Keith? You went to Keith about this, but you didn't come to me, your best friend?"

"I knew you would tell me to go see her."

"You mean like he did?"

I know she's upset and I understand why. I trust her more than anybody in this world, but I know it's a touchy subject with her. "I'm sorry."

She rubs her forehead and pulls her hands down the side of her face. I'm terrified of what she's going to say. I blew it. I should have come to her, and now I probably lost her. I can't. She is all I have.

"Don't worry about it." She picks up her knife and starts carving again, and I'm relieved I'm in the clear. "How did she look?"

"Fine. I can barely tell she was a drug addict. Her hair is really thin and so is she, but that's probably from her illness. With all the drug she's done, she's contracted HIV. It serves her right."

"How can you say something like that?" She tosses the knife down and flies across the table. I'm grateful I'm not sitting on the other side because it might have hit me. "Do you know what I would give to have my mother here with me?"

This is why I didn't want to tell her. Her mother died three years ago after an infection took over her body. The two of them were close. Like best friends. The kind of relationship I wish my mother and I had. "I understand, but our relationships with our moms are entirely different. I would have loved to have had a mom like yours when I was growing up. You hit the jackpot. My mom didn't even know what it meant to be a mom. Why does she get a second chance now?"

She slams her hand on the table, startling me. "Because people deserve second chances! When she's gone, you're going to regret that you didn't do more to spend time with her or be with her. You're going to wish you had taken the time to work through your problems. As much as she ignored you, you'll realize you still love her and that she *did* love you." She starting to cry and speaking so quickly I can barely understand her. "One day you're going to look at your children and wish you'd made it work."

She covers her face with her hands and I realize she's no longer talking about me or our mothers. I grab a tissue and bring it to her. "What's going on, Shannon?"

She wipes her eyes and blows her nose, her breathing heavy and fast. After a few sniffles and deep breaths, she manages to speak. "Ben has been discussing the possibility of separation."

I know she's waiting for me to say something, but nothing comes to mind except the fact that this is one of the reasons I don't like marriage. Now she may lose her husband and her kids will be affected. It's not a good situation. "I'm sorry. Is there anything I can do?" This is all I can offer her, and I hope it's enough.

She shakes her head and blows her nose again. "No. We'll figure this out, I'm sure. At least I hope so. I'm tired of us either fighting all the time or him completely ignoring me. I know you think I'm joking when you're on your tablet all the time, but that's the same to me as when Ben is staring at the TV. My husband ignores me. I don't need my best friend to as well."

I'm a terrible person. It's not a secret that my technology is an extra limb to my body. It's who I am. It's my job. It defines me. Of course, maybe this is why I'm so blind to human emotion. I'm a robot, just like my iPad. Hell, Siri may show emotion better than I do. Even *she* takes a break sometimes.

"Point very well taken. I'm sorry if you've ever felt like I've ignored you. I've never intended for it to be that way. And I had no idea how things were between you and Ben. Whenever you mention things like that, I always think you're joking. I look up to you two as a couple. You've been in love since college. I've had as many boyfriends for as many years as you two have been together. And you have two beautiful children. I envy you." I do in a way. I don't want marriage or kids, but I also don't want to be a forty-year-old without anyone in her life.

"Sometimes I envy you."

"Envy me? Why in the world would you envy *me*?"

"You're single. Unattached. I love my children and my husband. Sometimes, though, I think how life would be much easier if it were just me. I could do whatever I want, whenever I want." She points to my penis pumpkin, "Whomever I want."

I laugh silently. "You don't want my life. You may think you do, but I don't wish my life on anybody."

"You're an independent, successful woman."

"So are you, whether you realize it or not. My life can be pretty empty sometimes. You have a full house to come home to. I don't even own a cat."

"You don't want a cat. If you want anything, you want a dog."

I rub her back up and down and she takes a hold of my hand so it's resting on her shoulder. "The point is you have a home. A family. You may think you envy me, but it's pretty lonely being me."

And that's the truth. I throw myself into my work, because honestly, what else do I have?

She shakes her body and pretends to wipe something off her shoulder. "Enough with this. This isn't about me. Ben and I will get through this. I know we will. You, on the other hand, should really try to have some sort of a relationship with your mom, even a small one. An occasional cup of coffee, maybe a phone call here and there. I don't want you to have any regrets in life."

"I won't."

"You don't know that."

"If I do, it won't be for not seeing my mother." I think it may have more to do with not allowing myself to be happy if I even deserve that.

Chapter Twenty-Two

I can't believe this is the last class at the library. What began as a one-month class has turned into more than three. Everyone had so much fun they wanted to continue. Luckily, the library didn't need the space, and I was able to utilize it. I'm having a good time getting to know all the people. Even Stan, the man who kept falling asleep, has stolen my heart.

I skipped Thursday's Dating for Decades meeting, and I switched back to my previous yoga studio. I can't see Keith. Not yet. I need time to process that amazing kiss. And Shannon has me rethinking the whole situation with my mom. I'm not used to being pulled in so many directions. My focus remaining on work and work alone allowed me the liberty to go on about life as if I didn't have a past and not worry about a future. Day by day was how I lived, and now I find myself worrying about what the next year holds. The only thing I saw in my future was the big 4-0. Now I'm saying goodbye to a room full of people I've grown to love, I'm avoiding any opportunity at the possibility of romance, and I'm trying to remember a time when my mother didn't cross my mind.

Snow is falling now, a valid reason in my mind to hate November, and soon the temperatures will drop, and I'll switch out my short boots for my knee-high ones. That's something to look forward to, I guess. I need something to keep my spirits up.

I swing the door to the library open, ready to face the day. We'll finish up our last lesson on Facebook and then I'll introduce them to games. Even if I can't stand them, that doesn't mean the class won't enjoy the games.

The door to the community room is closed. That's weird. It's usually open. I can see the light is on so I open the door slowly. I don't want to interrupt a presentation if for some reason one was booked here. Of course, they should have told me before I wasted my time coming here today.

Once the door is open fully, I'm greeted with a big sign across the whiteboard that says "Thank You" with balloons taped to the side. Lucille is standing by her computer with a bouquet of flowers.

"Surprise!" The group shouts and I can't help but smile. I really never liked surprises, but as I fill with joy looking at all their faces, I think maybe I understand why others do.

"What's this about?" I set my things down at the desk and Lucille hands me the flowers. They smell beautiful like wildflowers in a meadow.

"We wanted to thank you for putting up with us old folks. We know sometimes it's hard for you young whippersnappers."

"Lucille, I'll be forty years old in a few months. I'm not exactly young either."

"Forty is the new twenty."

"Well then maybe I'm actually turning sixty because I sure do feel like I'm forty."

I don't really know what being forty feels like. I've never been forty before. All I know is I feel old. *Really* old. When I was in my early thirties, I didn't think twice about turning forty because it seemed so far away. Now it's staring me in the face in a couple of months. How on earth did that happen?

"My forties were some of the best years of my life." Lucille hands me the flowers. "You need to approach life differently. You're not dating or settling down, and you think marriage is some horrible thing. And children. You have absolutely no desire to have children. I don't understand it, but I'll respect it. But you need to promise me you're going to work toward a future you can be proud of."

I've never taken lightly to somebody telling me what to do or how to live my life, but Lucille is different. She hasn't a clue about my life or what I've been through and what I've struggled with, and she doesn't care. All she cares about is happiness. We all should go through life with happiness as our only goal. Forget about money or stature or what happened in the past. Just be happy. "Thank you, Lucille. I will." I clap my hands together to get everyone's attention. "Thank you so much everyone, and now it's time to get to work. Today I'm going to teach you about playing games online."

"Do you mean like Candy Crush?" Buddy, who sits next to Lucille, calls out.

"Unfortunately, yes."

"I've been playing that since the first class. I'm already on level 400 and something."

I wonder if Buddy has been playing every class, not even paying attention to anything I've tried to teach them. "Well then maybe *you* can help me teach the class," I say and we all laugh.

Twenty minutes later everyone has picked their poison and are playing the games. I sit down next to Lucille. "Seriously, though. Thank you for the flowers. That was very considerate. I've never received flowers from anybody before."

"Never?" She places her hand on her heart like it's the worst thing in the world.

Sasha has before, but that doesn't count. "I don't think I've been in a relationship long enough for anybody to *want* to give me flowers."

"I don't understand young folks these days. What's so hard about commitment? You find somebody, you fall in love, and history writes the rest of the book."

"If only it were that simple. I've come to realize that things in my past are what hold me back from living my future."

"Why? Stop it. Change it. Only you hold the true key to your future. Turn it. Unlock what awaits you."

Lucille is such an intelligent and charismatic woman. I can see why her husband fell in love with her and it's too bad for Billy that he moved away. Speaking of. "Did you find your long-lost love?"

"I thought you would never ask. I found him a few weeks ago, and we've gone on a few dates."

"What? Why didn't you tell me?" I thought for sure she would tell me the minute she found him on Facebook. She must have figured out on her own how to send him private messages. I'm happy for her.

"I don't know. But it's going very well. His wife passed away about ten years back, and apparently he's been looking for me as well." She pulls her shoulders to her ears and quietly says, "We're talking about getting married."

Lucille, an eighty-year-old woman, is talking about getting married. At her age. And here I am, half her age, and it's something I can't, and won't, even consider. *Is* there something wrong with me?

"That's wonderful, Lucille. I'm very happy for you."

"I'm glad my daughter and granddaughter made me do this. And I'm very glad that I've met you."

I never thought I would be friends with an eighty-year-old woman. But I like her. She's spunky. And as close to a motherly figure as I'll get.

"Did you find a game you want to play?"

"Hell, no." She waves her hand at me. "I don't have time for that." I love she said that. "I've got better things to do. And his name is Billy."

I could die laughing. When I think of someone her age, a dirty mind isn't a way I would use to describe that person. I seriously thinks she's me forty years in the future. "You're pretty sassy."

"I know. That's why the men love me."

It's amazing to me how much fun she puts into life. She toots her own horn and doesn't care who knows it. It doesn't matter, either, because she really doesn't give two shits what anyone thinks and the confidence she carries with that really brings out a likable side to her.

"I'll miss you, but I know we'll be friends on Facebook." She places her hand over mine and her touch warms me.

Facebook. I haven't gone on since the day I found my mom. And I didn't intend to go back on. "That sounds great." I want to see Lucille again. I don't plan to lose touch with her.

"And I want to see your status change to 'in a relationship' soon."

Facebook official. I think about Keith and how much I would love to tag him in such a change. I think I screwed things up with him, though, and my status will forever be 'single.'

Chapter Twenty-Three

I can't breathe, my eyes burn, and my head is throbbing. I can't remember the last time sickness took over my body like this. I don't even want to move. I think it's been about four years since I've been sick. Anytime I've felt something coming on I fend it off with essential oils. Not this time. I went to bed Sunday night in a perfectly healthy state and now it's Monday morning and I feel like death. I can't make it into work today. I'm not even sure I can find the strength to open my laptop. I better write this day down or let Shannon know. A full day without accessing work? She'll never believe me. Of course, I have my iPad, so there's always that.

I need something to help me out, so I take some non-drowsy cold medicine. Though knocking myself out seems like a pretty good idea right now. I may have just woken up, but I could go for another eight hours of sleep. I make my way back from the bathroom to my bedroom and almost forget where I'm going. I'm off to a wonderful start. I guess I'll watch some television. I flip through the channels. What the heck is on Monday mornings? Apparently a whole bunch of talk shows about current events or the latest diet trend. Or Judge Judy, Jeff, or Steve. If there's a chance someone will watch it, it's a guarantee it will become a show.

After about forty-five minutes of listening to a group of women rant and complain about who knows what (I really wasn't listening), I can't keep my eyes open anymore, much less put up with their asinine comments. I practically pass out the second my head hits the pillow. So much for non-drowsy.

My cell phone ringing pulls me out of my sleep. I sit up and realize as I almost pass out I can't get up that quickly. Very bad idea. The caller ID shows me it's Sasha. Great. I've avoided her calls since the fiasco at her house. I suppose I should own up to it and face the music. Maybe since I'm sick, she'll have a little sympathy for me.

"Hello?" I moan into the phone, hoping by doing this she'll immediately know I'm sick and do me the courtesy of not chatting too long.

"Why have you been avoiding my calls?" She starts to question me immediately. I shouldn't be shocked or anything. I deserve it. I hate when people ignore my texts. I mean, who calls people anymore anyway? No one wants to talk on the phone. Maybe if she texted me I would have answered.

"I'm sorry, Sasha. I couldn't deal with it."

"So you shut everyone out?"

I seriously don't want to deal with this right now. I want to lay back down and sleep for another hour, at least. "Everyone? I talk to *you* in the family. That's pretty much it."

"You know who I mean."

My head can't handle this. I'm cold, stuffy, and my brain hurts. I haven't eaten a thing this morning so I probably should try and consume some type of food. "I don't want to talk about her." Although good thing I *do* have an empty stomach because the thought of my mother right now may make me throw up.

"Well, too bad. I need to talk to you."

What now? Did she find my great great aunt by my mother's aunt's uncle's son's friend? I know that sounds ridiculous, but what the hell could be so damn important? I've got better things to do. Like sleep. And sleep some more. After I take more medication.

"Can you make it quick? I'm a little under the weather." And by a little, I mean a lot. Like I'm practically dying over here.

"I can tell. You sound stuffy." *Geez, thanks.* "It's your mom."

"I said I don't want to discuss her. What part of the sentence don't you understand?" I pinch the bridge of my nose, shut my eyes, and try not to scream. I'm a broken record with this one.

"She's in the hospital with pneumonia. It's pretty bad, actually. Her HIV has complicated things. She's very sick. The doctors are doing the best they can."

I should react, say something, but I'm ... indifferent. Am I supposed to feel something? What? Right now all I can feel is this pain in my head. It's pneumonia. People get that every day. It's not like she has an untreatable disease ... well, okay, maybe she *does*, but I'm sure she'll get over this pneumonia and continue to live her life with her husband, Dave. I think that was his name? Or did she call him David? Either way, same person.

"Cassie?"

I'm here, but I don't have anything to say. She's given her information to me. Let's move on.

"She's been there a few days already, and she's going to be there a lot longer. I've been to see her twice now and she doesn't even know I'm there. All she's doing is sleeping."

Like I wish I was. Let's wrap this up. Even if I *did* want to go see her, which I don't, if she doesn't know Sasha is there, she won't know I'm there either. Can't she tell her I came and be done with it?

"I can't believe you won't even talk to me. Your mother is *sick*, Cassie. What if she doesn't make it?"

Huh. *What if she doesn't make it? As in, what if she dies?* Well, what if? I never thought about it. I guess a majority of my life now I've already considered her gone, non-existent. Would the finality of death make any difference? Would this change how I feel about her? Would it change how she was to me as a child? Can seeing her *now* bring any closure and make everything all right between us? Sasha thinks so, apparently, and I'm sure Shannon would agree.

"Cassie? Are you there? What if she doesn't make it through this?"

"What if she doesn't? What does that have to do with me?"

She gasps on the other side. I can picture her hand reaching up to her mouth in horror, the sheer implication of my not caring burning a hole into her naive heart. "I can't believe you said that. You should be ashamed of yourself."

Should I? Maybe I should. Maybe I shouldn't, and I should flip my middle finger up to the world. Hell, I should make all my fingers dance in a bouquet of fuck offs. I don't even care. My life was getting along just fine until my mom forced her way back in, which, by the way, Sasha had a part in. My past with her was practically erased. I'm on my own, and I've *been* on my own and doing well for myself. I don't *need* her in my life. I didn't when I was a child, a teenager, and now as an adult. "Well, I'm not. She's no one to me."

"You'll regret it if you don't see her, Cassie."

"Why does everyone feel the need to judge what I will and won't regret in life? First Shannon and now you." My nose clogs up and I can't speak until I clear it. I blow rudely into the phone and toss the tissue on my end table. "I'll be the one to decide who I want to see and when I want to see them."

My phone dings. An email. I don't listen to whatever Sasha is saying and quickly check my message. It's Lucas.

Missed you at work today. Do you need any soup? A foot rub? I'm here if you need anything.

Sweet. Finally, someone who doesn't care about my relationship or lack of one with my mother. *He's* a friend. I'm sick and he wants me to feel better, not worse, which Sasha is doing right now. I reply I'll be back on Tuesday and thank him for his offer. I may take him up on the soup some day, but not the massage though it *does* sound appealing since I'm aware of what his hands can do.

Sasha is still talking, going on and on. "I know she wasn't the best parent in the world, but she wants to try now. You owe her that much."

I roll my eyes back and push my head further down on the pillow. I can picture myself at that library years ago, standing in the entryway, wondering if she would show up. Wondering if I walked out the door and never came back, would she even care. Now it's *my* turn not to give any fucks.

"I don't owe her anything."

Chapter Twenty-Four

I'm glad to be back at work, even if I still want to be in bed. My head feels as though I am floating through the day, and I'm nursing a small sniffle, but compared to yesterday, I'm on top of the world. It could be all the cold medicine I took this morning, but I don't care. I'm physically present and need to finish these reviews.

Sasha tried calling me back a few times after I hung up on her. I came close to blocking her number, but even if I hate that she orchestrated my whole failed meeting with my mother, she's the closest one I have in my family. Unless there is some big event planned, I don't show my face around too often. I'm surprised some family members even remember my name.

Today my priority is finishing the performance reports and catching up on all the emails I left sitting in my inbox yesterday. The fact that I haven't responded to them is driving me crazy. My inbox is *always* clean. Not having things in order in there is how I'm sure parents feel when their kids leave toys lying around.

The building feels empty, much like my heart. With Thanksgiving nearing, people are spending time with their families and some are taking off to go hunting. We have more people here than we do the week of Christmas, though, when we practically shut down as most take small vacations to warmer places. I normally spend Thanksgiving with Sasha, but not this year. I'm steering clear of her for as long as I possibly can.

Lucas is the next person on my review list. I'm not sure if I'm the best one to write this. I have a much more intimate take on his abilities than the review calls for. I open his file and begin typing:

Lucas has done an excellent job excelling in his area of expertise. When he came on board, he was placed into a large project already in production. He rose to the occasion and helped build out new server space and clean up files — not an easy feat. His demeanor is very professional and he takes the lead when needed.

I reread my words realizing how true they are when applied to his skills in the bedroom as well. I still don't know what I was thinking. Even if he's a fifteen on a scale of one to ten, I put my job in jeopardy. I need to be smarter about these things. I press print on his file so I can hand it into Terrence with the others on Friday. I'll grab it and put it with the others later. While I'm on a roll, I might as well get them all finished. I only have two more left to write.

Terrence interrupts my rapid pace when he enters my office as though he's walking on stage. "I have wonderful news!" He sings, something I've never heard him do. He's beaming and I can't imagine anything that would make him so happy. He's a great guy and a solid worker, but he keeps his fun to a minimum at work.

"Good morning to you as well," I return his invisible greeting.

"Are you feeling better?" He takes a seat across from me, crosses his legs and folds his hands on his lap. I couldn't even slap this smile off his face if I tried.

"Much. Thank you."

He snaps his finger. "Glad to hear it!"

"What is this news? Are you hiring on a niece, too?" I make the joke, though I'm partially serious. Wouldn't that be awesome? Working with Terrence's nephew *and* niece. Together they could take over the company.

"Very funny, Cassie, but this is even better!"

To be honest, I don't even know if he has a niece. I never bothered to ask Lucas if he has a sister and I don't know if Terrence has any other siblings, much less siblings with kids.

"Our firm has been chosen for an Innovation Award."

"That's wonderful!" The Innovation Award is big in our IT world. Every year a different IT consulting company wins. We're not a consulting firm, we're the IT department of a law firm, which is rare for a win, even a nomination. Terrence must be so pleased.

"I told you I had great news and I didn't lie!"

Terrence lives for awards. He likes to be recognized. I suppose who doesn't. It's a nice feeling to be rewarded. I hoped with the Pilot Project we would be afforded the opportunity. No such luck. "Congratulations."

"I'm not done." He rubs his hands together. "You might be getting an award!"

"What?" For what? What did I do? What award could I possibly be receiving? The Manager Who Refuses To Delegate So Her Manager Hired His Nephew To Clean Up After Her Award?

"Yes! You've been nominated as IT Manager of the Year!"

IT Manager of the Year? Did I hear him correctly? I can't believe it. Even after losing the Pilot Project to Lucas, working on my tiny projects and day to day management paid off. Something *good* is actually happening. Between my crushed heart with Keith and my anger toward my mother, I finally have something to be happy about.

"Congratulations! The ceremony is next Friday night. Lucas mentioned he thought you were dating someone. Bring him."

My smile fades. I'm not dating anyone, nor was I ever. Was he talking about Keith? Why was I even the subject of their conversation, especially my love life? Terrence is waiting for me to respond. "Okay." Now I need to find a date. Where will I find a date, and on such short notice?

"Great!" He makes a fist and pumps it into the air. "Today is a terrific day! Back to work!"

I wish his attitude were contagious, but even if I wanted to be enthusiastic and cheery, this cold is still holding me back. I lay my head on my desk, deflated. Maybe I should go home. The day off was kind of nice up until Sasha ruined it for me.

"You shouldn't sleep while you're at work, especially if you're winning some award."

My head pops up at Lucas's voice. He's tossing a stress ball in the air. If I had that thing, I'd pop it with one squeeze. "You heard, huh?"

He puts the ball in his pocket and shuts the door behind him. Do we have a meeting? Why is he closing the door? "Terrence told me last night right after he got the news. Great job. You deserve it."

"Thanks." I'm not sure if I'm being sincere. Besides, I haven't won anything yet. I've only been nominated.

Silence bounces between us, and I'm apprehensive to begin a conversation. What do I even say? Is he okay with the nomination? Does his opinion matter to me?

He steps closer and hesitates before he talks. "I missed you yesterday."

"*Please*. Thanks for the email, though. It was kind of you to offer to bring me something."

He comes around to my side of the desk and leans back against it. This is the closest he's been to me since that night. Now that I can smell him, even the cotton fabric of his shirt, I'm reliving that evening. Our hands, our lips, him inside of me. It's weird. Even a week ago this would have brought tingles, but today, well, today nothing. I really want a bed and a pillow and to close my eyes. That's all.

"Are you sure you don't want that foot massage? I can give one to you now."

"No!" I slap my hand to his chest. "That's so inappropriate."

"And what we did wasn't?"

"Yes. It *was* inappropriate. And a mistake."

He crosses his arms and lifts a brow, curling his lips up into a smile. "Was it?"

"You're twenty-two years old, Lucas."

"Age is only a number."

"And my boss' nephew."

"He loves you!"

Is he going to have a comeback for every reason I give? I'm trying to let him down easy, but he's making it difficult. "Listen, you're a great guy —"

"Don't say but. I won't let you. That night was amazing. I can't stop thinking about it." He notices the paper on my printer, grabs it, and reads what I typed. "Nice review." He puts it back down. "Do you need me to take the lead now?"

"What are you talking about?"

He races in and kisses me, his hands on either side of my face. I'm wobbling on my chair, trying to keep falling over, so I grab onto him, though this is not what I want.

"Lucas —" I mumble through my lips, my nose still slightly clogged and I can barely breathe.

"Oh, Cassie," he responds, misreading his name as a sign of passion.

"Mmm." I press my hand against his chest and shove him off. "Lucas!"

"What? I thought you wanted that, too?" He adjusts his shirt which I inadvertently pulled out while trying not to fall out of my chair and onto my ass. "Did I misread you?"

I grip my chair handles. I want to run out of here, but this is *my* office. "Yes. You completely misread me. I'm trying to tell you that this isn't going to work, not to mention I'm still a little sick."

"You're making excuses."

"No, Lucas, I'm not."

I've said about all I can say, and I can't be much more forward than I already am. Neither of us is saying a word, and while his eyes are sinking in confusion, mine swim in regret and apology.

He hikes the sleeves up on his shirt and backs up. "This is about that Keith guy, isn't it?"

My throat drops into the pit of my stomach. "What?" I can't find enough oxygen to breathe. "No!"

I'm a horrible liar. It's not *entirely* about Keith. We're not dating, either. It's more that my attraction to Keith is more appropriate than mine to Lucas. And now I feel a little gross about what happened with Lucas, and I don't want to give any opportunity for it to go further.

"Sure," he says as he clicks his teeth and pulls the stress ball back out of his pocket. This time, he isn't tossing it. He's squeezing it.

I feel bad now. I shouldn't, but I do. "Lucas, look, I'm going through a lot right now. I don't want to add something so complicated into the mix."

He clutches the ball and doesn't let go. "Do you want to talk about it?"

He says the words but his clenched jaw and stiff posture say something else. "No. Thank you, but no."

Lucas nods and I can tell he's looking for a way to leave without seeming rude. "If you need to talk, you know where to find me."

"I appreciate it."

And I do. Even when everything is falling apart in your life and the last thing you want to do is discuss it with someone, sometimes all you need is the suggestion the option is there.

Lucas leaves the room, and I'm left at my desk, trying to figure out what just happened. I sensed maybe he was a little more into what happened than I was but not to this extent. I hope he doesn't think I'm a horrible person for turning him down.

Keith enters my mind, and I replay the moment when I turned him down. Why did I refuse to give him a chance? Because he's part of Dating for Decades? So what? He's handsome, smart, employed, and makes me smile. I'm tired of spending my days and nights alone and now that my Facebook class ended, I don't even have that to cling onto. I don't even know if he'll have me. The way we left things I'm not sure if he's interested or not. I haven't been to a meeting and neither of us has made an attempt to contact one another. But, I need a date for this awards ceremony next week, and Keith is the only person I want to bring. It's time to swallow my pride and make a phone call.

Chapter Twenty-Five

My dress flows down my hips, hugging me in all the right places. The black is slimming and allows me to wear my favorite red heels. A pearl necklace plunges down my neckline. I managed to pluck every last hair from my chin and swept my hair up in a way it disguises the gray. These past months haven't been kind to me in the aging process.

Keith agrees to meet me at the venue. Calling him took a lot of courage, but he welcomed my phone call. Neither of us mentioned the absence between us, and that's fine. It made the conversation much less awkward. I'm more than anxious to see him tonight and spend time with him outside of the working relationship and group sessions.

I asked him not to go to the hassle of picking me up. I think this is a date, but we didn't define it as one and me driving with him only confirms it is. I want to see how the night goes before deciding to take this any further, so he meets me outside the double doors to the venue.

He stops me in my tracks when I see him. He's standing at the doors, a sleek peacoat buttoned up disguising the suit he's wearing underneath. The charcoal tone alerts me to his eyes, and his smile when he makes eye contact with me starts a fire inside me, a pleasant one, warming me to the core. I take my time up the steps, but I want to run straight to him. Wow, I've missed him.

Keith reaches his hand out to me, and I take it as he helps me up the last two steps. He's such a gentleman.

"Good evening, Cassie. Fancy meeting you here."

I laugh at his greeting as he opens the door for me. I step in and he follows behind me. "Thanks for coming."

I begin to take off my jacket, and he finishes the job for me, pulling his off as well and handing them both in at the coat check. I now get a full look at him, matching every description of the word sexy in his two-button slate suit, plaid purple shirt, with a narrow matching tie. Before I only had ever seen him in work clothes or gym wear. I'm taken away by what I see.

"Of course. You look incredible," he says as he begins the walk into the ballroom, his hand flush against the small of my back.

"Thank you." I whisper this, for some reason afraid to fully accept his compliment.

The ballroom is exquisite. It seems to go on for miles, ending at a window overlooking Lake Michigan. Round tables are placed throughout, each table seating eight. The milky linen is offset by turquoise napkins, bouquets of white roses as the centerpieces. The chandeliers hanging from the tray ceilings give an elegant glow with their gold lighting.

"This is amazing." Keith moves his arm a tad further down my back. "Shall we find our seats?"

I glance around the room, and my shoulders tense when I spot Lucas, an attractive little number at his side. This won't be awkward at all.

I motion to Keith I found our seats and he follows me to the table. I'm flattered when he pulls my chair out for me. After we're seated, I say hello to Lucas.

"I didn't know if you were going to make it." Lucas swipes a candy off the table and pops it in his mouth. "I wasn't sure you'd find a date."

I stiffen more as I anticipate an uncomfortable evening. I didn't come here to play childish games, a tug of war between Lucas and Keith with me being the rope. Lucas can pull all he want, but I'm not coming over to his side.

"Lucas, right?" Keith reaches his hand out and offers a handshake, which Lucas eventually accepts.

"Yes. And you're ... Keith?" Both cock their heads in some sort of a manly competition. "This is Nicole. Nicole, this is Cassie and Keith."

She offers a nod but no other words. Instead, she pulls out her phone and starts typing. Her blond hair falls in curls over her excessive cleavage and I imagine her skirt is probably so short I could see her underwear, if she's even wearing any. "How do you know Lucas?" I ask Nicole. I might as well start up some sort of conversation.

She glances up from her phone long enough to answer. "We've known each other since back in the day. We're old ... pals." She nudges him and I know exactly what she means. She's pals with Lucas the same way I was. Suddenly casual sex seems so dirty to me, knowing we've both slept with the same man.

"When is Terrence getting here?" Keith jumps in and saves the day.

"Soon. He had some issue at home. My aunt is sick or something."

Great. At least Terrence would have acted as some sort of a buffer. If he doesn't show, this will make for the world's most uncomfortable evening. "I hope she's okay. I was sick last week. It really brought me down. I haven't missed work in damn near fifteen years until I got that cold."

"Fifteen years? Damn, how old is this lady?" Nicole thinks she whispers to Lucas, but I hear every word she says.

Keith slips his arm around the back of my chair like it's always belonged there. "Would you like a drink?"

He read my mind. An entire bottle of wine would be nice. "Sure," I answer. "Something light." If things keep going downhill, I may step up the drinking, but I don't want to be too drunk before I accept my award, if I win.

Keith leaves me at the table with Lucas and the bimbo. This will make for great conversation. The air between Lucas and me is tense, and I'm positive Nicole and I have nothing in common. I hope he hurries back and brings something strong, even though I said not to. I honestly don't think I'm going to make it through this night.

I cup my elbows, rubbing my arms as though I'm cold, but I'm not. I glance table to table, scoping out the competition. Men mostly populate the tables, some with their wives or girlfriends. Women are making a lot of headway in the Information Technology field, but I still don't meet as many women as I'd like. Most I come in contact with are secretaries and administrative assistants. I'm anxious for the day we have an even playing field or, better yet, overtake it.

"So, you and Keith, huh?" Lucas rips me away from my people watching.

We had this conversation last week and even if I were with Keith, it's really none of his business. "I guess." For tonight anyway. We'll see how this goes.

"Are you okay?"

I gaze past him, contemplating the question. The nominations for this award is incredible, but right now I'm hating myself for being in such an odd situation. I could've come up with some reason not to come. When Terrence told me about the nomination, he was so high on excitement, that he would have accepted me not attending. My phone vibrates in my clutch purse. I wanted to not take it out tonight and prove to Keith that I'm not all about the technology, but answering my phone will provide a much-needed distraction right now.

Please call me. It's about your mom.

Sasha. Maybe looking at my phone was a bad idea. This is supposed to be an exciting night, and now not only do I have Lucas questioning my intentions with Keith, but now Sasha is starting in on me again. I understand her motives to put me back in contact with my mother, but we've been apart for such a long time. She's been absent from my life for so long, that she's now just somebody I used to know. A person who lives in my past. A person who has no right to be in my future. I don't wish anything bad upon her, but I have no desire to see her or make amends. I dismiss the message and put my phone away. "I'm fine. How are you doing?"

"Good. We're good." He glances over at Nicole, whose cat-like eyes are turned back at him seductively. I think I know what he sees in her. Pure sex, I'm sure.

"How long have you two been dating?" Keith better return soon with my drink. My throat is dry, and my sober self can't handle this. Is it too late to change seats?

He slides his hand off the table. I don't need to imagine where he probably placed it based on the small jump from Nicole. "We've dated on and off for many years."

"High school, really," Nicole leans into him. "We were high school sweethearts."

I hardly see her as a sweetheart. Anything but. She and I wouldn't have been friends back in high school. She's too prissy, too likely to stab someone in the back. "How nice."

Keith returns what feels like hours later. "I hope a martini is okay."

"Perfect." I almost spill it taking the glass from him, but I don't skip a beat and start drinking. I'll drink about anything right now.

"What were we talking about?" Keith's arm rests on my chair again, and he scoots in a bit closer. This is good. I like this.

"Oh, did you know Lucas and Nicole here are high school sweethearts? How romantic. Back together after all these years." A whole four, maybe five, years. I've been out of high school, let's see, five, ten. No, I don't want to do the math. It'll only depress me and require another drink to get the number out of my head.

Nicole turns and plants a kiss on Lucas, never even putting her phone down. Even *I'm* not *that* bad. I turn and look at Keith because I can't even watch this. As soon as my face is level with his, he closes the gap between us. What's this? A kiss off? I kiss him back, though, and am transported back to that night in the basement. My body weakens and my heart is pounding. This kiss is going on for a while, and I'm pretty sure people are watching us.

"Ahem."

We break apart and Terrence is standing next to us, Lucas and Nicole are watching us. "Terrence!" Keith and I both stand up.

"Please, sit down." He takes a seat. "Looks like I missed quite a show." He chuckles.

My embarrassment hits the highest of all time. I can't believe my boss caught me making out in the middle of a work event. Even if it's not his nephew, it doesn't change the fact that I'm humiliated and it was unprofessional. "That won't happen again."

"No, it's fine, Cassie. Don't worry about it. Thanks for joining us, Keith. You did a fine job at the office."

"Thank you." The two shake hands like old pals. "I take a lot of pride in my work."

"Well, it shows."

We chit chat for awhile, my favorite, and I learn Terrence's wife hurt her back and that's why she isn't there. I ignore a few more texts from Sasha before I finally do the unthinkable and turn my phone off.

The ceremony begins about fifteen minutes after Terrence's arrival. I'm grateful for the silence at our table. A few comedians make an appearance putting in jokes about all the different phone competitors and the commercials between Mac and PC. We all share a few laughs. An hour into the ceremony, I'm practically nestled under Keith's arm.

When it comes time to give out the IT Manager of the Year

award, Keith grabs my hand and holds it tight. I'm nervous. Maybe the martini and the few drinks I had after weren't the best idea because I'm starting to get dizzy as the emcee announces the nominations.

I'm on the edge of my seat when it comes time to announce the winner. My name comes over the microphone, and I can't move. My butt is glued to my chair, and I'm repeating the name in my head. Did he really say *my* name?

"Cassie!" Keith nudges me. "You won! Get up there!"

I pry myself off my chair as the applause echoes in my ears. As I stand, Keith grabs my hand and pulls me down for another kiss. I'm taken by surprise, and I think it shows because it draws a small laugh from the crowd. I glance over at Lucas, who's glaring at Keith.

I ignore them both and head to the stage. The presenter hands me my plaque. It's lighter than I expected. Not that I thought the gold plates were *real* gold or anything, but I expected it to be a tad heavier. The crowd quiets as they wait for my acceptance speech. All the speeches before me thanked their companies, their co-workers, and their parents. I've got two of the three.

"When Terrence Rhimes told me I was nominated for this award, I was more than a little shocked, to say the least. What I do, well, I love it, and I would do it whether or not this award existed. Thank you, Terrence, for believing in me." Short and sweet is the best way to keep this. Besides, I hate it when acceptance speeches go on and on, so I don't want to be one of those people. I nod my head to signal the end of my words, and the crowd applauds as I make my way back to the table.

"Well deserved, Cassie. Congratulations." Lucas nods toward me.

"Thank you. Maybe one day you'll be getting an award." I'm giddy with excitement now, and I hold the plaque against my chest.

Keith touches my knee, and I allow another kiss. I close my eyes, and I'm smiling inside.

"Excuse me," Lucas says as he stands up and takes a quick drink. "I need to get some fresh air." Nicole stands up to join him. "No, you can stay here. I'll be right back."

He takes off out the exit and leaves the four of us in confusion. "What just happened?" Nicole asks, embarrassed her date took off on her.

"Do you think I should go after him?" I whisper to Keith.

"Why?"

Because I'm sure it has everything to do with me. Because I'm certain seeing us two together hurt him. "He's a friend. He needs a friend."

"Sure. Do what you have to do." There's a cold insinuation in his voice, but I rush outside anyway.

Snow has started to fall, and neither of us is wearing our jacket, not having taken the time to grab it from the coat check. The precipitation is cold against my skin, and I can see my breath as I yell his name.

"Cassie, go back inside. I need a minute. I'll be fine."

"What upset you back there?" I step down the stairs and meet him at the bottom.

"What do you think?"

He's pacing the sidewalk of the venue, his arms crossed in an obvious state of anger.

"I told you, Lucas, we can't be a couple. I like you. We had fun that night. It can't go beyond that." Never in my life did I expect things to go this way. All I wanted was a night to feel young again, and Lucas gave that to me. I didn't expect this.

He tightens his fists and races toward me. I step back for a second until he grabs me and pulls me to him. The snow falls onto my face as he kisses me, dipping me into the flurries. He lets go and steps back. "You don't feel anything?"

I stand there, watching him plead with his eyes, telling me with sheer emotion he wants to be with me, and it kills me inside to hurt him. Is this how it's been with every man I've dated? Have I never even considered their emotional attachments? Have I hurt every single one of them and walked away without any guilt? Lust and love are two completely different emotions. They're two separate roller coasters. If having a strictly sexual relationship with him is only one-sided and he's returning more than that, well, I can't string him along any further.

"No. I don't."

He stomps his foot on the ground and snow kicks up from under his shoe. "Damn it, Cassie!" He curses me as he whips past me and back into the building, leaving me in the shadow of the moonlight, the heartless person that I am.

Chapter Twenty-Six

All I wanted to do was get out of there. I couldn't stand to sit at a table with Lucas knowing I had broken his heart and there was nothing I could do about it. He shrugged it off as though he didn't give a damn by groping Nicole every chance he had. He could've left just as easily, but Keith suggested we stroll through the lights at Red Arrow Park, and I couldn't refuse.

The park, only a few blocks away from the venue site, is quite busy tonight. People are crowding the area and taking in the holiday lights. "I think tonight was the tree lighting ceremony," I tell Keith as we walk hand and hand through the walkway that curves through the park.

"I think it was on Tuesday. Have you ever been to one?"

"No, but I come see the tree every year. You?"

We squeeze past a young family of four as we continue down the trail. "I used to go years ago with my parents and brother. It was kind of a tradition."

"Oh." I didn't have any traditions, even around the holidays. On Christmas morning, my mom gave me something she picked up from the dollar store, usually a coloring book or a plastic toy, and then we headed off to her flavor of the week. I wanted to put up a tree, decorate it with handmade ornaments, but we couldn't afford one.

He stops and faces me. "I'm sorry. I wasn't thinking."

"It's fine. It's not your fault my mom was a drug addict."

His eyes widen and I realize this is the first time I said anything about her addiction. I kept that part out of my discussion with the group, plagued by embarrassment and wanting to avoid judgment.

"I didn't realize ..."

"I didn't tell you." I take his hand back and start walking again. "It's a part of my past I prefer not to discuss. In fact, I prefer to keep it *all* in the past. When I found out my mom was looking for me, it brought all the anger back. She's in the hospital now, and I don't even know how I feel about it."

We approach a band playing classical music. I really should make it a point to come down here more often. The vibe is so positive and energetic, and there are so many different types of people. I lock myself in my office most of the time, and when I leave the office, I drive my fifteen minutes out of the city to go home where I turn my laptop back on and do more work. I'm here with this wonderful man whose hand I'm holding and I'm crushing on, and that's all I want to think about right now. I want to stand here and lean against him, take in these spectacular musicians, and not talk about my mother. This atmosphere is meant for fun and excitement, not sadness and resentment.

"It's okay, Cassie. It's normal to be confused."

I run my hand up his arm and he squeezes me tight. "Thank you, Keith, for being so understanding."

"About that," he begins and my head shoots up from the comfortable position it was in only seconds before. "What happened that night? Why did you kiss me and then want to take it back?"

"*I* kissed *you*?" I pull back and narrow my eyes. "*You* kissed *me*, Mister."

"Either way. *We* kissed and then *you* told me the timing was wrong. Now here we are. What changed?"

I should have known this would come up. I thought when I called him and he accepted my invitation with no explanation it was too good to be true. I'm not even sure I know what changed my mind.

A crowd begins to gather around us and the band. The interruption allows a distraction from Keith's question. Under the sparkling holiday lights and an orchestra of saxophones and piano, a man who must be no more than twenty years old kneels down on one knee in front of a woman with flowing dark hair tucked under a bright pink hat. Her hands cover her mouth and she's visibly shaking and nodding her head. The onlookers burst into applause as the man stands up and kisses his now bride-to-be.

"How sweet," I say as I try and pull Keith along. "I wish them luck."

"You really don't like marriage, do you?"

"Nope. I mean, it's fine for other people. I really do wish them luck. The whole thing never did it for me. I wasn't the girl who dreamed of her wedding day. Not the gown, not the reception, not even the honeymoon."

"That's the best part."

"Hey, I can have sex without a big party beforehand." I blush when I say this, but it makes him laugh.

We come across a bench and sit down, huddled in close together. I like this. We're connecting, and it feels nice. I'm not used to this, this closeness, and even though it's new and scary, I'm not shying away from it.

"You never did answer my question. What changed?"

Here we are again. I doubt he'll let it go until I respond. I lay my head on his shoulder. "I don't know when it changed. It just did. I enjoy time with you. I miss you when you're gone. You're easy to talk to. You make me feel ... wanted."

He kisses the top of my head. "That's nice to hear coming from the woman who turned me away from her group."

I lift my head and shove him away. "Stop it. I'm being serious."

"So am I! You kicked me out!" He holds his hands up in surrender, and as he chuckles, his breath meets the air and I can see it. "So, what is this, what is this between us?"

"Do we need to give it a name? Do you want me to officially ask you to go steady?"

"No, and even if I did, that's the man's job."

"Whoa! If you're some sexist man who can't stand a woman taking control and being successful, this will never work." He may think I'm joking, but I'm quite serious. I spend my days fighting for recognition in an industry dominated by men, and I'm not about to do so in a relationship. Yes, a relationship. "I want a partnership. I want romance and I want conflict. Like you. I don't want to be bored."

"And married?"

"Never." He was engaged once, so it may be something he's not willing to give up. "Are you okay with that?"

He takes my hand and interlaces our fingers. "Yes. I loved my ex, but I only proposed because I thought that would make her stay. I can get married, I can stay single, or I can live in sin my entire life. It doesn't really matter to me, as long as I'm happy."

"I like that."

He inches toward me and touches his lips to mine. He's slow to pull away, and when he does, it's as though an invisible force has to pry us apart. "But..."

It can't ever be easy. There has to be something that will throw a wrench in my happiness. "But what?"

"It's just that I thought that she and I were on the same page and after years together, it shocked me to find out that we weren't. I've had a thing for you since the second you tried to shove me out the door at your meeting. I've been patient waiting for you to come around and realize we'd be great together. When you told me it wasn't a good time for us to start anything, as much as I hated to, I accepted it. I know it seemed as though I didn't care, but I did."

Our hands are still stuck together and I'm squeezing his so tight I'm afraid I may break a finger. "I thought you didn't."

"When my ex left me I was devastated. I couldn't go through that again."

"You won't. I want this." I let go of his hands and wrap my arms around his neck, pulling him toward me. "I want you." As quickly as I shoved him away last time, tonight I close the gap before there's any chance of anything coming between us. He covers my ears with his hands, and within seconds, I'm losing my breath as we both hold on for dear life, our kiss consuming us, fulfilling an emptiness I've had inside of me for years.

Right now, in this moment, I'm whole again.

•••

The shelf right next to my television is the perfect spot for my award. It sits nicely there, dominating the space as it should. I can see it every day when I walk through the living room and catch glances of it while watching *Dancing with the Stars*. I could bring it to work and put it on my desk, but Terrence will surely be crushed since we didn't win the Innovation Award and displaying my award at work may be like a slap in the face for him. I never understood his obsession with awards, but now that I have one, I kind of get the desire for validation.

I wanted to go home with Keith. I really did. All of our kisses and hand holding brought me back to my high school years, and I didn't want to ruin that feeling. This time, I'm taking it slow. *We're* taking it slow.

I've missed a few Dating for Decades meetings, so I think it's about time I show up. I'll go on Thursday, but I'll need to explain my absence to everyone. I'm sure they're pissed, and I can't blame them. Attendance at the meetings has always been a big thing for me. And now here I am, hiding behind my own shame and fears when they're the ones I should be looking to.

I kick off my heels and trade my slinky evening wear for a pair of sweatpants and a sweatshirt. After the night I just had, I still feel beautiful, even in these frumpy clothes. I pull the clips out of my hair and let it fall to my shoulders, the slivers of gray sneaking within my eyesight. I twirl a few strands between my index finger and thumb. How long does it take for your entire head to turn gray? Will they fill my hair like highlights? Will they eventually turn all white and I'll prance around work with a cotton ball on my head like Olympia Dukakis? My mom's hair isn't a solid color, so maybe I'll be lucky. With my fortieth coming up, I wonder if I should dye my hair a natural shade of brown, embrace the grays and leave it as is, or say screw it and put on a hat. I drop the hair from my fingers. I have a few more months to think about it.

My phone vibrates again and this time, it's a phone call and not a text. Like I'm really going to answer the phone? I glance at the screen and it's Sasha again. She really refuses to give up. I'm sure she's festering with anger that I'm not responding. I had a wonderful evening; albeit, it started a little rough, but the ending has been perfect. I don't want her to bring me down off this high. I haven't responded to a text or phone call from her for quite some time. I guess I owe her that much. I ignore the phone call and click to send her a text instead. I thank her for her last update and to let me know if anything changes. I can at least give the impression over a text message that I'm somewhat sympathetic.

I toss my phone onto the coffee table and at the same time, sirens blare outside. My neighborhood is fairly quiet and any type of siren is rare. The lights are flashing practically right outside my window when the siren stops. I find my boots and rush to get my jacket on and race outside.

I'm not the only one who has come outside. Almost every resident on the block is standing at the end of their walkway watching whatever drama is unfolding across the street. An ambulance is parked outside the house and paramedics are rushing inside.

To the left of me, my neighbor watches with her children. I waved to her before, but I realize I don't even know her name. I slowly make my way to her driveway and asked her if she knows what happened.

"Mrs. Clarington. I think she had a heart attack." There is a kid on each side of her, and neither can be much older than six or seven.

I'm ashamed to admit that I don't even know who Mrs. Clarington is. The best I can gather is she lives across the street from me, and she's a woman. That's about the extent of it. "That's a shame."

"She's well over ninety. I'm surprised she's not in a nursing home. I don't see her outside very often, and people come to mow her lawn and plow her driveway. She's weak and she lives alone. I suppose her kids didn't want to foot the bill, though." She tightens the belt on her robe. She must be freezing. "Her kids should be ashamed of themselves, letting her live alone, and probably die that way too."

I resent her words. She's not talking about me, but I can't help but feel though she is. Maybe Mrs. Clarington wasn't a great mother. Maybe she pushed her kids away. Maybe she was mean and was never around. She shouldn't judge unless she knows the facts. And even then she shouldn't judge. She may know this woman, but she doesn't really *know* her. There are many things I want to say to this neighbor of mine, but then I suppose I'm not being any different than I think she is.

"Either way, I hope she is okay and pulls through." I mean that, I really do. I don't know Mrs. Clarington, and from the outlook of things, I probably never will, but it's sad to see something like this.

My phone vibrates in my pocket. I don't even have to look and I know that it Sasha. Again.

Things are looking bleak. Please come see her. They don't think she's going to make it.

As the sirens start up again and the ambulance takes Mrs. Clarington away, I shudder, thinking of my mom in the hospital, possibly taking her last breath. If Mrs. Clarington were a bad mother, would her children want to say goodbye? Would they mourn her death and be sad at the loss of their mother? Or would such a tragedy instead be a blessing in their eyes, free of all of her wrongdoings and harmful ways?

Months ago, before any of this happened, Sasha told me I should work towards forgiveness. Forgiveness is freeing, she said.

How can I offer forgiveness to someone who hurt me so badly? Do I want to have some sort of closure before it's too late? And if I try, will I succeed?

The ambulance turns off the block, and all of my neighbors retreat back into their houses. They rejoin their families and I'm sure will spend the next moments of their lives discussing what they just witnessed and how much they mean to each other, how each day isn't guaranteed. I live every day of my life lately despising my mother and wanting to hold onto my anger towards her. Do I want us both to be at peace with each other before I no longer have a chance?

The truth is, I don't know.

Chapter Twenty-Seven

After a very eventful weekend, Shannon invites me over for Jake's birthday on Tuesday. I haven't heard a word from Sasha, so I assume there hasn't been a change with my mother. Keith landed a job, so he's keeping pretty busy too. I'm glad I can spend the evening with Shannon and her family and celebrate Jake's birthday. At least it isn't mine.

Jake is into video games, like any boy his age I'm sure is, so I went to the easy route and picked up a gift certificate to Game Stop. This way he can pick out whatever he wants, especially considering I have no idea what games or even what gaming system he owns. I don't doubt he'll be happy with the $100 gift card.

I arrive shortly after they finish dinner, but right before cake. "Happy birthday, Jake!" I give him a big hug as I walk in the door and he pushes me away.

"Auntie Cassie, I'm too old for hugs."

"Maybe you just don't get this then." I hold up the envelope with my card and the gift card inside. He tries to snatch it from me, but I go in for another hug. When he finally gives in and lets me squeeze him tight, I hand him the card. "Enjoy." He takes off into the other room.

"Thanks for coming. Even though he doesn't show it, it means a lot to Jake."

"Of course. I had to clear my busy dating schedule, but I fit it in."

"Are you still dating *both* those guys?" I follow Shannon into the kitchen so she can put the candles on Jake's cake.

"I never was dating Lucas, but I *am* dating Keith now."

"When did this happen?"

"Yeah, when did this happen?" Ben touches my back and offers that as a hello.

"Ben! I haven't seen you in such a long time. How are you?" He rests against the counter next to me. I think he's gained a few pounds since the last time I saw him, and I can now confirm I'm not the only person I know turning gray.

He shrugs. "I can't complain." He and Shannon exchange glances, and I can't quite interpret this secret code in their eyes. "I wanted to say hello. I'll let you gals get back to it."

"I'm sure there's a football or basketball game or something on." Shannon picks up the cake and sets it in the center of the table. "Give us five minutes and we'll blow out the candles."

Ben exits the room with a salute to his wife. The vibe in the kitchen makes me shiver, but before I can say anything, Shannon is on me again about Keith. "Tell me! Details!"

"There isn't much to tell. We went out the other night, and I really like him. We're going to see how this goes."

"Oooh, Cassie may get *married*."

"Um. No. We're both in agreement on that. But, I think it may be time to give this commitment thing a try."

"Good for you!" She searches the drawers for something, slamming them open and closed. "I have no clue where the lighter is." In a matter of seconds, she's gone from happy to aggravated. I've never seen her this way before. "Anything new on the Sasha front?"

This is her roundabout way of asking about my mother. "She won't stop texting me. My mom is in the hospital with pneumonia."

"Is she going to be okay?" She finds the lighter and sets it on the counter.

My eyes glaze over and everything becomes a blur. "She tells me no, that I should go see her and possibly say my goodbyes."

"Cassie ... I ... I don't know what to say." She puts her arm around me, but I barely feel it.

"There's nothing really *to* say."

"Are you okay?" Her hand cups my shoulder and she gives it a squeeze. "Do you want me to go with you to see her?"

"I don't think I'm going."

As fast as she put her arm around me to soothe me, she drops it and places her hands on her hips. "You're *not*?" Her tone is condescending, judgmental. "How can you *not* go?"

"Easy." I slap the counter with my hand and move to the other side of the kitchen, leaning against the refrigerator. "I just don't go."

I cross my arms against my chest, making my stance on the subject known.

"I know I said this before, and obviously, it went in one ear and out the other, but you *need* to go see her."

I push off the fridge and begin pacing the room. "No, I don't. You have *no* idea how I'm feeling inside. My mom abandoned me my whole life, and now because she's on her deathbed, I'm supposed to forgive her?"

"Yes! At *least* go see her. Your mom had a *disease*. She was *addicted*. Whether or not you believe it, or *want* to believe it, the fact remains that she did, and *does*, love you. The drugs got a hold of her. But now she's clean and wants the last opportunity with her daughter. Don't you think she deserves that?"

I'm staring at Shannon, this perfect mother in my eyes. She loves her kids more than life and would do anything for them. Birthdays, Christmas, sports, school events, she's there for it all. Her mom was there for all of her big parts of life, too. Mine wasn't even there for the little ones. "I don't know if she deserves it. I didn't deserve *anything* I was given in life."

She steps in front of me to stop my pacing. "Yes, you did and you do. No, you didn't deserve a shitty childhood, but despite that, you managed to get through it all. You're successful and a great friend and a wonderful person. Show her that. Show her that despite her shortcomings, you came out a wonderful human being. Let her die knowing that she wasn't a complete failure, despite what her actions may imply."

She's shaking me and I'm letting her. I want to cry, but I can't let the tears come out. I think I lost my ability to cry years ago.

"Damn it, Cassie, I would give anything to have my mother here. If anything, do it for me."

Sometimes I resent Shannon, and everyone else I know who had a mother in their lives. Why was I the one to be put through all this hell? Why did I have to stand through all these tests? Why couldn't it be easier?

She lets go and turns her back to me, pressing her hands onto the counter. "Ben and I are going to marriage counseling. I'm not sure we're going to make it."

I never realized it was that bad between them. The weird looks in the kitchen before, the awkward exchange between them, that's why. They're one step closer to losing each other. She swings around and points her finger at me. "But do you know what? At least we're trying."

Her face is reddening and any minute now she'll burst into tears. She's fighting to keep everything she has, and I'm trying my damnedest to let go of my past. *Forgiveness is freeing. Forgiveness is freeing.* These words keep haunting me. Maybe it's time to wake up from my nightmare.

"If I go see her — *if* — will you get off my back?"

A tear falls from her eye and she smiles. "You've got a deal."

Chapter Twenty-Eight

Basketball isn't one of my favorite sports. Next to golf, it may be the most boring sport on television. When Keith suggested we go on Wednesday night, I thought why not give it a try live? The atmosphere of a live sporting event is much different than on TV, and I want to share something he loves.

The BMO Harris Bradley Center is busier than I expected, though the seats aren't filled to the max. This isn't like a Packers game where unless you're a season ticket holder or willing to pay out the ass to get tickets you're not going. Seats are still available the day of, and great ones at that. But Keith got the tickets from a client so while I don't mind the nosebleeds, I'm not complaining about the lower level. We're only about five rows back from the floor, so it can't get much better than this.

We arrive at our seats, each with a soft pretzel and a beer. My tray is almost overloaded with cheese. I always request extra. Cheese is the best. *The best.* I guess that's how you know I'm from Wisconsin.

I balance the food on my lap, stiffening my legs and wiggling my butt on the hard seat. How long is a basketball game? About two or three hours after half time and all the breaks? My backside will probably be numb by the time this is done. I look over at Keith and he smiles at me. Okay, maybe he can massage it after. There's a silver lining.

Once I'm finally settled in and comfortable, we're told to rise for the National Anthem. I slide my food under my seat so I have my hand free. I cross it over my heart and listen to the song, Keith belting it out next to me. After it's over, he waits for me to sit and then hands me my food.

"Thanks. It's difficult to sit with this. Next time I'll opt for cotton candy."

"Nah, you're too sweet for that. The arena can't handle both you and the cotton candy."

I roll my eyes at the corniness of what he's said, but it's adorable he's trying to be so romantic with his words. "I can't believe these seats."

"They're awesome. I'm usually way up there." He points to the balcony. "I don't think I'll ever come to a game again unless I have these seats. This is how it's meant to be seen."

The man next to me knocks my elbow as he jumps up to cheer the Bucks as the first basket of the game is made. My pretzel goes flying, the tray flips over, and the cheese collects on my lap. "Damn it!" I stand up as Keith takes my tray from me and sets it on the floor.

"Oh man, are you okay?"

"Yeah." I take a napkin from him and wipe it up. "Thankfully the cheese cooled down enough it didn't burn me."

The guy next to me offers no apology as the others surrounding us whisper and discuss the situation amongst themselves. "Here. You can have my pretzel." Keith tries to hand me his food.

"No. That's fine. I'll go buy a new one once this dries." My jeans now have streaks of yellow running through the material, but thankfully the damage is more on my leg than my crotch.

"Here," he rips the pretzel in half. "We'll share."

I give him a closed-mouth smile, and inside I'm relieved and thankful for his gesture. "I'd like that." Our hands touch as he hands me my half and he takes this opportunity to steal a kiss. The crowd is cheering, and I know it's for the game, but I can't help but imagine it's for us.

The person behind me taps me on the shoulder. I turn and it's a young man, probably a teenager, his Bucks hat turned around backward on his head, a buzz cut underneath. "You're on the jumbotron."

"What?" Both Keith and I look up at the big screen above the court and there we are, staring dumfounded at ourselves. Keith takes this opportunity to lift his beer to the crowd, grab me, and kiss me like it's going to soon be forbidden. Once we're off the screen, he pulls away and I need a moment to catch my breath.

"Wow. That was … "

"Sorry. I may have gone a little crazy, but that was pretty cool."

"Yes, it was. I'm not upset."

"Good. Then now may be the perfect time to tell you something."

After a kiss like that he can't be breaking up with me, but what else could it be? He butters me up and then gives me bad news. He must be a pro at this. "What is it?"

He puts his beer down and turns toward me. "Remember my brother? I told you about him. He's got two kids and lives in London."

"Yes." I swallow. Hard. Is he about to invite me to Europe with him? Wow. This is too soon. I'm not opposed to a weekend trip, but traveling over the Atlantic together?

"He's invited me to come see him. I leave tomorrow."

Tomorrow? He leaves *tomorrow*? As in less than twenty-four hours?

"I know this is short notice, but he's never invited me and my parents are going, too. I thought it was a good time."

So he's *not* inviting me. This is definitely a family event.

"Are you okay with this?"

"What?" He ducks his head to look into my eyes. "Oh, yeah. That's wonderful! How long will you be gone?"

"Ten days. And we can FaceTime and text and chat on the phone. I'll miss you."

I'll miss you. I'm not sure anyone has ever said those words to me. I've never been with anyone long enough to even have the chance for him to miss me. "I'll miss you, too. I'll let the group know tomorrow that you'll miss the next two meetings."

"Are you going? You haven't gone for awhile."

A vendor calls from the aisle interrupting my train of thought. The aroma of buttered popcorn is appealing. "I know. I think I should go. I'm ... I'm going to see my mom. On Friday."

"You're what? I should go with you. I'll cancel my trip."

"No!" I yell out the response so quickly he's taken aback, literally pulling away from me and tightening his lips. "I mean, I appreciate the offer, really I do, but this is something I need to do on my own."

"Are you sure? It's not a big deal. I can go see my brother another time."

"No, you can't. You waited this long for an invitation and can you imagine how much it would cost to cancel or change that ticket now?" I can't be the reason he misses this trip. Or this game. "Let's get back to this game. The first quarter is nearly done and you've barely seen any of it."

"Cassie, don't do this."

"Do what?"

"Don't push me away. You need someone at a time like this. I want to be that person." He's pushing his lips together, the creases next to his eyes deepening as he pleads with me.

"Did you see that shot?" The man next to Keith shoves his arm and Keith ignores him. The crowd is starting to chant as the end of the quarter nears and it's difficult to hear each other.

"I'm not pushing you away." I take his hands in mine and set them on my lap. "My past with my mother is anything short of complicated and I want, no I *need,* to do this on my own." I can see he's listening, but I don't think he's really hearing me. "Please. Go to London. Don't stay for me. I'll still be here when you get back. If you cancel that flight and show up at my door, I'll never forgive you." Water pools in my eyes and I'm afraid of how he'll respond. I don't want some big romantic gesture where he'll meet me at the hospital and it'll be him pronouncing his love to me. No. I am doing this on my own, whether he wants me to or not.

He lifts his right hand and touches my cheek. "Are you sure about this? I don't care about the money." His finger traces my lip. "I care about you."

For once in my life, I'm happy with someone, and I want something to come of this. I don't want this feeling to disappear, and I think he's on the same page as me. The fact he's offering is enough for me. I've gone my whole life not needing anyone, and I can get through seeing my mom without anyone, too. The buzzer sounds, I jump, and reply, "I'm sure."

I've never been so sure about anything before in my life.

•••

I'm apprehensive to attend tonight's meeting since I haven't gone to the last few. A lot has changed since the last time I attended, mostly my relationship with Keith. He's been gone all of six hours, and I miss him already. We haven't slept together yet, but the second he gets back from London, that's first on my list. Right now, I'm craving his touch, his lips, the salty taste of his skin. I'm ready for more.

I arrive at the meeting five minutes before start time, and I'm the last one to walk through the door. Everyone stops their conversations and stares in my direction. I'm on display and they're not happy with me.

"Look who decided to show." Luna leaves the refreshment table avoiding eye contact with me. She plops down on her chair, crosses her legs and her arms.

"Cassie, glad you decided to join us." Cheyenne greets me with a slightly more polite attitude while Noelle and Monica take Luna's lead and take their seats with the frustration clear on their faces. "No Keith?"

Her voice rises in accusation. Has he told them anything about us? I never even thought to ask. I'm the one who ditched the meetings, not him. I should have prepped myself before I came. "He's in London visiting family."

"Here's your bell, if you want to call the meeting to order." Cheyenne sticks it out to me, but I instead turn and sit down in the spot Keith has occupied in the past.

"No. I assume you've been taking the lead while I've been gone. You can do it."

She snaps her mouth shut and sticks her nose in the air as she rings the bell. "This meeting of Dating for Decades is hereby called to order." She places the bell on the floor next to her chair and sits down. "Now —" She clears her throat and wipes a strand of hair from her face. "— is there anything anyone wants to discuss today?"

The room is quiet, something that doesn't happen too often. Are they all waiting for me to say something? Is this where I inform them of my relationship with Keith? I can foresee it already. They all bet how long it would take for us to get together and now it's happened. They win. I realize they will find out somehow, though, so I would rather it came from me.

"I guess I can go." Everyone's eyes dart to me. I tug at the sleeves of my jacket and pull it off, swinging it on the back of my chair. No one's attention has moved from me in the time it took me to straighten my coat and turn back around. "I wanted to let you all know that I'm dating someone."

Noelle's eyes light up. "Dating, dating? Or like Cassie dating?"

I want to be upset with that question for clarification, but I understand why she asks it this way. "Dating, dating. It's new. *Very* new, like only a few weeks new." And I don't want anything to ruin it.

"Is this why you haven't come to any meetings?" Luna interjects with pain in her voice.

I've hurt the group. I've let them down. They deserve an explanation. "I'm sorry about that, Luna. I owe you all an apology."

"No phone call, text. Nothing." Luna points her finger at me, her nose crinkled and eyes shrinking to slits. "You would have had my *ass* if I pulled that."

I nod my head. "You're right. I'm really sorry. There isn't anything more I can say. I've been going through some things with my mother and thought I needed time away."

"Time away? We're here for you." Monica, oh, Monica. I miss her motherly ways. "You can always come to us. Tell us what's going on with your mom."

I don't know if I want to do this, but they want to help me. When people extend their hand to me, I push it away. This time, I won't. So this time, I don't. I break into the tale about my mother, my childhood spent in a furniture absent home and random homes of men I didn't know. I dive into the details of her addiction and her sickness. I exhale deeply, but the weight isn't off my shoulders. I still feel like a boulder is on my back, and I'm trying my best not to let it crash down on me.

"Wow," Cheyenne's mouth drops open. "We had no idea."

"How could you have known? I didn't want you to know about this part of me. I kept this part of me locked up, this past I've moved on from, and now it's haunting me again. Even though I'm going to see her, I'm still unsure if I want to." I shake my head and focus on my nails as I pick at the cuticle. "I'm not even sure what I should say to her."

"Speak the truth to her, Cassie. Tell her how you feel." Monica rises from her chair and kneels next to me, resting her hand on my knee. "You have years of pain tucked away inside of you. This is your chance to speak your truth."

I nod again, placing my hand on top of hers. This is a level of closeness I've never experienced in all my years running this group. As fast as I nodded, I'm now shaking my head. "I can't." My lips quiver as the tears release from my eyes. "I want to, but I can't."

"You'll only regret it if you don't." Luna offers the words, and I'm cautious to accept them as advice. I really upset her with my absence.

Raising my head and the tears still falling, I say, "Am I a horrible person if I do?"

"No one is telling you to go in there and rip into her." Noelle joins Monica at my side. "But you need to say what you've been thinking all these years, what you've been feeling."

I huff in some air as I swallow my tears. They're all staring at me, the care evident in their eyes. My lips are trembling, and while I'm surrounded by support and love, I can't imagine feeling more disconnected than I am right now. My mother is dying. *Dying.* And I'm entirely lukewarm about the situation. I'm the worst person in the world. "I'm broken."

Monica cocks her head and runs her hand up and squeezes my knee. "Cassie, we're all broken in some way."

"You know I have nothing but baby daddy drama," Luna says.

"And my ex-fiancé thought it would be a wonderful idea to sleep with my sister." Cheyenne smiles.

For some reason, Cheyenne's comment makes me laugh, and we all burst into chuckles. The tears are sticking to my face and drying to my cheeks. "Thanks, guys. I appreciate it." Cheyenne offers me a tissue, and I gracefully accept.

"We're all here for you." Cheyenne puts her hand on my shoulder. "Now tell us, who are you dating?"

I exhale and gather myself for a moment before I reply. "Keith."

"I knew it!" Monica hops up and claps her hands together as she breaks into a little dance. This is a side of her I've never seen.

"Okay, okay, you all predicted it would happen and it did. Happy now?"

"Yes, as a matter of fact we are." Noelle says this proudly as though it were always meant to happen. "You know, you're not the *only* one with a steady man in their life now."

"Really, Noelle? Did you meet someone?"

She shakes her head. "Not me." I wait as they all take their seats again. "Cheyenne."

"Cheyenne?" I wink at her. "Good job! When did this happen? Tell me about it."

"Well, I met him while pumping gas of all places, and we exchanged our cell numbers. At our last meeting, Keith encouraged me to put my fears aside and call the guy. So I did. And we've actually been on four dates in the past week."

"Four in a week? Wow! That sounds pretty serious to me."

Cheyenne squeezes her shoulders together. "I guess sometimes you know when it's time to let go and no longer let your fears hold you down, but instead drive you forward."

"That's a very interesting view."

"Those are Keith's words. And they really stuck with me."

"Good for you, Cheyenne. I'm very happy for you. Luna, what's going on with you?"

"Not a whole lot on the dating scene. I've had a little bit of drama with my son's father, and that's held me back a little bit. But I'm making a New Year's resolution to put myself out there and try something new. I think I might give online dating a shot."

This makes me think of Lucille. I wonder if she's spending her Christmas with Billy, or if they decided to tie the knot. She's a successful story of online dating if I've ever heard one. Sure, they weren't strangers, but considering the number of years from when they saw each other last, they might as well be. "I think that's a great plan," I encourage her. "Just be careful. There are some crazies out there."

"Not any crazier than me!" Luna's dig on herself draws out a series of laughs we can't stop. For the first time in a long time, maybe ever, I feel as though I'm in the company of friends, and for a while I'm able to forget about what awaits me tomorrow.

A harrowing truth.

Chapter
Twenty-Nine

I don't belong here. Of all the things I could be doing today, visiting my mom in the hospital is not top on the list. I shut off the car and lay my head back on the headrest. Was I stupid to deny Shannon, Sasha, *and* Keith's invitation to come with and support me? As much as I want to do this on my own, the last time I saw her I acted like a child. If I can't be an adult about this, maybe I shouldn't even be here.

I yank my keys out of the ignition. Damn it, I'm doing this. Noelle, Monica, Luna, and Cheyenne all have confidence in me. *I* should have confidence in me like I do in everything else. Sasha said she's in a pretty bad state, not even able to respond at this point, so I won't have to deal with her comments back to me. I can say what I need to say and leave.

I enter the hospital and check in at the front desk. The person hands me a Visitor sticker with my name and the room number on it. "Fifth floor," he tells me as I slap the sticker onto my jacket. My knees shake as I wait for the elevator, and when I finally step on and the door closes, my stomach drops to the floor. Not the normal stomach dropping when the elevator takes off feeling, but an *Oh my gosh I'm about to see the woman who screwed up my entire life and never gave a shit about me.* Should I have brought something? Is there a protocol for the ICU? Will she be expecting anything? And what do I say when I get in there? I want to turn around, but I can't. I promised Shannon. I gave my word to the group. And Keith will be disappointed. If there's one thing I'll never do, it's break a promise.

The doors open and I'm face-to-face with the sterile area, a large corridor before me. I maneuver my way through the halls following the signs for ICU. When I finally reach it, I'm in open area with five rooms with clear glass and a nurse station in the center. I put one foot in front of the other because that's all I can remember to do. My hands are in front of me, and I'm picking at the skin, yanking at it and pulling out it, until I eventually pull the arms to my jacket down so I'm holding a wad of cloth in my hand.

The nurses at the desk are chatting, throwing their heads back in laughter and typing on their computers. I'm slightly irritated by this. Isn't an intensive care unit supposed to be somber? Patients lie on their death beds, and they're out here joking and going on about their lives. I shake my head before bypassing them to my mother's room.

I take my time and the closer I get to her room, the harder my heart beats. She's in the fourth room. I can see her lying there, tubes coming out of everywhere. Her head is turned to the left, away from me. David is at her side, reading her a book. I remind myself to breathe. David notices me and puts the book down. I watch as he leans over and kisses her forehead.

I'm standing outside the room, David coming toward me. I guess he's my stepdad? If I wasn't uncomfortable before, I sure am now. I try to swallow and panic for a moment when I can't. When I finally manage, he's in front of me.

"Are you Cassie?"

I nod, unable to form any words. He's shorter than I expected. The pictures made him appear taller, and he's much less radiant. I suppose his wife is dying behind that glass so he wouldn't exactly be cheerful.

"I'm David. David Heckler."

My mother married someone with a last name like that? I imagine his grade school years. He probably was called Heckles, or Hickey, or maybe even they manipulated it into David the Pecker. No wonder she didn't change her last name. Noble is a bold name. Proud.

"Hello. How ... how is she doing?" Dumb question. She's doing crappy. But what else am I supposed to say to him?

He's blocking the doorway, holding the door slightly shut. "She's heavily drugged. They can't keep her blood pressure up so they've laid her flat on her bed and have her on Levophed and Neosynephrine."

These terms mean nothing to me. All I hear is Leo and Neo and I gather they do something for her blood pressure.

"When you've been here as much as I have, these drug names roll off your tongue."

I bet he's been here almost every minute of every day and I only cared to show up when she's close to taking her last breath. Here's a man standing before me who committed to my mother after all the drugs, after the HIV, after all of it. He's looked past it all. Why can't I? "Is she speaking?"

He shakes his head. "No. Besides the low blood pressure, her kidneys are shot. She's unresponsive. The machine is doing her breathing for her. You're not too late, but ..." he trails off and gazes past me. "She doesn't have long."

I swallow again and this time, I'm mourning for his loss before she's even gone. Through his tired eyes, his love shines through, bringing light to a place that only darkness can typically consume. "Thank you for being there for her." I shift my weight from one leg to the other and with every ounce of pride swallowed I add, "since I wasn't."

I allow him to put his hand on my shoulder. "She loves you, Cassie. She wishes she could do everything over. She can't, and she's accepted that. Please go in and see her. Say your goodbyes." His hand releases. "She wouldn't want to live like this. I waited for you, so you could say goodbye. I'm ... we're ... the doctors."

He doesn't need to finish his sentence. Once I say what I have to say, he's taking her off the machine. She'll be gone. He's strong, David. I admire he shares this with me and does it without shedding a tear. It's not that he's not sad — I know this — he's her rock. And he's exhausted. "Thank you. Why don't you get yourself some coffee? You could use a cup."

He doesn't open his mouth when he smiles or laughs, but he seems pleased with my suggestion. "I sure could. I'm fine, though. I want to stay close. I'll give you two some private time." He reaches out and touches my arm. "Look, don't be a stranger. I'm glad we finally met."

She's talked about me before with him. A lot. It's obvious through this short conversation. I never had a dad in my life and I don't need one now. But maybe I have room for a friend. "Me, too." He moves out of the way so I can enter my mom's room. I wait for him to be out of my sightline before I step through the large entryway to the room.

I'm in shock at what's before me. She lies in the bed, tubes coming out of her nose and chest and a huge one attached to her mouth. The room is silent except for the beeping of the machines. Standing outside the room, it didn't seem this bad. I cover my mouth at what I'm seeing. Her eyes are closed and she looks at peace, though she's much thinner than when I saw her last. I wonder if she is in any pain.

I gently step beside her, trying to be as soft as I can with my steps. "Mom?" I can't believe I'm calling out to her. I haven't called her that with such a soft, pleading voice in decades. I say it again, but she doesn't move.

I keep my jacket on but unzip it. I'm a little hot even though it's only twenty-something degrees outside. As I approach her, her chest is moving up and down, but I know the machine is doing it for her. When they take all the tubes out and stop the machine, will she just stop breathing? Will she gasp for air, or maybe even wake up and see me? It's too much to think about, too much to handle. "Mom, it's me, Cassie."

I swear she tries to open her eyes, but I know this isn't possible. Did I see her index finger twitch? I'm sure it's a reflexive action if I did. Sasha said that she was in a bad state, but I didn't expect to not be able to have her talk back to me. She's lying there, helpless, unable to speak or barely move, and her eyes open barely to a squint. Sasha should have said it was this bad. *She's sleeping a lot* she told me every time I texted with her. She clearly isn't sleeping. She has no idea what is going on around her.

I pull one of the chairs over by the window to the bed. When I sit down, I go to touch her hand, but then quickly retreat. I want to be with her, I want to say so many things, but I'm not ready for that. I try to gather my thoughts, but all the words are floating in my head, bumping into each other as they try to formulate into sentences. I close my eyes and lean my head back as I take a deep breath. *One, two, three, four, five.* I exhale on the same count before I begin to speak.

"I'm sorry it's taken me this long to come see you. You can understand, though, why I didn't. Our last meeting didn't go so well, and well, you know about everything before that."

She doesn't offer any type of response. Not in the form of a head nod, shake, blink, or even the raise of a finger. This may all fall on deaf ears, and maybe that doesn't make it relevant. I may say all of this and it won't mean a thing because if she can't hear a thing I say, maybe it's like it didn't even happen. But, it doesn't matter. I have to say it. For me. For the little girl in me.

"I'll be forty in a couple of months. Can you believe it? I made it, Mom. After everything, I made it." I picture myself on the living room floor, keeping warm with a waffle blanket and space heater. I'm curled up into a ball, calling out for her, crying, and she isn't there. I wonder if it's like this for all ten-year-olds. I wouldn't want this for my kids. And in that moment, I vowed I would never have any.

"I'll be forty years old and be childless. Much how you are today." Even though I'm still her daughter, I certainly don't see myself that way. "I don't understand why you chose the drugs over me. How did they get a hold of you? What was so great about them? What could they offer you as a high that I couldn't as your daughter? I watched my entire childhood pass me by. My friends were going to dances and Girl Scout meetings and doing things with their moms, and I was left in the care of whatever guy you were hooking up with that month, while you went off and did your drugs. How did you really expect me to react to all this? Did you think once I became an adult I would know how to automatically take care of myself and then I would be grateful to you as though all of these instances were chances for me to learn to be out on my own?"

I suck in air and hiccup as I push back the tears. I can't lose it. I must be strong. Resilient. The Cassie Noble I've grown to be. "No. It doesn't work that way. Instead I was left to find myself a job and make money so I could go to college and struggle to get where I am today. I didn't have anyone to help me through it all. Sure, there was Aunt Dorothy, and Sasha, but they had their own thing going on. Sasha's dad was away on business trips, and they were trying to hold it together. Did you expect Aunt Dorothy to raise me, too? Obviously not. I don't think they even knew what was going on half of the time." My mom had an Oscar winning performance keeping her lifestyle under wraps for so long and feared me into thinking I'd end up in foster care if I told anyone. I managed to keep it a secret most of my life. I should get an Oscar, too.

She's motionless, except for the machine. The hum of the heater buzzes in my ears, a reminder of that space heater. I bolt upright when someone marches into the room, a teenager. She stops in her tracks when she sees me. She has dark hair outlining her face and black eyeliner I think she used a marker to put on.

She tightens her lips and nods at me, and I think this is her way of offering sympathy. "Sorry. I thought this was my mom's room. She's the next one over."

I watch as she leaves and disappears to the room next to me. She didn't look distraught. She didn't look like she wanted to get away from her family. She probably has a close relationship with her mother and wants to sit at her side while she's in the hospital. She's more than likely been at her mom's side through whatever illness brought her here, and wishes more than anything she'll be okay. Here I am, and I barely even know my mother. I can't hold it in any longer. The tears start to fall from my eyes and drip down my nose into my mouth. I sniffle as I try to control myself from breaking down into a hyperventilating state.

"All I ever wanted was a mother. I didn't need to have the latest and greatest things or anything special. I only wanted *you*. And that was too difficult for you to give me. Between me and the drugs, you chose the drugs. When I left, you didn't try to find me for how many years? Forgiving you, it's too difficult. I can let go of it all. I have to. But I can't forgive you."

After all these years, it feels good to be saying all of this. This is what I should've said to her at Sasha's house, but didn't. Am I a cruel person for choosing to tell her all of this now? Perhaps. But I need to lift this boulder off me. I'm suffocating. I need to find peace within myself.

"I'm not saying I don't love you. Those words never came out of my mouth. And I hope you're okay with the kind of mother you have been, even if I'm not. And I hope that you're happy in your new marriage, and you are truly clean and going forward can live a proper life. Right now, at least, I don't think I can be a part of that. But maybe someday."

I stop what I'm saying, realizing she *won't* be there. She *can't* live a proper life. I can *never be* a part of her life. She's not going to recover from this. Ever.

What if by some miracle she *did* hear everything I said? I'm a horrible, horrible person and daughter and I should take it all back. I don't want the last thing she hears from me to be that I hated her. I didn't outright say that, but I didn't say the kindest things either. I'm glad I shared my honest feelings with her, but at the same time, I should say something else.

Forgiveness is freeing. There's Sasha in my head again. She'll forever be screaming this in my mind until I finally take a chance and do it. And mean it.

The machine she is hooked up to is beeping at a more rapid pace. Should I call someone in here? Is she going to be okay? I peer out the glass window in front of me and one of the nurses points to the monitor and leaves the desk and comes into the room.

"Is everything okay?" I rise from my chair and David follows behind the nurse.

"I'm Bridget. I've been taking care of Claire." She doesn't hesitate when she comes to my mom's bedside, and doesn't give me a second glance. She's focused on my mom and pressing buttons on the machines. A tinge of jealousy jolts through me when she places her hand on my mom's forehead. "Everything is okay, Claire. I'm here. So is David."

And her absent daughter. I don't fit into this equation. David is her life now. Or was. His eyes meet mine, and I know it's time. He's ready, or at least as much as he can be, because my mom is.

This machine is what's keeping her alive. She's no longer in there. Her chest is rising and falling, but only because a machine is telling it to. David waited for me and it's time. He needs to move on, as do I. She's already gone, she's waiting for us to let go.

"I'm sorry, David. I can't be here for the final ..." I choke on my tears to keep them in. "Thank you for allowing me to see her."

I take a step back and stare at this woman, this person I could have given a second chance to and refused. I stare at her and think of what David said, how she would change it all if she could. She can't change the past, but I can change the future and my response to this situation. I step out of the room and before I turn to leave, I touch my hand to the glass and mouth silently, hoping she hears me, "I forgive you."

Chapter Thirty

What happens when someone dies? Does her soul leave her body and she floats above herself, waiting for her invitation into Heaven or does she listen to a list of all the ways she did people wrong on the long trip down to Hell? Does she reincarnate into a butterfly or a lamp or a spoon, or even a new human being? Is she able to watch the people around her, read their minds and understand their emotions?

My mother died tonight, and I have no way of knowing if she heard me forgive her.

My visit to her was supposed to be enlightening for me, a chance to say what I've been feeling and lift this burden off my shoulders. I told her I forgave her, and I really believe I do, but now I'm ridden with guilt. Guilt that I didn't say these things sooner. Guilt that I thought these things at all.

I didn't go into work at all today. After witnessing death, as much of it as I allowed myself to watch, it sort of takes the energy out of you. I comforted David the best I could, as someone who barely knew the deceased despite our blood. He told me this was what she wanted. She didn't want the doctors to spend time trying to revive her if she lost her battle. My mom *was* happy, and she and David loved each other. Even if things didn't go well between us, she felt blessed she had an opportunity to see me at Sasha's.

And I threw spaghetti at her.

It's six in the evening, and I can't remember the last time I ate. I think I had a handful of cheerios around noon when Sasha came by, and Shannon tried to force-feed me a bowl of chicken noodle soup at around four. I drank the broth, that's it. I'm sitting on my couch and that's all I'm capable of right now. I've cried — *cried* — like my eyes hurt and I'm so tired but they're wide open. The stickiness of my tears is holding them hostage, and I don't know if I'll be able to close them again.

I'm dried up. I don't have any more tears to give. I'm ridden with shame and guilt, and I'm the worst person in the world. Sasha told me to go weeks ago to visit my mom, and I didn't. Even when she texted me, she probably wouldn't make it, what did I do? I waited three more days to go see her.

My phone chimes next to me. I don't think I've picked it up the entire day. I called Terrence and said I wouldn't be coming into the office. He offered his sympathies, and I accepted, though I think David is owed them, not me. The rest of the day I've been sitting in practically the same spot, staring at a blank television, trying to process this.

I pat the couch until the phone is underneath my hand. I'm expecting this time for it to be Aunt Ella or Aunt Dorothy, or maybe Sasha or Shannon again. The screen is flashing and it's not any of them. It's Keith and he wants to FaceTime.

Keith. In all of this, I've forgotten about him. Add onto my list of ways I'm a shitty person that I didn't even call my boyfriend to tell him my mother died. My face looks as though I've been crying for months, not hours, and I'm not much in the mood for talking. I can't ignore him, though.

I press the button to accept and when his face fills the screen, I forget for a moment about the pain, and my heart is together again. "Keith." I can't say his name with enthusiasm. I can barely move, much less talk. "What time is it in London?"

"It's one in the morning. I wanted to talk to you. I didn't want to bother you at work and figured you would be home right now." He squints and eyes my face up and down. "Are you crying? Did things not go well with your mom?"

I bite my lower lip as I shake my head. "She ... she ... she's gone." That's easier to say than the D word.

"Cassie, I'm sorry. Why didn't you call me?"

"I ... I've been sitting here on the couch all day, thinking. I said mean things to her before she ... well they weren't the kinds of things daughters say to their mothers before they pass away. I'm such an asshole." I can't keep eye contact with him. I'll cry even more.

"You're not an asshole. A lot of people wouldn't have even gone and you did."

"I forgave her, Keith." I bring my attention back to him. He's sitting up in his bed, his head against the headboard. "I said the words before they took her off the respirator. But she didn't hear me."

"You don't know that. You went, and that's the important thing.

I'm hopping on the first flight in the morning and coming home."

"No, you're not." I sit up for the first time in hours, and my tired back almost forces me back down again. "Stay with your family. There's nothing you can do here." I don't want to be a burden on him.

"Yes, there is. I can be there for you, offer you comfort, and attend the funeral with you."

"There isn't going to be one."

"What?" The space between his eyebrows shortens. "Why not?"

"She didn't want one. She'll be cremated, and David is taking her ashes. You have to understand that she wasn't the most favorite person in our family."

"That doesn't mean no one would attend her funeral."

"It's exactly what it means. Sasha, David, and possibly me and my aunts. That's it." I think about when I die. I can't say I'd have many more people at mine. "Besides, this is what she wanted. She and David discussed it. She has it in her will. So no, don't come back."

He's fixated on my face, and sympathy is written all over his. "No. I'm coming, Cassie. Nothing can keep me away from me when you need me."

I don't expect him to come. I don't expect anyone to do anything for me. I can't believe I've found someone who cares for me so much he's willing to cross the Atlantic at a moment's notice to be with me.

I don't deserve this.

Chapter
Thirty-One

A little more than twenty-four hours later, I'm at the airport, picking Keith up. He wanted to take a cab, but I insisted. While he spent fourteen hours on a plane, I spent those same hours trying to sleep. I tossed and turned all night, incapable of falling into a slumber. Anytime I closed my eyes, there lay my mother, machines attached to her, unable to communicate. It's funny how many times as a kid I was in her presence when she was so doped up she passed out on the floor. This wasn't the same. Not even close.

When Keith meets me at the front entrance, he drops his bags down and runs to me. I don't move. My favorite black boots are glued to the ground, unable to process that this man came to me, came to rescue me like my Knight in Shining Armor, something I never in my life thought I wanted or deserved.

"Cassie," he says when he reaches me, throws his arms around me and presses his lips to mine as though it's the last kiss we'll ever share. The familiarity of his kiss breathes me back to life, and I embrace him too. I never want to let him go. When we pull apart, I bury my head in his chest and sob.

"I'm sorry, Keith," I mumble into his jacket, and he holds me tighter.

"It's okay. I'm the one who's sorry." He kisses the top of my head, and I hold him for a moment longer before we grab his bags and go back to my car.

"You didn't need to pick me up." He slams his car door, and I flip on the seat warmer for him. Once he clicks his seatbelt in, I pull away from the curb.

"Yes, I did. I had to get out of my house. I had enough of that place." I crack the window and inhale loudly. "The fresh air is good. I'm only sucking in the circulated heat in the house. This is nice."

"Are you okay? Did you make any plans to spread the ashes with your mom's husband?"

David asked me before I left the hospital. I think he wanted to wait to approach me, but I sensed he wasn't sure he would see me again. He probably won't. I didn't know him at all. I only learned his last name yesterday. Even if he was married to my mom, we hardly have a connection or a reason to keep in touch. "No. I told him he can do it. Find somewhere special that they loved, or keep them in a beautiful urn. I left the choice up to him. I shouldn't be involved."

Keith doesn't respond, and I think he realizes I'm right. I may have been stubborn about seeing her and people may have fought like mad for me to swallow my pride and visit her, but the line is drawn here. "When are you going back to work?"

"Terrence doesn't want me back to the office for two weeks. *Two weeks.* Can you believe that?" I put my attention to him for a moment to gauge a reaction, but he doesn't seem too surprised. "There is so much to be done at work. It's the one thing I can always count on to be there. Regardless of what's going on in life, I'll always have an email to respond to, a coworker to assist, or somebody who needs my expertise. It's nice to feel needed and wanted."

Keith reaches his hand out and rests it on my knee, moving it up slightly on my thigh. He doesn't move it too far up to be sexual, but it's not far enough down to be a friendly gesture. "I need and want you, Cassie. Don't forget that."

And it is so easy to forget. This romance between us, I'm not used to it. We've been together only a few weeks, and it's the longest I've dated anyone, I think, *ever*. Being part of a couple is different for me. I need some time with it. "Am I taking you straight home?" We hadn't discussed if we were going to do anything first, or maybe tonight would be the first night for us to be intimate. I want and need the comfort right now. Before he left for London I made the decision when he came back I wasn't going to hold out. I want to take things slow, but a few weeks is slow enough for me.

"Do you want to go on a date?" He removes his hand from my knee. "I mean, are you up for a date?"

"Yes. Please. Take me out and show me a good time. Anything to take my mind off of things."

"Hm." He rubs his chin and I now notice he hasn't shaven in some time. I kind of like the scruff. "How about ice skating?"

Eek. The one time I went ice skating I fell pretty hard and split open the skin by my knee pretty bad. I didn't need stitches, though I have a scar. "Like on skates and everything?"

"That's usually what ice skating entails."

I love to hate his attitude. "I'm not the best at it." Maybe I can think of something else. Would he like laser tag like I did with Lucas? No, scratch that. Bad idea to do something with Keith that I did with Lucas, unless it's sex.

"You don't have to be. I can help you."

He will, too. I'm positive he'll hold my hand and make sure I don't fall and hurt myself like I did when I was a little girl. "I'm not sure about this."

"What's there to be sure about? It's ice skating. It's two people going out in the cold and having a good time together. Maybe we can get some hot chocolate afterward." He crosses his legs and twiddles his thumbs up.

I'm being standoffish. He wants to take me out. I should let him. Ice skating could be romantic, and I'm in desperate need of romance.

Chapter Thirty-Two

I don't completely despise the cold. Winter is at the bottom as far as favorite seasons ago. I tolerate it. I've lived in Wisconsin my entire life, and I honestly can't imagine living somewhere where I never see snow. Snow and the cold have become such a part of my life that I would miss it if it were gone. Besides, winter is the best month to wear the cutest boots and find the most adorable jackets to keep me warm. And don't even get me started on the purses. The more pockets, the better.

The place to ice skate is Red Arrow Park, the same spot we went after the awards ceremony. I exit the interstate and maneuver through the one-way streets. "You must be exhausted." The few times I've been out of my time zone have given me massive jet lag. I can only imagine what being out of the country does to you.

He opens his mouth and a yawn comes out. "Come on now, don't mention anything even related to sleep. I *am* tired, but spending time with you is much more important than sleep."

My pulse races as I hold a grin back. I don't want to come across as a giddy school girl, though I very much feel that way when I am around him. "If I weren't out with you I'd either be sitting on my couch moping or trying to find a way to work without Terrence knowing I'm doing so."

"Do you work *all* the time?"

"Not *all* the time. Maybe *most* of the time." We exchange smiles. "Though, in the wake of everything, I think it may be time to reevaluate a few things."

"That's good. I believe it's important to take a step back every so often and observe everything in life with a fresh viewpoint. You don't want to stay in a constant state of standing still. Get moving, change things, mix things up. You never know what you'll discover and what you like to do."

"Is that how you became an electrician?"

"As a kid, I loved building things. The wires and light bulbs and the science behind it all fascinated me. This path felt natural."

"Do you know what doesn't seem natural?" Keith shakes his head as I pull into a parking spot a block away from the rink. "The fact that I didn't have to park in a garage and found a spot this close."

"I suppose that doesn't happen very often."

Downtown Milwaukee is bumper-to-bumper cars parked on the side of the streets and during special events the parking lots fill up quickly and it cost a lot of money. Scoring a spot where we did makes me want to buy a lottery ticket. Although with Keith beside me, I may have already won.

"Stay right there. I'll get the door."

He surprises me with this gesture, especially since I'm the one driving. I think back to all the dates I've been on in my life and not one man has ever opened my car door for me. I could definitely get used to this.

"Thank you very much," I say with appreciation as he takes my hand and helps me step onto the curb, his hand supporting my lower back.

He shuts the door and doesn't let go of my hand. I feel a little silly holding his hand. I don't think I've done that since high school. At the same time, it's kind of nice. Though we're both wearing gloves, the pressure of his hand on mine is helping keep me warm. We're like the teenagers already on the ice, young and in love.

I wait at the bench while he rents skates for us. They aren't the most attractive things, certainly not as stylish as my Stuart Weitzman over the knee boots, but I can pull them off. Once I'm all laced up, I stand and nearly fall right back over. Keith catches me, and we're practically in a hug.

"Be careful!"

"Thank you," I say as I catch my breath.

"Why don't I hold onto you until we get on the ice?"

"I'd like that."

His hand is tight around my waist, and I'm glad I wore a jacket that covers any excess muffin top I may have. There's nothing worse than a man holding onto your fat.

Once we're on the ice, he lets go of my waist but grabs a hold of my hand again. Despite my fear of ice skating after such a hiatus, I pick it right back up as though riding a bike. We glide across the ice, our skates leaving imprints. After a while, I don't even notice the cold air hitting my face. I'm warm inside. I'm warm everywhere. After probably about a half an hour of skating, he leads me to a bench to sit down and take a rest. "You're actually pretty good."

"I'm really glad I didn't fall. I worried about that the entire time."

"Don't worry. If you started to fall, I'd catch you."

I don't doubt that he would.

We lean back against the bench and he puts his arm around me. I'm watching all the couples and families and children on the rink. They're all having so much fun without a care in the world. "Wait a minute. Is that..." I squint my eyes until the face becomes recognizable. "Lucille! Lucille!" I wave my hand, and as soon as she sees me, she and her skating partner glide towards us and off the ice.

"Cassie, dear! How nice to see you!" She intertwines her arm with the man beside her. "This is Billy. My husband."

"You two got married? Congratulations! Nice to meet you, Billy." The class hasn't even been over more than a month and Lucille already is married?

"Pleased to meet you. Lucille has said quite a lot about you." I kiddingly glare at her. "Good things. All good things. I should thank you for putting us together after all these years. We can attribute our marriage to you."

Billy is sweet. He is a lot shorter than I imagined, standing at least a couple of inches shorter than Lucille. His hair, what I can see underneath his hat, is all gray. He also wears circle glasses. He almost reminds me of an elderly Harry Potter. All that's missing is his magic wand.

"I'm glad I was able to help. This is Keith." Everyone exchanges their hellos. "Lucille was in my class at the library," I explain to Keith, confused as to why this woman and I have a connection.

"Was Cassie a difficult teacher?"

"Be careful, Lucille. It's not too late for me to change your grade."

Lucille smiles and turns her body so Billy is now hugging her. They remind me of a young couple who just found love. I suppose they kind of are. "She was great." She begins to pull Billy back to the rink. "We should get back on the ice." As she offers a wave to me, she says, "It was so nice seeing you, Cassie. And it was absolutely wonderful to meet you, Keith." She winks at him. We say goodbye and even though Keith is beside me, I'm a little envious of Lucille. It took me months to even admit I had feelings for Keith, and here she is, twice as old as me and she married the man of her dreams in a few short weeks.

"She was an interesting lady. They met in your class?"

"No. She searched for him on Facebook. They went to grade school together." The story still amazes me, even more so saying it out loud. "She was my favorite in the class. Teacher's pet, I guess."

He pulls me close and whispers in my ear, sending shivers through my body, "What does one have to do to become the teacher's pet?"

"Mmm," I groan as he kisses right behind my ear. I squeeze his arms tighter. "Buy me a cup of hot chocolate."

"You bet."

The Starbucks across the street is the perfect spot for our hot chocolate. I've come here before for business meetings. On a typical day, it's filled with either business people or college students. Tonight, it's hopping with couples, loners, and families. Everyone has come in to warm up from the cold.

I wait at the table, watching Keith as he places our order. Every so often he looks behind and steals a smile from me. This evening couldn't be better than it already is. If I went home right now, I think I could fall asleep, content and filled with love inside me. This is the perfect end to a few not so perfect days.

He arrives back at the table with our order. "Hot chocolate for my lady." He slides the cup to me, a large hot chocolate complete with whipped cream on top. As I bring the cup to my mouth, the cinnamon surprises me, but I love the extra sweetness.

I pull off my gloves and set them next to my cup. "Thanks so much for this."

"Of course. Hot chocolate was always one of my favorites in the winter. My brother and I used to go ice skating and then get a cup."

"Did you get to spend a lot of time with him while you were there?"

"Some. I hung out with my nieces a bit."

I picture him playing Barbies and putting pigtails in their hair, and them taking turns covering his face in make-up. The image makes me giggle.

"What?"

"Nothing. You're just nothing short of amazing." He reaches across the table and takes my hands. Now I'm picturing us strolling through Paris, hand-in-hand, taking in all the scenery and everything the culture has to offer. "I've never been out of the country. Hawaii, once, on business, if I can count that since I flew over open water."

"Nope. Doesn't count since it's still the US."

"I'm grasping at straws here. I'm not well traveled."

Keith rubs his finger on mine where a wedding band would go. "I'll keep that in mind. I would love to take you to London. Or Italy. Anywhere, really."

I want to take him straight to my bed, but I don't say that. I hold my breath, keeping myself from saying exactly what's on my mind. Darting my tongue out and licking my lips, I release my breath. "This is nice."

"Yes," he pushes our fingers closer together, "it is."

Even though I'm warm from the hot chocolate, goosebumps take over my body, and I'm sure my skin is flushed. "I kind of don't want the night to end."

A smile slowly builds on Keith's face, and he leans forward, closer to me. "It doesn't have to." My eyes are locked on his, and I'm speechless that he's reading my mind.

This is the next step, the one I've been waiting for, the one I promised myself when he left for London. I think of Lucille and Billy, and Cheyenne and the gas pump guy, and even my mother and David. They didn't deny themselves love. Why should I?

I don't say anything. I only close the gap between us, telling him yes with my lips.

•••

This is the first time I've been to Keith's place. I assumed he lived downtown for some reason, but he doesn't. He lives about fifteen minutes away, nestled in a small neighborhood on the south side of Milwaukee. While it's urban, it definitely has a suburban feel with the wide street and trees lining the sidewalks. They're all bare now, but I'm sure in the summer the greenery is magnificent. However, I don't envy him when fall comes and he has to rake all the leaves.

The outside of his ranch is decorated for the holidays, strings of lights hanging from the garage and the outlining the windows.

When we exit the car he flips a switch in the garage which turns on the lights.

The garage is small, fitting only one car. It's neat — too neat for a garage! Storage units outline the entire thing and the floor is spotless.

We enter the house through the attached garage, directly into the kitchen. I gasp and cover my mouth when an orange tabby cat jumps past me and hops onto the kitchen table.

"Now, Einstein, you know you're not supposed to be up there." Keith picks up the cat gently and holds him, stroking his fur. "This is Cassie. Cassie, meet Einstein, my partner in crime."

"Hi, Einstein." I reach out to pet him expecting him to run away, but he doesn't. He lets me run my hand down from his head, over his back, and to his tail. "You're sweet."

"He is." He gives him a quick smooch on the head and sets him on the ground. Once his paws hit the floor, he takes off. "I won't see him for another few days, probably. He has a mind of his own."

I didn't picture Keith as a cat person. Dog, *maybe*, but not cat. All those times I joked about becoming a cat lady and here's Keith with the necessary piece. I laugh inside, and my heart smiles at how gentle he is.

I make my way into his living room, which is filled with homemade bookcases, a coffee table, and I believe his mantel on his fireplace as well. The pieces are definitely handmade, the craftsmanship unbelievable. "Wow. These are incredible." I run my hand over the coffee table. "You have quite the hobby. Why aren't you doing this instead?

"Instead?" His eyes open wide and he grins. "Why choose when I can do both?"

He makes a point. "I don't have any hobbies, really."

"None? None at *all*?"

Taking care of myself as a kid never lent me much time to discover any talents I may have. I loved reading. Escaping into someone else's world was the perfect way to forget about my life. I can't do much with that. I never was that great of a writer, though I tried. "I guess I can sew." I had to fix any of my clothes with holes in them, hem clothes for my mom, and when I needed a costume or something for school, I was always on my own.

"Well, there you go! That's something."

"I haven't done it in ages, though. I used to scribble designs in a notepad I carried around." Wow. I haven't thought about that notepad in years. I shoved it between my textbooks at school. I didn't think there was much I could do with sewing, so I pursued a more promising career in technology. It's paid off, though now that I imagine my thread and needle, I kind of miss it.

"Maybe some time you can show me your designs. You've seen a lot of mine."

I want to see a lot more of him, too. "So this is what you do to relieve stress? Woodworking?"

"Yep. I blast Blake Shelton and create."

"Blake Shelton?"

"Yes, Blake Shelton. Do you have a problem with Blake?" He shifts his head to the right and winks as he approaches me. I allow him to unzip my jacket and help me out of it.

"Blake? You two are on a first-name basis?"

"We're like brothers," he teases as he brushes my hair aside and kisses my neck. I shiver at the touch of his lips. His tongue touches my neck, and I want nothing more than to be with him.

"Enough talk about brothers." I wrap my arms around his neck and we're entangled in each other. A tide of euphoria rushes over me, and I'm afraid I may flood his living room with tears of joy. We're breathing heavily through our noses as neither one of us wants to stop where this is going. "You still have to show me your bedroom." I keep pecking at his neck while he begins to step back, pulling me with him.

"I'm not sure I can make it there." He shifts his movement from backward toward his bedroom instead to the right and guides me to the couch. "Is this okay?"

I grip his jacket collar and yank the coat off him, tossing it to the ground. "I really don't care where it happens, as long as it does." I shove him onto the couch and straddle him, cupping his face in my hands. "Welcome home, Keith."

•••

I wake up to the sound of Keith's voice. He's wrapped me in a blanket and the fireplace is burning. I pull the covers to my chin and stretch my legs. The only thing that could make this better would be if he were next to me.

"I know, Mom. But you have to understand —"

He's pacing in the kitchen, his phone stuck to his ear. He hasn't seen I'm awake yet. His parents are still in London with his brother. I squint to see the time on his microwave. The bright green light reads 8:14. Wow, I don't ever sleep this late. My body must have needed it. I'm shocked he isn't still sleeping after his long flight yesterday.

"You've never met her so it's not fair for you to talk about her like that."

I snap my eyes shut when he glances my way. Is his mom talking about *me*? What is going on? I swallow hard and concentrate as I try to hear what he's saying.

"You'll meet her eventually." He pauses. "I had to come back. She needed me." He's silent for a few moments so I assume she's saying something to him. "Well, have it your way then. We can talk when you return to the States." I listen as he says goodbye and hangs up.

I don't want to cause a fight between him and his parents. What would have brought up him discussing me? I wonder if he called her or she called him. I suppose it doesn't make any difference, but I really want to know what this is about.

I take my time opening my eyes so he doesn't realize I was listening. When I finally have them open, he's sitting at the kitchen table, his head in his hands. He's in a t-shirt and boxers and his hair a tangled mess. That's my fault. He senses me watching him and lifts his head. "Hey you." He stands from the chair and makes his way to the living room.

I hold the blanket over myself as I sit up. "Hey. Did you sleep okay?"

"Yeah." He plops down next to me, grabs me and pulls me onto his lap. "You sleep like an angel."

I kiss him, never mind my morning breath or his. I don't know what an angel looks like when sleeping, but he obviously thinks it's sweet. I hope I didn't snore. I've been known to do that.

"Did you want some coffee and breakfast? I can make a hell of a bagel."

"Isn't that taking it out of the package and putting it into the toaster?"

"Sure is, but I'm bad ass at it."

I imagine how he can make it look tough, maybe flexing his

biceps as he pushes the handle down. Sigh. I can't stay. I shouldn't. That phone call didn't sound good. I should have known opening myself up to a real relations go would only result in failure.

"Thanks for the offer, but I think I'll run through a drive thru and head home."

"A drive-thru? You would rather have fast food than a home cooked meal from me?" He playfully pushes me off his lap.

"How do I put this lightly?" I tap my finger on my chin. "A frozen bagel and a K-cup is hardly a home cooked meal."

"You've got me there." He steals another kiss from me. "Besides, my mom, now *she* can cook. You'll have to try her chicken and waffles sometime."

I'm not sure why he's anticipating me ever meeting his mother after the conversation I overheard. He mistakes my lack of response as offense.

"I'm sorry. I keep mentioning my family."

"So?"

I tense as he places his hand on the blanket covering my knee. "With what just happened, it's insensitive of me."

"You don't have to walk on eggshells around me, Keith." I stand and allow the blanket to fall off me, paying no mind to my naked body that I'm sure he's checking out. I find my underwear and bra and put them both on as I continue. "If you don't remember, my mom was dead to me years ago. Now it's only the truth."

Out of the corner of my eye I see his mouth fall open. Once my shirt and pants are on, I slide my boots on and grab my keys. "This was too soon. We moved too fast."

"Cassie, take a deep breath and let's talk about this."

"My whole life is a series of deep breaths. I inhale pain and exhale poison. It's probably best you stay away from me before I infect you, too."

He bolts from the couch and slaps my hand away from the door. "That is not true and you know it. You're a beautiful person full of kindness and love, and the shit you dealt with as a kid formed a protective glass around you."

"Please. Let me leave. I need time. Christmas is coming up. Spend time with your family. I'll see Shannon. Let's end this before it's too late."

"You're talking crazy, Cassie. Let me break that glass around you."

I wrap my hand around the door knob and allow tears to fall. "That's the problem with glass, Keith. When you break it, it cuts you." I swing the door open. "And pieces are left shattered everywhere that you can never put back together. "

Chapter Thirty-Three

The wind is whipping outside, and the snow is coming down hard. The meteorologists say that the worst of it will be over by one o'clock, which allows the plows four hours to get the job done so I don't have to spend three hours getting home. I don't mind the cold, and the snow doesn't bother me that much, except when it makes for such a long drive home. I'm glad to be back at work, though, and this first day has been busy.

Keith mostly honored my request to give me some time. He texted me on Christmas, and I replied with a smiley face and wishing him well. He misses me, he said, and I'd be lying if I said I didn't miss him. Shannon kept my mind off of him, though, and even Sasha. We have a Dating for Decades meeting tomorrow, and I fully plan on attending. This is the first after the holidays, and I think I need the group right now.

A meeting request pops up on my computer. Terrence has called a meeting of the entire help desk, me, and Lucas. I glance at the time. Crap. He wants to meet us now. Good thing I'm at my computer.

I shut my laptop, grab my phone and meet everybody in the conference room, taking a seat next to Lucas. We haven't spoken too much since the awards ceremony, but in the few times we have, we've been friendly. I think he's finally accepted I'm not interested. Well, and since he began dating Kimmy, I think it's safe to say he's over it.

"I wonder what this could be about. He never calls meetings on such short notice." I set my phone down on top of the small notepad I brought with me.

"I guess we'll see." Lucas has his hands folded and is sitting with the straightest posture I've ever seen on him. He's ready for business.

Terrence strolls into the room with a large smile on his face. Okay, that's good. Good news. If he walked in with a frown or his lips pursed together, I'd be concerned. Maybe we're hiring more lawyers and will need more staff, which I will oversee.

"I apologize for the short notice on the meeting. I have a lunch appointment and want to make this announcement before it makes its way through the grapevine." He's looking straight at Julian, the department gossip.

He unbuttons his suit coat and hugs his hips with his hands. "As you know, Lucas has spent the past couple of months with us helping out on the Pilot Program. Thanks to both him and Cassie, everything is running smoothly. Thank you both."

Lucas and I exchange a smile, and I'm thankful for the sincerity behind it. Things may have been rocky to begin with, but together we pulled it off. I tried like hell to keep him from stealing my job, and that was never his intent. He's an ethical worker, and a better man.

"You also may know that Lucas is my nephew. His plan never was to stay with us very long. He sets his goals very high, and he doesn't want to give the impression his uncle paves the way." Terrence walks behind Lucas' chair and puts his hands on his shoulder. "He doesn't need me to help him. His talents speak for themselves."

Lucas pats his uncle's hands. "Thanks, Uncle T."

Uncle T? He's getting pretty personal, a no-no in Lucas' eyes. Terrence continues around the table until he ends up back at the head.

"He planned on staying for longer than he is, but his father has asked he move forward with his career goals."

His father. I remember Lucas saying he was sick. I guess he isn't any better, but Lucas is moving forward.

"Lucas's last day here will be on Friday. He's accepted a job in San Francisco and starts on Monday."

Everyone starts to congratulate him, and I want to punch him in the shoulder. How could he *not* tell me? I've finally gotten used to having him here and our friendship is in tact, and now he's leaving? I look over at Kimmy, who doesn't look surprised, but somewhat sad. She's a good girl. I wonder where this leaves them.

Terrence congratulates Lucas and dismisses the group. I ask Lucas to stay behind.

Once everyone is out of the room, I jab him in the side. "Why didn't you tell me?"

"Ow!" He pretends I've hurt him while laughing. "Do I have to run everything past you? I accepted the job while you were out. And my uncle wanted to wait until you returned to announce it."

"You still could have texted me."

"Okay, one, you suck at responding to text messages. And two, he didn't want me saying anything. I only told Kimmy."

For some reason, I'm a little jealous when he says this. I don't like Lucas in a sexual way, and I'm so happy for him and Kimmy, but his face lights up when he mentions her name, a twinkle in his eye that could light up the night sky.

"She's awesome, you know. You hold onto her." I suddenly feel like a mother looking out for her child. All the young adults at the help desk, they're people I've help mold into professionals. I want them to be happy.

He moves from the table to the doorway. "I'm going to try. We've come up with a plan for the next year and hope we can make it work."

Remaining in my seat, I nod. "Good." I gaze past him into the hallway, the doorway to the server room in my view. God, I miss Keith. Me and long-term relationships don't work, though. His mom doesn't even like me and she's never even seen a picture of me. I rake my fingers through my hair, around my neck, and as my hand slides off my chin, I tickle a hair. Those damn chin hairs.

"Look, I want to mention the elephant in the room here. I'm sorry about what happened at the awards ceremony. Keith's a great guy. You two are good together."

We were. We would be. Even if I had the chance to make things work, he wouldn't take me back. "Thanks, but we're not really together."

"Oh?" He slides his hand up the door frame as he furrows his brow. "Well, if you want my opinion, you should be."

•••

Spotted Cow is my favorite beer, when I actually drink beer. After the day I just had, I want to bathe in it. My spectacular first day back after a hiatus and it's ruined by Lucas leaving. Keith is gone, my mom is gone, and now Lucas.

I'm almost through my third beer when someone taps me on the shoulder. I turn my head to see Lucas sliding onto the barstool next to me. "What are you doing here?"

"It's The Spot, right? *The* place to be."

"This dinky old bar?" The bartender gives me a stink eye, and I shy away, not wanting to start anything.

"You seemed upset in your text."

"I texted you?"

"Are you *that* drunk that you don't remember texting me?" Those eyes that twinkle for Kimmy are now filled with concern.

"Nah, I'm joking. I remember. I'm only in for three so far. Did my text convey my emotion that well?"

"Well, you sent me a red angry face and a poop emoji, so I kind of figured." He orders a Pabst and I giggle. No one drinks that except old men. "What's got you down? Keith?"

He doesn't waste any time getting to the point. I can't believe I'm going to discuss this with him. Lucas, who I've seen naked and done things with that I'm ashamed to even mention. Lucas, who is seventeen years younger than me rocked my world like it was the end of it. Being friends with him is proving to be a little awkward.

"I guess."

"Did you talk to him?"

"In the few hours since I last spoke with you? Nope." I take a swig of my beer, the bottle popping on my mouth. "He's done with me. I said some pretty shitty stuff to him. Why bother? He's done with me. I'm done with everything. With everyone."

"Don't say that."

"It's true. What's the point, Lucas? *Everyone* leaves. I shouldn't even bother anymore. This is why I never bothered in the first place. Then Keith had to come along and screw everything up."

He takes my beer and moves it aside. "I don't know how many you've had, but you're being unreasonable."

"Do you know what's unreasonable? Expecting someone to want me." He's watching me, listening, and those eyes start to comfort me. I flash back to that night at his apartment. What a tremendous night it was. He wanted me. I pushed him away. Why? Because he was young? Because I was afraid of what my boss would say? Terrence loves me! He probably would have welcomed the relationship with open arms.

"You were a good one," I tell him. "I let you get away." Maybe it's the beer talking, I don't know, but I can't control myself and lean in, planting my lips on Lucas. For a brief moment, he kisses me back before he grabs my shoulders and pushes me away.

"Cassie, don't."

"What? Don't you want me? Don't you find me attractive?" I want to cry, to drown myself in my tears, rid myself of all my pain. A few months ago he couldn't keep his hands off me, groping me with his eyes at every chance he got. I touch my chin. No hairs. Maybe it's the gray in my hair. Or the wrinkles. Am I getting a double chin? I don't even want to check my arms. I bet they're disgustingly flabby.

"It's not that."

"It's because I'm going to be forty in two weeks, isn't it? FORTY! As in four zero. In two damned weeks!" I lift three fingers, then put one down and show two to emphasize. "Forty years old. I'm not married, no kids, and I pretty much think I'm stuck in my job now unless Terrence retires. Lucas," I ball his shirt up in my hand as I make a fist, "I don't even own a cat! The cat ladies of the world are in a better place than me! *Keith* even has a cat!"

He's trying not to laugh. His head is shaking, and his lips are pressed together. I can make out a smile behind those thin lips.

"Fine. Laugh at me." I let go of his shirt. "Suck it up. Here's poor Cassie who can't even get laid by her old fuck buddy." My head slams onto the bar. "Ow." I massage my scalp.

"Cassie, you're drunk. And upset. It's not a good combination." He pauses. "And watch your language. We're in a public place."

I shake my head as I suck in the tears. I'm not lifting my head until they've dissipated. I can't look him in the eye. I'm so humiliated.

"Trust me, you're a great looking woman and you're intelligent and have yourself together ... well, not tonight, but most of the time." I smile through my tears. "I'm leaving in a few days. I don't want to go down this path again."

I wipe my face on my sleeve and lift my head. "This path again?"

"You know, the one when I fall madly for you and then we have a great night together and then you leave."

"I won't leave this time. I promise." I don't know why I'm pleading for him. I think right now I would plead with anyone, *anyone* to love me.

"No, you don't. Because you don't love me. And I'm with Kimmy."

"But I care about you. A lot. I should have given you a chance. Maybe this would have worked out if I hadn't been so scared."

"No, it wouldn't have."

My hands drop to my side and my heart goes with it. I'm being rejected. I'm throwing myself at this man and he's turning me down. What possible reason could there be? "Why not?"

He finishes his beer, stands up and pats me on the shoulder. "Because you're in love with Keith, whether you realize it or not."

Chapter Thirty-Four

Today's the day. It's the day I face my fears. It's the day I put it all on the table. It's the day I proclaim my love for Keith.

The Dating for Decades meeting may not be the best place to do this. But maybe it is. I'm in a safe place and can show the others that it can be done, that I can actually move forward. Cheyenne did it, Keith wants to do it, now I can. I can let go of everything, try in spite of what his mother says. I can do this.

I arrive early today, my nerves building inside of me and trying to talk me down. I won't listen, though, no matter how much they get to me. I'm determined.

This is the first meeting since before the Christmas break, so I bring cupcakes to welcome everyone back. This should score points with everyone, too. Who doesn't love red velvet? Besides, the fine cake represents love, in my opinion, and that's precisely what I'm here for.

I set the cupcakes up on the refreshment table, over the red tablecloth I purchased. It looks amazing, and the champagne flutes and sparkling apple juice were a fun touch. Okay, I *may* have gone *slightly* overboard, but isn't that what you're supposed to do when you're in love? Isn't that what romance is all about?

I pace the room for a solid ten minutes before Luna arrives. She strolls in, bundled up with a face that matches the inside of the cupcake.

"Could it be any colder out there?" She whips off her scarf and hangs it with her jacket. "Cupcakes? Thank you. Don't mind if I do."

I slap her hand away. "Not yet."

"You're denying me cupcakes? You do want to live to see tomorrow, don't you?" The space between her eyes shortens, but I ignore her empty threat.

"You can have one when everyone gets here."

"Three!"

Three cupcakes? *Really*, Luna? "How about two?"

She contemplates this for a moment, her head shooting back and forth between me and the sweets. "Deal." She shakes my hand and hers is so cold it sends shivers throughout my body.

Cheyenne shows up next, followed by Monica and Noelle. Everyone is getting ornery waiting to dive into the cupcakes, and I'll admit, I am too. I don't tend to eat sweets, but today they're calling my name. Maybe facing my fear of love is also expanding my need for sugar. I can't go down that road again. I'm limiting myself to one. That's it.

"I'm getting hungry." Cheyenne raises her voice as though she's a toddler begging for candy.

"We're missing Keith." I point to the empty chair.

Monica shakes her head. "No, we're not."

"What?" I shoot my head around. "What do you mean we're not missing him? This is the first meeting after the turn of the new year. He should be here."

"He texted me this morning he wasn't coming." Cheyenne pulls out her phone, scrolls through the messages, and hands it to me.

Can't make it tonight. Sorry. I'm not sure when I'll be back.

I lower the phone and Cheyenne has to reach toward me to take it before I drop it. "Why did he text *you*?"

"Whoa. What's the accusatory tone?"

"I'm not accusing you of anything. I only wonder why he told you and not me." He sent me one or two messages since Christmas checking in, but he never said anything about being done with the group.

"Beats me," she shrugs. "You're his girlfriend." She leaves her chair and steals a cupcake. "No reason to wait on these then."

Keith abandoned the group? He abandoned *me*? Without even so much as a goodbye? Don't I at least deserve that? My head is spinning and sweat is starting to seep through my shirt. I look over at Cheyenne, who is about to break into the frosting. "Put. The. Cupcake. Down."

I startle her and she stops short, slowly placing the cupcake back on the table while stepping away.

"Are you okay, Cassie?" Monica asks in that motherly tone I usually love but today hate.

"No. I'm not okay. Keith and I had a fight a few weeks back. We haven't really spoken. I .. I made a mistake."

Noelle retrieves a nail file from her purse and starts filing her nails. "So tell him."

"Don't you think I was going to? What do you think the cupcakes are for?" These cupcakes that *I* took the time to bake. Yes, I did this all on my own and every ounce of my heart is in them. He thinks he can walk away without saying goodbye? Well, I can do the same. I march over to the table, pick up the plate of cupcakes, and slam them into the ground. The floor is covered in white and red, pieces of glass nestled in between. Ironic.

"I'm done." I hold up both my hands. "I'm so done."

"With what? Keith?" Monica stands and tries to come toward me, but I take a step back.

"All of it. Keith. The group."

"Excuse me?" Cheyenne interrupts. "You can't just shut the group down."

"I sure can. I created the group. I can disband it." Time to move on. It's about time I accept my pitiful life for what it is.

Noelle stands up and stomps her foot on the ground like a teenager. "No. We *all* need this group. Even you. You're going to quit because of *him*? Forgive me, but aren't men the reason you started this group? So we can discuss and work through these things?"

"Even if I did, what does it matter? None of us are helping each other. We're a bunch of pathetic losers who sit around and bitch about men every Thursday night. I don't need this." I lost everything else, I might as well lose the group, too. I can start fresh. Make new friends. Form a new group. Losers Anonymous.

"Cassie, think about what you're doing." I give Cheyenne the benefit of the doubt and hear her out. "You've put so many years into this group. We're all friends. We need each other. If we didn't have each other, if I didn't have this group, I wouldn't be where I am today."

"You mean in a healthy, long-lasting relationship? I'm glad someone from this group found that. But if you're happy, why are you even here?" My voice is rising, and my heart is pounding. "Why are *any* of us in this group? No one wants us. Any of us. I'm sick of wasting my time here!"

"You don't mean that." Luna's eyes well up with tears as she whispers to me.

"I sure as hell do. I can't take this anymore." My voice has now risen to a level I'm making everyone uncomfortable, including myself. "When I created this group, I wanted to form relationships with other women, connect with them because we're the same age and experiencing the same issues. Everyone is moving on. Everyone is happy in their lives and have their boyfriends or their kids or their parents. Meanwhile, here I am with a dead mother, an ex-boyfriend who hates me, and a group of women whom I've grown to love who I can't even identify with anymore!" I snatch my purse off the back of my chair and it catches in the arm of my jacket as I frantically try to put it on. Noelle comes over to help me, but I shake in a way she can't get to me. "Leave me alone!" I cry. "Leave me alone!" The tears begin flowing out of my eyes, and I can't stop them. No matter how hard I try, they keep coming and coming, and there isn't a shut-off valve.

Noelle wraps her arms around me and I bury my head in her chest as I sob. Moments later, the arms of the other women are around me, and no one is saying a word, but they're proving one thing to me.

We're all broken, and we're all here to help put each other back together.

Chapter
Thirty-Five

January thirtieth isn't any normal day for me. It's the day I step over that hill and officially become an old lady. I want to spend my birthday with Shannon, but her son has something going on that day for school, so she's taking me out today, two weeks early. I would have been fine staying home, moping about Keith and drowning in my sorrows. But, it's Friday night and after my horrible Dating for Decades meeting, which honestly ended in a pretty cool way with solid friendships in tact, Shannon is forcing me out. Turning forty is a big deal, so she says, so she's dragging me to The Spot for some drinks and, if I get drunk enough, some dancing. I may be old, but I can still hold my liquor. I only hope I don't come onto some random stranger like I did to Lucas the other night.

She doesn't want to go out until nine. *Nine!* Maybe the fact that I'd rather be in bed at nine o'clock than out at the bar pledges me into the over forty club. Now I move up an age group in demographics, and soon I'll be getting my AARP card in the mail. Before you know it, I'll be sixty-five and retired. Okay, who am I kidding? I'll probably never retire. I'm addicted to working.

I'm feeling old so I need to feel sexy. I opt for tight, white pants with alligator skin heels and a long sleeve brown top that scoops down in the back. I know you're not supposed to wear white after Labor Day, but I never heard when it is okay to *actually wear it.* So it's my night out, I'll wear it if I want to. I leave my hair down but curl the ends. I finally went to the salon last week and my grays are gone ... for a least a little while. I find a thin gold necklace to wear as well. Even I'll admit I look pretty hot.

I'm about to text Shannon to forget the whole thing at 8:55 when she still hasn't arrived. She knows I'm a stickler for time so I don't appreciate the tardiness. She finally pulls up to my place at exactly nine. "I thought you wanted to *be* there at nine." If you're right on time, you're late in my book.

"It's not like we're on a schedule, Cassie. Ben is watching the kids, and I had a to-do list to go over with him. We'll get there."

She's wearing her favorite blue dress. I can tell with her jacket slightly unbuttoned. This is her favorite dress for going out. It's the one that slims her down and highlights her curves in all the right places.

"What kind of a to-do list do you have this late at night?" The kids should be almost ready for bed, and I don't know how much you can get done with the kids asleep.

"I always find something."

This is true. Shannon is never without a laundry list of things to get done, including laundry! I shouldn't have doubted her.

"Are you anxious?" She wiggles in her seat as she drives to The Spot.

"I'm forty. I'm devastated." There was a time in my life I wondered if I would make it to forty. I thought my mom would take me down with her, and I'd become addicted to drugs. I'm proud I never succumbed to it. I battled with my weight for a few years, but Shannon helped me, though. Now that I'm here, I'm grateful, but that still doesn't mean I'm happy about admitting it.

"It's not *that* bad. I survived my first year."

Shannon is a year older than me and she must have forgotten dealing with all these same emotions last year. It's not the end of the world to be turning forty, but it's not quite as exciting as turning twenty-one or even thirty. It seems so ... old. What comes next? I work for twenty-five more years and retire to Florida where I live out my final days? I think of my mom who never even saw sixty-five. She didn't even make it to sixty. *Shake it off, Cassie. Be happy you're here and healthy.*

We arrive at The Spot, and she parks right in front. I'm ready to *drink.* I unbuckle and reach for the handle, and she stops me.

"Cassie, I know turning forty has been difficult for you. Please know it's not a finality of anything. It's the start of a new part of your life. Welcome your forties. Embrace them. Fight *against* the current. If you're back starts to hurt, work out that kink. If you get tired, drink some caffeine. I have a feeling the best years of your life are ahead of you."

"Thanks?"

"Trust me, Cassie. It's not as bad as you make it out to be. You make a much bigger deal out of it than it actually is."

I make a big deal out of everything. Doesn't she know me at all? I filled her in on everything that happened with Keith, and while she thinks I should have stayed and worked things out, I don't have the time to be in someone's life who doesn't want me in his. It would eventually end up that way. His mother hates me already, and when I'd eventually meet her, she probably would convince him to dump me. I still have the group and Shannon. That's enough. That's all I need. So maybe this next year won't be so bad, considering I have everything I need. I open the door and step onto the sidewalk. "Okay, Chief. You've got it." I duck my head into the car and salute her.

"Stop it." She exits on her side and meets me around on the sidewalk. "Let's go." She hooks my arm with hers, and I enter the bar with my best friend.

Before we even get through the door, I'm inundated with people yelling. "Surprise!" I latch onto Shannon's arm to keep my balance, and I scan the group of people.

"Got you!" Shannon says as she embraces me. I tighten my hold on her and I'm squeezing her so tight I'm probably cutting off her air supply. I start crying as "Time Of Your Life" by Green Day plays from the jukebox. It's been rough, but I think it truly has been the time of my life.

I can't believe this. I've never had a birthday party in my *entire life*. My mom barely remembered my birthday, and on the years she did, it wasn't much of a big deal. I never really celebrated after we parted. Shannon always tried, usually inviting me over to her place for cake and a small gift, but that was it. She wanted to do that for me and I let her, though it was tough.

I peer around the bar, scoping out who is here. Terrence, Noelle, Luna, Monica, and Cheyenne came. I wave at Lucas who's holding hands with Kimmy. That's so sweet they came since he is leaving for California tomorrow. Sasha and Garrett are here along with Ben. "Who's with the kids?"

"We got a sitter! This is a night out for us, too!" Shannon jumps up and down, and I'm happy for her. A date night may be just what she and Ben need.

I continue to check out the faces, hoping to see one in particular, and my excitement fades when I don't.

"I tried to call him." She runs her hand up and down my back. "I managed to steal his number from your phone the other day. I left a voice mail. I assume he got it. This was before everything happened between you two."

"It's okay." I wipe my cheeks. "We broke up. I shouldn't expect him to be here. I guess I was holding onto hope."

"You can stop holding onto it." I recognize the gentle, smoky voice, and when I turn around, Keith is standing there, his normally smiling face a stoic statue. "Can I take your jacket?"

I allow him to pull it off me and his lingering stare on my back doesn't go unnoticed. Good.

"Happy birthday, Cassie." His lip is curled up in a half-smile now, but he isn't wide-mouthed like most would be when issuing such a greeting.

"What are you doing here? Shannon said she tried to call you, but you didn't respond."

"She did, did she?" They exchange winks. So they *did* have a conversation. Fine, but that doesn't change what happened between me and him.

He folds my jacket over his arm. "Can we talk?"

I want nothing more than to talk to him, to take everything back, but I can't. What's done is done. I said a lot of things to him, and they haven't changed.

"Sure." If I'm going to enjoy this party, we *should* discuss it, get everything off our chests, and then move on.

He surprises me by taking my hand and leads me to the back of the bar where it's a little quieter. No one seems to notice the birthday girl has disappeared. As we continue the walk to the back of the bar, I miss this touch more with every step. We stop at a high table and set our arms on the wood, and our elbows are almost touching.

"When Shannon called, I didn't get a chance to call her back until after our argument. I told her I had to think about it." He dives right into it, no warning or buildup. "I asked her not to tell you in case I decided not to come."

"I understand."

"You left me dumbfounded that morning. I still don't know what happened. The way you walked out on me was a pretty solid sign you're not ready for a commitment. What happened there?"

The morning is a bit of a blur, between dealing with my mother's death and our breakup. I cried so much over those forty-eight hours I didn't even know what tears were for what. "I heard you on the phone."

"Okay?"

He moves his hands so he's gripping the table. The dimly lit bar casts a small light on his face and I'm glad he's shaven. I enjoyed the scruffiness, but when he smiles, I want to see every crease in his chin and cheeks. Only he's not smiling.

"You were talking to your mom about me. She was saying things about me. She's upset you left to come see me. I know how this will go down. We'll date for a few months, she'll meet me, hate me even more than she already does, and then you'll break up with me. I'm ending it before it gets to that point."

"What?" He throws his head back and that smile I love so much comes through. Why is he happy about this?

"What's so funny?"

"Cassie, I wasn't talking about you."

"You weren't?" That doesn't make any sense. "Then who?"

He reaches over and takes my hand, and my heartbeat speeds up. "My sister-in-law is going back to work and they're hiring a nanny. My mom is up in arms about someone she doesn't know watching the kids."

"You told her that you came back because I needed you."

"*That*," he points to me with the free hand, "*that* I said about you. That's the problem with eavesdropping. You only hear one end of the conversation." He grabs both my hands and kisses them. "She's fine I came back for you. I'd always come back for you."

He's too sweet for me. He's considerate, gentle, loving. "I don't deserve you."

"What does that even mean? I love you, Cassie. I want to be with you."

"You what?" My heart is between my ears now, and I'm shaking. This can't be real.

"I love you. I get that you're scared. I am, too. But we're in this together. We can be afraid together and overcome our fears just the same."

Keith knows all my highs and lows and he still wants to be with me. He's seen me at my best and at my worst. And he still wants me.

"I got you something." He reaches into his pocket and pulls out a small box.

"What .. what are you doing?" He better not be proposing. I

thought we were on the same page with that. Yes, I love him, *love* him, but I don't want to get married.

"That night when you told me about your design notebook, your face lit up like nothing I've ever seen before. That's the same way I feel when it comes to my woodworking. The passion shot out of your eyes and how much you missed it was obvious to me, even if it wasn't to you. I think you should pursue that."

"I'm forty years old, Keith."

"Well, not for another two weeks." He smiles. "You have to start somewhere, so start here." He takes his hand off the box and hands it to me.

I snicker as I review the mini sewing kit, complete with a scissors, needles, pins, tweezers, and snaps. "Really?"

"Yes, really. See where this goes."

"Or sew where this goes." I cover my mouth as I accidentally snort when I say it.

"You're corny. I love your sense of humor."

"And I love you." This is the first time I'm now saying it to him and inside I feel amazing and full and like I can face anything.

"Cassie Noble," he says as he steps to the side of me and keeps my left hand in his. "Will you *not* marry me and be with me forever?"

A fortieth birthday party, a sewing kit, and an anti-proposal. I'd say this is the best night ever. "Yes, Keith. Forever and always."

The words leave my lips and seconds later he's dipping me, and I throw my arms around him. His lips are warm and inviting, and after years of being engulfed in pain and doubt, I'm finally overtaken by love and the belief of a future worth fighting for.

Chapter Thirty-Six

After almost a year of planning, the day has finally arrived. Despite a few hiccups in the beginning, the entire ceremony went well. The reception is booming, and everyone is out on the dance floor. Even though it's almost ninety degrees outside and the air conditioner is on the fritz, everyone seems to be enjoying themselves. A perfect summer wedding.

The Dating for Decades group is going strong again, and even though one of us is now married off, the group is far from disbanding. Every person in the group is now in a relationship (and one of us now married) so we're more of a group of friends than a group of older women (and man) who can't find love. It's been a good year and almost a half for all of us.

Keith convinced me to reach out to David and spread my mother's ashes with him. He said I've come a long way, and he believed I could do this. And I did. David held onto the ashes convinced one day I would come to him. I'm proud of myself for contacting him, for allowing him to see me in such a vulnerable state, and to welcome me even though I wasn't the daughter I should have been.

Now there's this wedding, and it's beautiful and fun, and I'm having the best time of my life. I'm free — free of fear. I'm not afraid to be in love, to be happy. This is the best feeling I could ever have in my entire life and while I wish I'd opened up sooner, I think my heart was waiting for Keith.

I'm careful not to snag my dress. It goes to my knees only, but there's a lace layer covering it. All the dresses are gorgeous. The bouquet toss arrives, and I remember the last time I was involved in one ended with a horny kid grabbing at me. I'm hoping there isn't a repeat.

I march in the circle, trying my best not to get dizzy. I'll tell you, while turning forty hasn't been the worst thing, now that I'm forty-one (yes, forty-*one*), I think my senses are disappearing, my knees are weakening, and I'm physically falling apart. That's what happens when you get older, right? I'm waiting for the music to halt so I can stop moving. When it finally does, I'm ready.

I lift my hands up and catch it. Cheyenne tosses it directly to me even though she knows I'll never walk down the aisle. Keith and I are happy and in love, and we plan to spend the rest of our lives together.

I'm always the bridesmaid. I'll never be the bride.

And I'm okay with that.

•••

Acknowledgements

I tend to write long acknowledgements, so I'll keep it short and simple this time. There are so many people to thank. First and foremost, my husband and family, for without you, I wouldn't have a spark to write. Stephanie P., for believing in this book and encouraging me to keep going. Christine A., for spending a weekend emailing me back and forth to assist with a pivotal scene.

There are a trillion more people to thank, so if your name begins with a letter of the alphabet, I'm thanking you! I'm so grateful to Chick Lit Chat, Chick Lit Goddesses, For Love or Money, Seasoned Romance, and Daily Author Goals. These are my frequented Facebook groups that get me through writing every book. I also have to give a shout out to Romance Authors Unite, Fast Draft Club, 10 Minute Novelists, and Sprint Buddies.

Karen B., thanks for basically writing the entire blurb for this book.

Najla Qambar Designs — thank you for an awesome cover.

A special thanks to Cameron Diaz and Melissa Stack. A simple line in a movie sparked the idea and title for this book. Inspiration comes from everywhere, and this amazing actress and screenwriter inspired me!

Last, and never least, thank you to every single person who picks up this book — or any of my books — and reads them. I hope they bring you laughter and tears and you enjoy them. Reading is so important to me and I was always told to write what you want to read. This is it, and I hope I've brought you joy!

About the Author

Tracy's love of writing began at nine years old. She wrote stories about aliens at school, machines that did homework for you, and penguins. Now she pens books and short stories about romance. She loves to read a great book, whether it be romance or science fiction, or any genre in between, or pop popcorn and catch up on her favorite TV shows or movies. She's been known to crush a candy or two as well. Her first romance novel, Pieces of it All, released in May 2014 followed in December with Caching In, a romance mixed with the hobby of geocaching. She also has written several short stories.

Thank you so much for reading DATING FOR DECADES. If you liked this book, consider other works by Tracy Krimmer. You can purchase the books and find out more about Tracy Krimmer at www.tracykrimmer.com. Sign up for her newsletter at www.tracykrimmer.com/newsletter.